Susan – thanks so much 88

enjoy

SISTER LOST

ALSO AVAILABLE BY BRENDA LYNE

Charlie's Mirror

SISTER LOST

BRENDA LYNE

Brenda
Lyne
Books

Copyright ©2021 by Jennifer DeVries
Writing as Brenda Lyne

All rights reserved.

Cover design by Susan@yuneepix.com
Book design by Jennifer DeVries

Published in the United States by Brenda Lyne Books

Printed in the United States

ISBN: 978-1-7376133-0-5

First edition: September 2021

brendalyne.com

For Price & Kendall, my constant inspirations.

And for Ken Ferk: your memory lives on. Rest in peace.

PROLOGUE

The little boy knew he was in trouble the second the bedroom door slammed behind him. The sound reverberated through the house and awakened the monster from her slumber. His sister sat on the floor, in the middle of a pretend tea party with her favorite orange-haired doll, staring at him with wide eyes that looked just like his own. She knew.

His feet were rooted to the floor in terror; he couldn't decide what to do. Hide in the closet? Crawl under the bed? Climb out the window?

The sound of heavy feet pounding across the floor grew louder outside the door. His heart jackrabbited in his chest and an involuntary *eek* sound escaped him.

The bedroom door flew open so hard and fast that the doorknob punched a hole in the wall. The monster stood there in her tattered bathrobe, panting, mousy brown hair hanging in greasy clumps around her pale face. She held a large kitchen knife in her right hand. The big brown eyes that she had passed on to her children were wide and wild, and they fell on him. "Did you slam the door?" she asked him in a calm voice that was utterly at odds with her appearance. He nodded slowly, mute. He knew better than to speak.

"Even though I told you I was taking a nap?" Her voice was still calm, but her eyes brimmed with barely-restrained madness.

His entire body began to shake. He nodded again.

"Do you know what happens to naughty children who don't listen? They get punished." She held the knife up and stepped into the room.

Sheer panic dropped over the little boy like a heavy curtain. "No!" he screeched. He finally found his feet and ran, quickly squeezing between the monster's legs and the door frame. He was halfway up the attic stairs before she could react.

"Get back here!" she roared.

He scrambled across the attic to the small door that opened to the long, slanted crawlspace where he and his sister liked to play. It was the best hiding place he could think of. He wrenched the door open and crawled in, closing it quietly behind him.

The monster prowled around downstairs, opening and closing doors and cabinets. He could hear her muffled voice through the floor. "Oh, you want to play hide and seek?" She grunted, and something slid back and forth across the wood floor in the living room. "Okay, we'll play hide and seek."

The boy leaned his shoulder against the wall next to the door and pulled his knees up to his face. He stared at the small metal doorknob and listened to the monster below him.

"Come on out, buddy," her muffled voice crooned from somewhere below him. He heard the distinct creak of the front door opening below him. "You want some ice cream? I'll take you to get a chocolate cone. Your favorite." The front door creaked and thumped closed.

"How about some candy?" This was much softer, as if she'd moved to the back of the house. "I got some candy." A couple moments of silence; he thought she might be searching for him in the basement. The attic would be the next logical place for her to look; his trembling turned to violent shakes as he thought about all the bad things she might do to him if she found him. Tears snaked down his cheeks.

"I know!" she said, her voice deceptively cheery. He knew she was standing in the kitchen again. "I'll take you to see your daddy. Wouldn't you like to see your daddy?"

He did want to see his daddy. More than anything. Life was good when Daddy was here, and it had been bad since he left.

But she always said that daddy went to heaven. He was only four years old, but he was pretty sure that meant he could never see his daddy again. Fresh tears coursed down his face.

"You can't hide forever!" she shouted. "Come on out, buddy. We'll just talk. I know you're sorry."

"Leave him alone, Mama!" His sister's voice floated to his ears from below him, and a small, grateful sob escaped him. She always was the brave one.

"Shut UP!" He was startled by a loud smack, and his sister cried out. "This has nothing to do with you, you little bitch."

"He didn't mean to wake you up, Mama!" The little girl wailed. "Don't hurt him, please, don't be a bad mama!"

The silence from below him was deafening. Then he heard the monster's footsteps move from the kitchen to the dining room. To his relief, the knife clattered on the table and something else slid across its surface. *Probably her medicine,* he thought. *The kind in the square bottle with that guy's face on it.*

It seemed she had lost interest in hunting him. "Get out of my sight." Her muffled voice was soft again. "Or you'll take the punishment that he's got coming."

His sister ran from the kitchen to their bedroom, and the house below him was quiet – save for the occasional *thunk* sound the monster's bottle of medicine made when she set it back on the table.

He didn't feel safe leaving the crawlspace yet. He suddenly found himself unable to keep his eyes open; they fluttered closed and before he knew it, he was no longer stuck in the dark and cramped crawlspace. He was riding the red tricycle he shared with his sister along the sidewalk outside his house, free as a bird. The sun shone, the birds chirped, and his little legs pumped as hard as he could make them. He could even feel the breeze ruffle his hair.

"Atta boy, champ!" Was – was that Daddy's voice?

I miss you, Daddy.

The squeak of the crawlspace door opening jerked him out of his dream; he scrambled away from the door in a semi-conscious panic. A hand appeared and he couldn't help but cry out; in his terror he was absolutely convinced that hand clutched a large kitchen knife.

His sister's blonde head appeared and he cried out again – this time in relief.

"You can come downstairs now," she said. She clutched Dolly in one hand. "Mama had too much medicine again and she's sleepin on her bed." He noticed that one of her cheeks was turning black and blue.

"Okay," he said. They crawled out and made their way downstairs hand-in-hand, as twins often do.

Soon there would only be one.

PART ONE:
LEXIE & AVA

1

The brakes squealed as Lexie pulled her old SUV up to the curb in front of the little house. She winced. *Come on, baby, hang in there a little longer,* she thought. *I just gave a fat cashier's check to the closing agent. The ol' bank account has nothing but dust bunnies in it.*

"Are we there, Mommy?" The tiny voice that sounded like fairy bells drifted from the back seat. "Is this our house?" She glanced in the rearview mirror to see Ava straining to see the house around the sides of her carseat.

Lexie smiled. "It sure is, pumpkin." She pulled the keys from the ignition and got out of the truck, then opened Ava's door and unfastened her restraints. The little girl climbed out and stood on the little patch of grass between the sidewalk and the street. Both gazed at the midcentury bungalow that now belonged to them. Ava's little hand sneaked into Lexie's, and she smiled down at her daughter. Ava grinned back, her bright blue eyes glowing in the June sunlight. A warm breeze blew her soft blonde curls around her pudgy cheeks.

"We have a HOUSE!" Ava suddenly screeched, shattering the moment and running across the sidewalk. She dropped on the lawn and rolled around in the shaggy green grass, giggling.

"We have a yard!" She sat up abruptly and gave Lexie a stern look. "Now can I have a puppy, Mommy?"

Lexie laughed, walked over to Ava, and scooped her up. She held her daughter's healthy four-year-old body in her arms and nuzzled her tummy. Ava kicked her legs and laughed brightly, her curly hair cascading over Lexie's right arm. "We'll see," Lexie said, and laid Ava back on the grass. Ava's blue denim biball dress had bunched up around her waist, laying bare her pink-and-white underpants.

"Is my Daddy coming to live with us?" Ava sat up and looked at Lexie with plaintive blue eyes.

Lexie should have been prepared for that question, but it caught her by surprise. Her stomach crashed to her feet. She sighed and resolutely sat in the grass next to her daughter. "What makes you ask that, pumpkin?"

Ava pulled a fistful of grass out of the lawn. "All my friends at daycare have daddies. Logan's daddy picks him up from Cindy's every single day." Another fistful of grass. "Nobody else but me only has a mommy."

Lexie sighed. *Bastard*. "Yes, but that means you're the only one at Cindy's with a mommy who is actually your mommy AND your daddy."

Ava inspected her mother's face closely for signs of parental bullshit: shifty eyes, corners of the mouth slightly upturned, or an unnatural lilt in the voice. Apparently satisfied that Lexie was telling the truth, she threw her grass to the side and pulled another chunk out of the lawn. "You're a mommy and a daddy?"

Lexie nodded. "I sure am. Not every mommy can do that, you know."

Ava blinked. "So you're...like a superhero?"

The mental image of her body, with its entire set of spare tires, stuffed into stretchy superhero tights made Lexie cringe. She did her best to disguise her distaste with a big grin. "You know it, babe. And this house is our new superhero lair." She gestured widely at the boxy story-and-a-half house. Built in 1955, one of thousands in Minneapolis built quickly and inexpensively for returning World War II soldiers and their growing families, it was simple on the outside, with two large gables and three windows in the front, bright white siding, and black trim. Save for a few modern fixtures, the house probably looked much the same as it had when it was built.

Ava, wide-eyed: "It is? Like...like Batman's cave?"

Lexie laughed, stood, and picked Ava up off the grass. "Yes! And you, my sweet, get your very own room in your superhero mommy's very own Bat-cave." She held Ava so that they were nose to nose and looked directly into her troubled little eyes. "So don't you worry about your daddy, okay? I got you."

Ava threw her arms around Lexie's neck and squeezed. "I love you, Mommy."

Relieved that this seemed to be the end of the daddy questions for the time being, Lexie hugged Ava back. "I love you too, doll. Now." She set Ava down. "Let's start moving our things in, what do you say?"

"Okay!" Ava took off running for the truck. Lexie followed her; they each picked up a box – Ava's was marked PILLOWS and Lexie's was marked PHOTOS & FRAMES – and carried them back into the house. She stopped just inside the front door and gazed into the empty living room; painted in neutral colors, it glowed in the sunlight that cascaded through the picture window. It was Lexie's favorite room in the house, perfect for sipping coffee and reading the newspaper every morning. She set her box on the floor, tore it open, and dove in.

Ava dropped her box next to Lexie; the boom sound it made echoed in the bare room. "Whatcha doin, Mommy?"

"Aha!" Lexie exclaimed, her head and arms emerging from the depths of the box. "Found it." She walked across the room and carefully placed a framed photo of her parents on the rustic wood mantel over the painted brick fireplace. *There. That ought to make Jane happy,* she thought.

"It's Gramma and Grampa!" Ava exclaimed. She stood in front of the fireplace and gazed at the drab church directory portrait.

Lexie went back to the box and pulled another framed photo from it. "Yep, and here's an even better, cuter picture." This one was of herself and Ava from last year's Christmas photo shoot, seated back-to-back in ugly sweaters and grinning goofily at the camera. Ava's blonde hair and blue eyes were a contrast to Lexie's dark hair and eyes; their identical smile was the only feature they had in common. *Is there such a thing as a sweater that doesn't show every hill and valley of my belly?* she wondered.

She placed the photo next to Paul and Jane and forced a smile for Ava. "Our bestest Christmas ever, right?"

Ava laughed and spun like a ballerina. "YES! 'Cept Santa didn't bring me a PUPPY like I asked!"

Lexie watched her daughter spin through the empty living room, blonde curls fanning out from her head, and her smile turned rueful. *She looks so like her dad.* The thought pierced her heart for the thousandth time, and tears tried to fight their way into her eyes. She blinked rapidly in an effort to hold them back. *Jake has no idea what he's missing.*

And then Lexie zoned out as the familiar internal battle between her pragmatic head and her sentimental heart began again.

Heart: *Maybe he needs a reminder.*

Head: *No. Have you forgotten what happened last time we called him?*

Heart: *Maybe all he needs is to see a picture of her. That would change his mind. How could it not? I could text him one of the pics I took at the zoo last weekend.*

Without realizing she was doing it, Lexie patted her legs looking for her phone.

Head: *You're kidding, right? Come on. Nothing is going to change Jake's mind. Especially not a picture of the kid he never wanted.*

Head: *You and I both know that Jake doesn't really care about anybody but himself.*

Heart (a tad stubbornly): *I want him to be a part of Ava's life. And...my life too.*

Head: *Never gonna happen. You're no longer useful to him.*

"Mommy?"

Lexie blinked, bringing the room and Ava back into focus. "Yes baby?"

"Were you hippopotamused again?" Ava asked. She had stopped pirouetting and was watching Lexie with a bemused look on her face.

"I think you mean hypnotized," Lexie said. "I guess so. I'm all right now. Should we go get some more boxes?"

"YEAH!" Ava bellowed and shot out the front door. Lexie followed. When they each came back in with another box, Lexie walked past the living room toward the kitchen. On the way she passed the stairs up to the second half-story and the bright dining room with its modern black metal and crystal chandelier. Lexie couldn't wait to host her first dinner party under that chandelier...as soon as she could afford a decent dining room table. She set her box on the kitchen counter and headed back the way she'd come, toward the front the door.

Something – or rather, the *absence* of something – caught her eye in the living room. She stopped and looked back. The mantel was bare; the photos she'd just put there had disappeared. She frowned. "What the hell?"

"What is it, Mommy?"

"The pictures I put on the fireplace. They're gone." She set her box down; still frowning, she went to the fireplace and looked around. She found the photos lying facedown on the floor. She squatted and picked them up.

"Are they broke, Mommy?" Ava watched her mom inspect the frames, brow furrowed with worry.

"No, they look okay." She stood and set the frames back in their places. "Weird, huh?"

"Yeah," Ava said.

"Come on, pumpkin. Let's try to get Mom's truck all emptied out before the movers come with all our furniture."

"OKAY!" Ava shot out the front door. Lexie followed her, smiling.

2

Finally, the movers were gone. The house was quiet. The beds were made, the TVs and coffeemaker plugged in, and the toothbrushes had new homes in each bathroom.

Lexie was famished, to the point that a headache had started creeping behind her eyes. "What do you say to a picnic right here on the living room floor, babydoll?" she asked Ava, who was sprawled on the couch with her tablet.

A perma-frown had settled over Ava's forehead as the afternoon wore on. Lexie chalked her crankiness up to the fact that they'd been on the go all day. "I'm hungry."

"Me too. How about a turkey sandwich?" Ava's favorite, sure to cheer her up.

"I don't want a sammich, Mommy," Ava whined. "I want pizza."

"I can't have pizza, babygirl. You know that." The headache ratcheted up a notch.

"You can just take the cheese off," Ava pointed out.

"Mmmm...floppy bread and red sauce. Sounds delicious."

Lexie's sarcasm was lost on Ava. "So we can get pizza?"

"No. We're getting sandwiches." Lexie went to the kitchen and lifted her purse from the cluttered countertop, then walked back through the living room toward the front door. "Come on, let's get in the car."

Ava stood stubbornly just outside the living room, next to the staircase that led to the master bedroom in the attic. Her little arms were crossed. "No."

Lexie turned toward Ava and assumed one of her Mom looks: this one said *Did you just say what I think I heard you say?* She gestured to the door. "Now."

"I said I don't want a sammich!" Ava screeched. She emphasized each word with a mighty stomp.

Temples throbbing, Lexie regarded her daughter like she was some new and exotic species of bug; this behavior was completely out of character for her sunny, precocious child. "Excuse me?"

Ava's scowl deepened, and her arms crossed a little tighter.

Something snapped in Lexie's brain. She went to Ava and grabbed her by the arm. "Get in the car. Now."

Ava jumped up and down and began to cry. "Noooo Mommy, let go of me, I DON'T WANT A SAMMICH!" Her voice shook with every jump.

Lexie dragged Ava, kicking and screaming, to the front door. "I SAID GET IN THE GODDAMN CAR! RIGHT NOW!" She swore she could feel her vocal cords tearing, she was shouting so loud. Her head felt like it might explode.

Something peculiar happened when they stepped through the front door and into the deepening summer dusklight. The strangest sensation came over Lexie – like static electricity had charged her blood and was coursing through her veins. Her knees buckled. She grabbed the iron handrail that lined each side of the concrete steps to keep from collapsing. Ava stopped screaming and her body went limp; Lexie barely caught her before she fell down the steps.

Lexie sat for a moment with her unconscious daughter in her arms, blinking and trying to understand what had just happened. Her legs felt like limp noodles; she wasn't sure they would support her weight if she tried to stand up. Strength gradually returned to her legs, but her brain felt...deflated. Sort of like a balloon that rapidly lost its air.

Ava stirred and her eyes fluttered open. She looked around with her typical curiosity; the stubborn, irascible Ava from a few moments ago was gone. "I'm hungry," she announced. "Can we get sammiches?"

Lexie helped Ava sit up, then attempted to stand. Her body seemed to be working as expected, much to her relief. She reshouldered her purse and locked the front door with her key. "Yes, baby. Let's go."

Later, after their living room picnic (something that Lexie and Ava would never be allowed to do at Paul and Jane's house) complete with twelve-inch sub sandwiches plus chips and fountain drinks, Lexie put Ava to bed with no argument at all. Ava watched with heavy-lidded eyes as Lexie made sure the closet door was closed and the nightlight was on, and then Lexie tucked the girl in and kissed her goodnight. *She's already asleep,* Lexie thought fondly as she quietly closed Ava's bedroom door.

Lexie was exhausted too, but she decided to decompress with some quiet time and a glass of wine. She dug a bottle of pinot noir out of a box, poured some into a glass foraged from another box, and sat on the couch in the living room. The evening light filtering through the unadorned picture window gave the room a gray hue that Lexie found comforting, like a fuzzy warm blanket. She looked around, held her glass in the air as if toasting the gods of good fortune, and took a sip. Her stomach immediately burst into flame.

"Whoa," she muttered, and placed the hand not holding her wine on her sternum. She picked up the bottle and looked again at the label, confirming that it was the pinot noir she always kept on hand. She hadn't had heartburn this bad since she was pregnant with Ava.

She sat in the dark and listened to the house make its old-house clicking and popping noises. She took another sip of wine, which seemed to fan the flames in her gut and made her belch. Acid licked at the back of her throat. She swallowed it back and turned her thoughts to the strange events that closed out their otherwise productive day. Ava's fainting episode on the front stoop was especially concerning.

I wonder what that was all about, she thought. *Ava has never thrown a tantrum like that before. Ever. And I can't believe I screamed at her like that.* Hot shame crawled up Lexie's neck and face. *I swore when she was born that I would never do that, no matter how overwhelmed I become.* The familiar rage at Ava's father started percolating in Lexie's chest; as far as Lexie was concerned, Jake Stratton was not only the reason she had Ava, but the reason she always felt like she struggled as a single mom. This was not the path she would have chosen for herself.

A noise that was different from the usual old-house pops and clicks she'd been hearing stopped her train of thought dead on its tracks.

It was a long, drawn-out creak. Like someone slowly stepping on an ancient wood floor. The sound made the hairs on Lexie's neck stand up.

There was another creak.

Lexie set her wineglass on a cluttered table and cocked her head, listening. Her heart pounded.

Another creak. It sounded to Lexie like someone was creeping down the stairs from the attic. Or up the stairs. "Ava?" Lexie called. "Is that you, pumpkin?"

No answer.

Lexie got up from the couch and tiptoed through the dark to the attic stairs. She peered up and saw nothing but pitch blackness at the top; she flipped the switch and then remembered that the light bulb at the top of the stairs was burned out. Suddenly she wished she'd left the lamp next to her bed turned on.

She doubled back and was headed down the hallway to Ava's room when two loud *SMACK*s startled her. Lexie ran back to the living room, heart racing. She flipped on a light, temporarily blinding herself; once her eyes adjusted, she could see right away what was amiss.

"Damn it," Lexie said. She went to the fireplace and picked the family photos up off the floor again. They had made the sound she'd heard when they landed on the hard oak floor. A horizontal crack in the glass stretched right through the middle of Paul's and Jane's faces. "These fucking things keep falling on the floor. Now this one's broken," she muttered. Out of patience and too tired to care, she tossed the frames on the coffee table and decided to go to bed.

She turned off the living room light and cautiously approached the stairs to the attic. She pulled her phone out of her jeans pocket and used it as a flashlight; the stairs were clear, no ghost or goblin in sight. Lexie took a deep breath and ascended.

At the top, Lexie felt her way to the bathroom and turned on the light. The half-story attic space had been converted into a cozy master suite. The long, narrow room with angled ceilings and knee-height walls along the sides was just large enough to accommodate a queen-sized bed under a window on one end and a dresser and small chair on the other. The small half bathroom jutted from the middle of the room at a ninety degree angle.

She reflected on the craziness of the day as she brushed her teeth, and all she wanted was to crawl into her own bed and fall into a deep, dreamless sleep. *Tomorrow we start anew.*

3

Lexie did not have the restful sleep she'd hoped for. Every time she drifted off, powerful images of an angry little girl and a sad little boy – twins? – flickered into her dreams, startling her awake with a heavy heart and a strange desire to cry.

She awoke for the final time when her alarm went off at 4:00 in the morning. Her eyes felt heavy and gritty as she dressed for the day in her medical scrubs and padded downstairs to start the coffee and wake Ava. *It's going to be a long Tuesday*, she thought, and yawned.

Ava was still out cold, but absolutely tangled up in her blankets as if she'd spent all night tossing and turning like Lexie had. It hurt Lexie's heart to wake her. In the dim glow of the nightlight, she smoothed Ava's messy hair away from her face and whispered, "Good morning, babygirl."

Ava stirred, and her eyes fluttered open. She blinked a couple times and finally focused on Lexie's face. "Hi Mommy," she mumbled.

"Time to get up. You're going to Cindy's today."

"Okay." Ava unwound herself from her covers, then slid out of bed and onto the floor while Lexie pulled an outfit for the day out of a box next to Ava's pink dresser. She noticed that

Ava's closet door was ajar. *That's odd*, Lexie thought. *I'm positive I closed that when Ava went to bed last night.* She peeked inside, saw that the closet was still empty, then closed the door again and gave it a little tug to make sure the latch was completely engaged.

As she got herself and Ava ready for the day, Lexie realized she should have taken an extra day or two off work to unpack and settle in. Now she was spending extra time to frantically dig through boxes to find everything she needed. A headache was beginning to form like a summer storm behind her tired eyes.

"I'm an eel," Ava said from the floor, where she lay prone with her arms clamped to her sides. "We learned about them at Cindy's, they're slippery!" She wiggled to show how eel-like she was.

Lexie forced a smile. "Come on, you need to get dressed."

While Ava dressed, Lexie made her way to the kitchen and her coffeemaker. She dug through another box until she finally found what she was looking for: a giant 100-ounce insulated travel mug with a faded "Cumm & Go" logo printed on the side. She'd grabbed it during a road trip fuel stop in Iowa many moons ago, unable to resist its sheer size and the juvenile humor behind the gas station's name. She had used it almost daily ever since. That mug, which had lasted longer in her life than the boy she'd been road-tripping with, was enough to keep Lexie caffeinated for an entire twelve-hour shift when properly filled with black coffee. She hoped it would keep the steadily increasing throbbing in her temples at bay enough to focus on her work.

She was fortunate; the headache eased as she left the house and loaded her mug, her kid, and her kid's bag of clothes and toys into her car and drove off into the darkness to Cindy's daycare.

Cindy lived less than two miles from Lexie, just a couple blocks from the hospital where Lexie worked as an operating room nurse. Cindy's specialty was caring for the children of medical professionals who worked long hours at the hospital. She was set up to watch up to four kids for up to twenty-four hours at a time, and she didn't come cheap. But to Lexie she was worth every single penny.

She pulled up to the curb in front of Cindy's house, her headlights carving a pair of bright cones in the predawn darkness. As soon as Lexie unfastened Ava's restraints, the girl shot out of the car and ran up the sidewalk toward the front door. "HI CINDY!" she bellowed.

Lexie winced at Ava's angelic little voice echoing off the quiet houses around them. "Ava!" she called in a sort of loud, hoarse whisper. "Be quiet! People are sleeping!"

The front door opened and Cindy stood there, framed by the interior light and dressed in her usual early morning leggings and oversized sweatshirt. Ava barreled into her; she scooped the girl up in a giant bear hug and took her inside. Lexie didn't know exactly how old Cindy was – she guessed late fifties or early sixties – but she marveled at the energy the woman had. She could easily keep up with her charges all day and night, and somehow find the energy to bake a couple dozen cookies and rearrange all the furniture in her living room. She walked into Cindy's house –

which was remarkably similar to her own – and found them on the couch. Ava sat on Cindy's lap, and they were deep in conversation about what Ava did this weekend.

"Our new house is smaller than Gramma and Grampa's big house, but we have our own fridgenator, and our own baffrooms, and even a big backyard!" Ava said, throwing her little arms out to her sides to illustrate just how big the backyard was.

"Is that right?" Cindy exclaimed, brushing her silver hair, cut in a wedge, from her forehead and tossing Lexie an amused look. Lexie smiled, shook her head, and set Ava's things on the floor just inside the door.

"Is Tyler here?" Ava inquired, anxious to see her best buddy.

"He's upstairs sleeping," Cindy said. She had converted her entire upper half-story into her daycare facility, complete with a bedroom with four bunkbeds, a playroom, and a full bathroom. "So you and I are going to have a little breakfast, and then we'll go see if those lazies are ready to get up."

"Pancakes, please," Ava said.

"You got it, kiddo." Cindy moved Ava from her lap to standing on the floor. "But give your Mom a hug first, because she has to go to work."

Ava ran to Lexie and threw her arms around her waist. "Bye Mommy, I love you."

"I love you too, babycakes. I'll see you after dinner, okay?"

"Okay!" Ava was already on her way to Cindy's large kitchen table to sit and await her breakfast.

Lexie waved goodbye to Cindy and went to work. Her morning was typical, assisting with an appendectomy on a little girl about Ava's age and a cholecystectomy, or gallbladder removal. Halfway through her twelve-hour shift she scrubbed out and headed to the hospital's staff cafeteria for lunch, accompanied by Sam Biondi, one of the other nurses in surgery that day.

They only had thirty minutes, so Lexie headed for the grab-n-go line and took her premade Cobb salad, packet of ranch dressing, and bottle of lemonade to a table in the corner farthest from the door and sat. She was ravenous; she'd forgotten to eat breakfast.

Sam appeared, holding a tray with a cup of chili and a packet of oyster crackers, and sat next to Lexie. "You know what I don't get?"

"What?" Lexie muffled through a bite of salad.

"Why Dr. Sloop has to be such a sexist jerk." Sam shook her head.

"Sloop. Isn't he the ENT?"

"Yeah. Routine tonsillectomy first thing this morning, and every time he called for an instrument or suction, I was 'sweetheart.' Pisses me off." Sam spooned steaming chili into her mouth, then popped an oyster cracker.

Lexie took a sip of lemonade. "Yeah, I know that guy. One time I said something about how hard it was to find a vein in a patient's arm because she was so overweight, and he told me I could stand to lose a few pounds myself."

Sam lowered her spoon. "Are you serious?"

Lexie nodded, teeth clenched. "Yep. I know exactly how you feel. He talks to you like you're eight years old and makes you feel about three feet high."

Sam sighed. "Doctors can be such assholes."

Lexie was about to wholeheartedly agree when the doors clacked open and the man who sat at the tippy top of Lexie's list of all-time asshole doctors strode into the cafeteria. Her heart stopped dead in her chest.

It was Jake Stratton, wearing clean light blue scrubs and gray running shoes. He moved quickly, with the easy confidence of the naturally athletic; Lexie would not be surprised if he'd gotten up early and run ten miles before coming to work. The surgical cap he'd worn during an earlier procedure had flattened the wavy blond hair his daughter inherited. Heart pounding and stomach churning – reminiscent of last night's crippling heartburn – she watched him make his way to the food lines, where he disappeared behind a soft drink cooler.

"Lex?" Sam said. "You all right?"

Lexie blinked. "Huh?"

"You were going to say something, and then your face went white. Do you know that guy?"

Lexie nodded. "Yeah. I've – ah, I've worked with him. I didn't know he was operating here again. I thought his clinic switched to doing all of its procedures at Methodist a few years ago."

"He's a surgeon?"

"Orthopedics."

Sam's green eyes studied Lexie's face carefully. "What's going on?"

What Lexie wanted to say: *Oh, nothing. It started with too-long, meaningful looks and "accidental" touches over unconscious patients. Then it was the occasional shared coffee break. Then grabbing drinks at the Eagle's Nest after shift. Until finally I brought him home with me one night after too many vodka cranberry cocktails. I didn't know he was married until it was too late.*

What Lexie actually said: "It's complicated."

Jake emerged from the food area holding a tray; Lexie watched him make his way to a table in the center of the dining room. Her heart slammed painfully against her ribcage. She took a deep breath, trying to steady her heart and her nerves.

"Complicated how?" Sam asked.

Lexie barely heard her. "Excuse me." Propelled by angry energy, she marched to Jake's table and stopped next to the chair directly across from him. Her heart pounded in her throat, forcing her to clear it with a low *ahem* before she could croak, "Is this seat taken?"

Jake glanced up. He froze in the act of removing the pickles from his hamburger.

Lexie didn't wait for an invitation. She pulled the chair out and sat. She folded her hands on the table to stop their trembling and regarded Jake with an expression she hoped was strong and steady – the opposite of what her body was currently doing. She was glad her knees were hidden under the table, where he couldn't see them shaking. His eyes, impossibly blue, still made her weak.

"Lex." Jake slowly lowered his hands to the table and stared at her in shock.

"Jake."

"What – what are you doing here?" His eyes flicked back and forth, up and down over her face as if he could not believe what he was seeing.

"I still work here," she said shortly. "I might ask the same about you. I can't believe you would show your face here again after the stunt you pulled."

Jake's face reddened. "I don't –"

Lexie held a hand up. "Spare me the bullshit, Jake. You disappeared. You switched hospitals. You changed your phone number. You're a fucking coward." Lexie had spent countless hours over the last five years rehearsing what she would say to Jake if she ever saw him again; none of this was in her script. She was acting on pure gut feeling, but she felt sure of herself.

Jake sat back in his chair and folded his arms across his chest.

Lexie leaned over the table. "You abandoned me, and you abandoned your daughter."

Jake's eyes widened. "You had the baby?"

"Of course I had the baby!" Lexie shouted, and hit the table with the palm of her hand. The sound was loud enough to silence the entire dining room.

Jake looked around and gestured frantically with both hands. "Sshh...would you be quiet, for god's sake?"

It was Lexie's turn to sit back and cross her arms. She glared at Jake. The hurt and the anger that had simmered under her surface for so long had finally boiled over.

Jake pushed his tray out of the way and hunched over the table so he could speak in a lower voice. "What the fuck is wrong with you?" His deep baritone didn't quite jibe with his baby blue eyes.

Lexie shrugged. "You first."

"Look. I can appreciate your situation, Lex. I really can. However. I already have a wife and kids..."

"A fact that would have been good to know before we slept together," Lexie pointed out.

It was Jake's turn to glare. "So I'm sure you can appreciate my situation."

"Your...situation." Distaste dripped from her words like bitter molasses.

"Kara doesn't know I cheated on her. If she finds out, she'll make good on fifteen years' worth of threats and take the boys and half of everything I own."

Lexie rolled her eyes. "So that's how you justify not being a part of your daughter's life. I always wondered."

Jake sat back in his chair again and held his hands up at shoulder height. "Hey. You decided all on your own to have the baby, Lex. Nobody forced you to have it."

The edges of Lexie's vision flashed red. "She is not an *it*, Jake," she snarled. "She is a little girl. *Your* little girl."

"What do you want, Lex? Money? Is that it?"

Incredulous, Lexie shook her head. "All I want is for you to be a part of your daughter's life, Jake. She deserves to know her father."

"Yeah. That's not going to happen." Jake pulled his tray back in front of him and resumed removing the pickles from his burger. "I'll write you a check." He looked up and coldly held Lexie's gaze with his blue eyes. "And then I never want to see your face again."

Lexie blinked to keep the tears back. *Cannot cry in front of him.* "Keep your fucking money. You don't want be in your kid's life? Fine." She stood and slid her chair back under the table. "Your daughter is an extraordinary little human. She has your blue eyes and wavy blonde hair. She loves sub sandwiches and pepperoni pizza and dancing like a ballerina. She's smart as a whip, and she can already read *If You Give A Mouse a Cookie* cover to cover. It's your fucking loss." She took a couple steps toward her table, where Sam sat watching with her eyes wide and mouth ajar, then turned back. "Oh. By the way. Her name is Ava. Ava Jacoba Novak."

Something in Jake's eyes changed subtly. The first tinges of regret, maybe? Satisfied, Lexie said, "It's too bad you'll never know her."

She turned and went back to her table. She sat in front of her partially-eaten salad and covered her hot cheeks with her hands. "Holy shit." Her voice cracked with the tears that threatened to burst their dam again. "Holy shit. I can't believe it."

Sam's eyes followed Jake as he quickly walked out of the dining room, then turned to Lexie. "Okay. You want to tell me what the hell just happened?"

Lexie took a deep breath, trying to steady her jackrabbit heart. Her eyes felt gritty. She shook her head. "Like I said, it's complicated." She looked at her watch, then started piling her lunch back on her tray. "It's a story that should be told over a glass of wine rather than a half-eaten salad with only about seven minutes before we have to scrub back in."

"Man," Sam said, picking up her own tray. "I've known you for, what, two or three years now? I had no idea there was such drama in your life."

Lexie snorted and dumped her tray in the waste bin. "Trust me, my life is not that exciting."

"Um. You had a baby with a hot doctor, that much I did hear. The very definition of drama." Sam said.

"We'd better walk fast or we're going to be late," Lexie said. She didn't know what was on her schedule for the second half of the day, but she was glad to have work to distract her.

Too much to think about.

4

As soon as Lexie clocked out at 6:00 p.m. and climbed into her car, the tears she'd been holding back all afternoon finally came like a tidal wave. She leaned back in her seat, covered her face with her hands, and wailed like her heart was being ripped from her chest. Her confrontation with Jake had not gone as she'd always imagined it would. Her Head had been right all along. The sight of Lexie and the mention of Ava's name did not convince Jake that he had made a huge mistake. He was not inclined to make room for them in his life. He wasn't interested in meeting, or even acknowledging, his fourth child. His only daughter.

She cried for Ava, who, through absolutely no fault of her own, would grow up without ever knowing her father. Even though it was Jake's choice, Lexie felt like she carried some of the blame too; she had chosen to bring Ava into this world knowing she'd likely be raising the child on her own. At the same time, she'd spent five years naïvely hoping he'd come around. All those hopes were dashed today, and her heart broken all over again.

Told you so, her Head whispered.

After several minutes the sobs subsided, leaving a snotty nose, swollen eyes, and hiccups in their wake. Lexie dug a couple tissues out of her purse, blew her nose, and wiped her face – she could not let Ava see her like this.

She glanced at her watch at the thought of Ava. "Shit." She fumbled her keys out of her purse and started the Explorer.

A few minutes later, feeling reasonably put back together, she pulled up in front of Cindy's house. Ava was drawing around Katelyn's sprawled body on the sidewalk with chalk while Cindy kept watch from a chair in the grass.

"HI MOMMY!" Ava bugled. "Look! I'm drawing Katy's syncopation!"

"Silhouette," Cindy corrected her.

"Good job, babydoll!" Lexie called as she walked through the grass toward the front door.

Cindy stopped her with an extended arm. "You okay, hon?"

Lexie looked at the ground and nodded. "Yeah. Long day, I guess."

Cindy retracted her arm, although she didn't look quite convinced.

Lexie went inside and gathered all of Ava's things. "Come on, Ava, we've got to get home," she called as she stepped back out into the yard.

"Okay!" Ava gave Katelyn a hug and then ran for the car. "Bye Katy! Bye Cindy!"

Ava never stopped talking in the car on the way home. By the time Lexie pulled into the back alley and parked outside the garage, she knew what Cindy served on her pancakes ("She said I couldn't have any more chockitchips"), who can count higher

("Tyler said he can count to TWENTY-FIVE, but he skipped a bunch of numbers so he's a cheater"), and how long today's nap was ("When I woke up Cindy asked me how my three-hour tour was, what does that mean?").

"Let's go inside and see what I can scrounge up for dinner. I'm starving." The half salad at lunch was the only thing she'd eaten all day.

Lexie unlocked the door and stepped inside; her empty stomach twisted in her gut and she gave a hot belch; the heartburn was back. She walked into the kitchen and looked around at the mess of boxes; she realized, rather belatedly, that she had no food in the house.

Ava's voice echoed from somewhere else in the house: "Mommy! I'm hungry!"

"Yes, Ava, I'm aware of that," Lexie called back from between clenched teeth. "I'm working on it."

Ava stomped into the kitchen. If Lexie were in a better mood, Ava's little sparkly pink cowboy boots would have made her smile. Right now she wanted to rip them off the girl's feet and throw them into the street.

Instead she listlessly poked around in random open boxes, hoping to find a lost box of spaghetti and jar of sauce, or something she could cook.

"I WANT PIZZA!" Ava bellowed, a mighty scowl on her tiny face.

Lexie could actually feel her blood pressure rising. The pain in her head throbbed to her heartbeat. A fog drifted into her conscious mind, weighing her regular jumble of thoughts down like a heavy blanket. Lexie welcomed the silence; without all that noise in her head, she could *focus*. She could make *decisions*. She could put that little shit in her *place*.

Ignoring Ava's outburst, Lexie opened a smallish box labeled UTENSILS. She pushed aside an assortment of large spoons, a whisk, several rubber spatulas...and found what she knew she would: the expensive kitchen knives she'd treated herself to back when she was childless and carefree.

A mischievous gleam ran along the wicked sharp blade of the large chef knife. She carefully took hold of the black handle and lifted it from the box. It had a sinister weight to it that made Lexie smile.

If I'm quick, she won't feel a thing. The thought, not quite her own but welcome just the same, floated unimpeded across the cavernous, foggy silence of Lexie's mind. Her smile stretched across her face, and she turned toward her daughter.

When Ava saw the large knife in her mother's hand, her eyes went wide. "What are you doing, Mommy? MOMMY!"

The panic in Ava's voice pierced the heavy fog in Lexie's head, and it broke apart like a summer thunderstorm. Lexie blinked and shook her head. "What?"

"Put it down, Mommy! Put it down!" Ava screeched, backing away from Lexie.

Confused, Lexie looked down and saw that she was holding her chef knife her clenched fist. She gasped and dropped the knife, and it clattered on the ceramic tile floor. She covered her mouth and nose with both of her hands. "Oh god, what was I doing?"

"Were you going to hurt me?" Ava's eyes brimmed with tears.

"No, baby. No, no, no." Lexie fell to her knees and embraced Ava. Pain still pulsed in her head, but at least she was thinking clearly again. "I don't know what came over me. I'm sorry."

Ava leaned her head against Lexie's shoulder. "It's okay, Mommy."

Lexie took a deep breath and covered her forehead with a hand – and then inspiration struck. "Come on, kid. We're going outside. We'll order a pizza and eat it on the picnic table."

Normally the idea of a picnic in the backyard would send Ava into a fit of cheers and jumps; she just shrugged and trudged to the back door. Lexie grabbed her phone out of her purse and followed her. She felt a faint *zing* in her head when she stepped outside, and her stomach quieted. She sat at the picnic table and took another deep breath, then called and placed an order for a small cheese pizza for Ava and a half dozen chicken wings with a salad for herself. Then, smiling, she watched a much perkier Ava run in a big circle with her arms straight out at her sides, then collapse on the lawn and roll around in the fairly shaggy green grass.

"What in the hell did you give her?" An unfamiliar voice startled her a bit, and she turned. A man stood on the other side of the chainlink fence that divided her backyard from the next door neighbor's. He appeared to be a few years older than Lexie, well-built and of average height, and wore a ballcap turned backward and a pair of reflective sport sunglasses. His gray t-shirt did a poor job of hiding his chest and arm muscles. He held a garden trowel in one hand and watched Ava with an amused look on his scruffy face.

Lexie chuckled. "Oh, this is her normal setting. The only time she sits still is when she's charging at night."

The man smiled, revealing strong, slightly uneven teeth. "You got a wireless model, then. Very modern." His throaty voice reminded her of some actor she couldn't quite place.

Lexie stood and moved closer to the fence, smiling. "Worth every penny."

"I'm Ryan Laughlin," he said, transferring the trowel to his other hand so he could extend his right hand over the fence. "I live there." He pointed the trowel at the blue house next door.

She shook his hand and said, "I'm Alexis Novak. Everybody but my mom calls me Lexie." She gestured toward Ava, who had launched into a solo game of her own invention, which she called Pirate Princess Fairy Dogs. Lexie could never tell if it was so much a game as it was Ava prancing around the yard, pretending to lead a gaggle of chihuahuas on sparkling leashes. "That's my daughter Ava."

"Welcome to the neighborhood, Lexie and Ava." He watched Ava for a moment longer. "Appears she has an active imagination."

"You have no idea," Lexie said, gazing fondly at her daughter.

"How's it going in the house so far? Getting settled all right?"

Lexie shrugged. "It's only day two, so kind of hard to say right now. I didn't get a ton of sleep last night." The mere mention of it made her yawn. "Sorry. Old house, strange noises, you know how it goes."

Ryan nodded. "I get it."

"Have you lived here long, Ryan?"

"Just about six years now," he said. "I bought this place right after my divorce, and it's taken me that long to remodel it. Did all the work myself." She sounded like a proud papa.

Impressed, Lexie said, "Wow. Do you have a day job too?"

"Yes, and that's why it's taken so long to fix the house up. I teach physical education and coach football at Edison High School over in Northeast."

Lexie smiled and said in that peculiar Minnesota way, "Summer break for you then, huh?"

Ryan nodded. "Yep." He held up his trowel. "Hoping to get some landscaping done over the next few weeks. What do you do for work, Lexie?"

"I'm an operating room nurse at North Memorial Hospital," she said. "We moved here because it's so much closer."

"Where did you come from?"

"Minnetonka."

Ryan nodded. "And your husband? What does he do?"

"Oh. No husband." A nervous laugh escaped Lexie. "Ava and I lived with my mom and dad. It...it's a long story."

"Mommy!" Ava stood on the sidewalk and pointed toward the front yard. "I think the pizza man is here!"

Lexie saw a small red coupe sitting at the curb and smiled at Ryan. "Excuse me, I'll be right back." She grabbed her wallet on her way through the house and paid the pimply teenaged delivery guy. On her way through the house to the back door, a small girl's voice stopped her dead in her tracks. It was so clear that at first Lexie looked to her left to see who was standing next to her.

"We can't have a picnic without Michael, Mama."

Lexie blinked and scanned the kitchen for the source of the voice. Although she was quite sure Ava was still in the backyard, she tentatively called her daughter's name. A bolt of white pain shot through her head like a meteor streaking across the sky. Lexie cried out and covered her eyes with her free hand.

Then the pain was gone as suddenly as it had come. She slowly moved her hand away from her eyes and blinked. *What the fuck was that?* Her legs felt wobbly. Her racing heart started to slow. She went to the kitchen sink and splashed cold water on her hot face.

"Where are you, Mommy?" Ava's voice drifted in through the back screen door.

"I'm coming, babydoll." Lexie wiped the excess water from her cheeks with a towel, then took the food outside to the backyard picnic table.

Ava was standing at the fence, inviting Ryan over for dinner. "We're having pizza. And chicken wings!"

Ryan grinned at Lexie. Something in his eyes faltered when he looked at Lexie's face, but the smile stayed on.

I'm sure I look like a complete wreck, Lexie thought, then smiled back and held the boxes up. "I don't have much, but we're happy to share."

Ryan considered for a moment, then deftly hopped over the four-foot fence. He sat on the bench next to Lexie and took off his sunglasses, sliding them on top of the crown of his cap. His eyes were a deep chocolate brown that Lexie found entrancing. "Thank you," he said.

Lexie arranged the boxes on the table and pulled paper plates and napkins from a paper bag while she listened to Ryan and Ava talk.

"How old are you, Ava?" Ryan asked.

Ava held up her thumb, pointer, and middle fingers. "I'm four," she said.

"Wow, that's pretty awesome," Ryan said, grinning again. "What's your favorite food? Is it pizza?" He gestured at the pizza box in front of Ava.

"Yes, and mac and cheese. I like them both the same."

Ryan nodded. "I like mac and cheese too. How come you're not having mac and cheese for dinner?"

"My mommy can't eat mac and cheese," Ava said. Then she leaned across the table and said in the tone of someone sharing confidential information, "She's lab-ratory installation."

"Lactose intolerant," Lexie corrected her.

"She is?" Ryan asked conspiratorially. "Well, I'll tell you what. Now that we're neighbors, maybe someday you can come to my house for lunch. We'll have mac and cheese, and put some extra cheese in it too."

"YAAAAYYY!" Ava jumped up from the table and ran in another big circle with her arms straight out at her sides, then collapsed on the lawn and rolled around in the grass.

"Come on, pumpkin, your food is ready. I know you're hungry."

Ava hopped up to standing and faced Lexie, pulling a pretend pair of sunglasses down her snub of a nose with one finger. "Yes, dahling, I'm stahving."

Lexie and Ryan laughed. "Is that how pirate princesses talk these days?" Lexie asked.

"No, silly, it's how souvenirs in New York talk," Ava said. "Like Holly Golightly."

"Do you mean socialites?" Lexie asked.

"That's what I said," Ava said, and took a bite of cheese pizza.

"I take it she's been watching Breakfast at Tiffany's," Ryan said, still grinning.

"It's her favorite movie," Lexie said. She held up her carton of chicken wings in front of Ryan, who took one and thanked her. "I don't think she understands anything going on in the movie, but she just sits and stares at Audrey Hepburn. Sometimes I'll catch her walking around with a pencil sticking out of her mouth, pretending it's Holly Golightly's cigarette holder. It's pretty cute, actually."

"Call me Holly from now on, okay Mommy?" Ava had already moved on to her second piece of pizza.

Lexie could relate; she had demolished half of her salad. "I'm not sure I can remember, but I'll try."

"Holly it is," Ryan declared. He gestured toward his yard. "I'm going to go finish cleaning up my pesky hostas." His smile climbed all the way up his face and settled in his eyes, crinkling the outside corners adorably.

She smiled back, her heart skipping a beat or two. "Sounds like a plan. Thanks for saying hi; it's nice to meet a new neighbor."

Ryan gave her a nod. "It sure is. Thanks for the chicken wing." He turned to Ava. "Bye Holly. Will I see you around?"

"Of course, dahling," Ava declared, then bit into her third slice of pizza.

Ryan shot Lexie another grin and a quick wave, then hopped back over the chainlink fence, walked around his house, and disappeared.

Lexie and Ava ate in silence for a few seconds, then Ava said, "He's verrrry nice."

Lexie nodded and gazed at Ryan's house without really seeing it; she was thinking about his chocolate brown eyes, and how easy it might be to get lost in them. "He sure seems to be, doesn't he?"

Ava set her half-eaten slice of pizza on the table and yawned. "I'm tired, Mommy."

Lexie felt the stress of the day in every one of her joints. Her arms and legs still trembled with adrenaline left over from the episode in the kitchen. After that she wasn't at all sure that going back inside was a good idea, but she didn't really have another option; going back to Paul and Jane's house in the suburbs was out of the question. *I suppose we'll give it a shot*, she thought, glancing at the western horizon. *Eight o'clock-ish, close enough.* "Me too, babydoll. Let's pick up this stuff and go to bed."

She hoped tonight would be less eventful – and more restful – than last night.

5

Lexie slept fitfully again, her dreams plagued by the same flickering images of the little girl and little boy. The images were snippets; scratchy, black and white, and they looked like they came from old film reel movies. They flashed back and forth to reveal each child in a different moment in time: the little boy sitting on a tricycle, the little girl on a swing. The children, both with identical blond bowl haircuts – one in a little calico dress with a ruffled collar, the other in a red t-shirt and shorts – were never pictured together. Always separately.

Lexie tossed and turned all night, with a pit of churning lava in her stomach and that strange, inexplicable desire to cry. Not just cry; weep. Sob. As if a phantom sadness might sweep her away like a tsunami. She awoke for the last time at 5:00 a.m. No alarm today; it was Wednesday, her day off. She dragged herself into the bathroom and checked in the mirror to make sure she did not have tiny weights tied to each of her eyelashes.

Lexie wrapped her robe around her and stumbled downstairs to the kitchen. She regarded the coffeemaker for a moment, then decided against the usual cup of joe; her stomach felt like she'd had burning embers instead of chicken and salad for dinner. She dug a glass out of a box and filled it from the kitchen faucet. A couple gulps of cold water calmed the fire in her belly somewhat. She took her glass to the living room and sat on the couch. The sky outside her picture window was slowly transforming from the gray of dawn to the orange and pink of a summer sunrise. She gazed around the room, its carefully neutral beige walls still bare, marveling at the fact that she finally had a place of her own again after living in her parents' house for five very long years.

I did what I had to do for my baby, but man, giving up my apartment and moving into Mom & Dad's basement was a bitter pill to swallow. Her stomach reignited, and Lexie took another sip of water in an effort to extinguish the flames. *Fucking Jake. Knocks me up and then leaves me to deal with it all on my own.* Stomach churning, she thought back to when it all started: when she invited him to see a band with her and a few friends at the Eagle's Nest one Saturday night.

Excerpt from Lexie's diary: November 8, 2015

Ugh. I haven't spent such a hungover day in a long time. I'm feeling better now, but man, what a harsh day. This is why I don't drink like that much anymore.

I have so much on my mind after the events of last night.

I don't know how much real estate I've devoted to the subject of Jake Stratton in these pages. I wouldn't be surprised if it hasn't been much, since he pretty much qualifies as an untouchable in my mind. We've known each other a couple years now, and we've always gotten along so well. He and I had an instant connection the moment we met. Our working relationship has evolved into a great friendship. And, I must admit, I developed a bit of a crush on him. More than once over the years I wished he would see me as more than just a friend, you know?

I hang out with him, and talk to him, and I watch him, and I can't help but love him. He's just such a nice, genuine, sweet, funny guy. I've noticed that the dynamics between Jake and me have subtly changed over the last couple months, but I didn't think anything of it. Truly. He started dropping strange comments ("As usual, I am putty in your hands."), and I played along, felt flattered, but didn't put any stock into them. But they did get me thinking, sort of roused my dormant feelings for him.

Tell you what. The stakes just went up. Big time. Huge.

Earlier this week, while Jake and I were having drinks at the Eagle's Nest, I had a brainstorm: he should come out with me and Sarah and Jessica on Saturday to see our favorite band. So invited him out, and he happily said he'd come.

By the time he got there last night I was well on my way to wasted. Him coming along and buying Jägermeister shots and more drinks didn't help. "I was hoping to get you loaded so I can take advantage of you," he said. "I'm most of the way there," I told him. I was really excited to see him, gave him a huge hug when I turned in my chair to find him standing behind me. And from that moment on it was pretty fucking obvious that he wanted me, and that I wanted him.

I don't remember much from the last hour or so at the bar. I do remember dancing with him there at the table. He was behind me, and I leaned against him and moved to the music. His hands roamed over my body, my arms, my hands as I moved. We kissed a couple times. I was completely focused on Jake. I was also completely drunk. After all that fooling around, both of us totally turned on, he brought me home.

And we made love. Many times. What strikes me most about it is how sweet and attentive he was. During sex, yes, but also in general. I got sick and puked...I was so sick I couldn't even leave the bed. He was there with something for me to puke into, and after going out to dump it, he came back with a wet towel for my face. He never stopped kissing me, never took his hands off me.

He was, and is, amazing. I could imagine going home to that every night.

We got up early so he could take me back to my car and then head home. I saw him off before coming home to crash again. I can still smell him in my bed.

I'm not yet sure how I really feel about what's happened. It doesn't change how I feel about him, but it does complicate things. I do want to do that with him, lots more, and I do remember him saying the same. It felt wonderful to hold him in my arms, to feel his lips caress my body. I don't know that it's right, because we work so closely together, but I think that's something else I need to come to terms with. It's a delicate balance, and maybe it's not about that. Maybe it's about saying "fuck it" and doing what feels good for me. And that felt damn good.

Excerpt from Lexie's diary: November 15, 2015

Jake and I met up last night for a couple drinks, and had a really good talk. And then he came over last night and rocked my fucking world. I couldn't wait to experience him as a sober woman, and every moment was fantastic.

Afterward, while we cuddled, I asked him what he thought about maybe making things between him and me official. He asked me what my hurry was, weren't we just having fun? Then he said that we can't be seen together at work. I asked him why, and he gave me some long, rambling answer saying it's because we work together and hospital policies and who knows what else. It seemed a little weird, but I went along with it and said okay. But I gotta be honest, I felt kind of icky. I certainly do hope we aren't jeopardizing our friendship by doing this, and of course I hope it'll grow into something more.

Unfortunately, I can't know that now. Can't know the end of the game without fucking playing it. I made the decision, the choice, and now I gotta ride it out. And maybe ride him out in the process, haha.

Lexie sighed and took another drink of water from her glass as she remembered the internal battle she constantly fought with herself over whether or not she was doing the right thing, carrying on with Jake. She didn't recognize the signs that she was being played. Not yet. All she saw was someone who seemed to want her and made her feel good, but he still seemed somehow unavailable. Just when she'd finally settled on feeling okay about their affair, she missed her period – and everything changed. The day she confronted him was one she would never forget.

Lexie had been looking for Jake at the hospital for nearly a week; this was a conversation that needed to be had face-to-face, no matter what his issues were about being seen with her around the hospital. Finally she found him in the staff cafeteria, eating a turkey sandwich with the gusto of someone accustomed to short meal breaks and looking at his phone. Hands shaking and heart pounding, Lexie slid into the chair next to him. The steaming bowl on her tray might as well have been filled with sawdust instead of chicken noodle soup, for all the appetite she had.

"Hey," she said quietly.

Jake looked up, his blue eyes meeting hers and sending a shockwave through her. Her mind flashed back to the last night they spent together, how intense his eyes had been as they'd made love, and warmth flooded her entire body.

And then she remembered why she was sitting there next to him. Her blood turned to ice and her heart slammed in her chest.

He leaned closer to her. "What the hell are you doing?"

A flush crept up her neck and face. "Jake –"

"I told you we can't be seen together at work, Lex." His voice was low.

"This is important." Lexie's tone matched his.

"Yeah, okay, what is it?" he asked dismissively, turning his attention back to his phone and taking a bite of his sandwich.

Lexie had been debating for days how to say what she needed to say to him. Now that she was here, she forgot all the words. What fell out of her mouth: "I'm pregnant."

Jake choked on his sandwich, triggering a violent coughing fit. Just as Lexie was beginning to wonder if she should perform the Heimlich maneuver on him, his coughing tapered off and he composed himself.

"You're...what?"

Lexie fiddled with her fingers. "I'm pregnant."

"How?"

A surprised laugh escaped Lexie. "And yet you are a doctor."

Jake shook his head, irritated. "Are you sure?"

"Half a dozen pee sticks, Jake. All positive. My period is three weeks late. I'm sure."

Jake rolled his eyes, sat back in his chair, and covered his face with his hands. "Fuck. FUCK." He threw his hands up in the air let them fall into his lap. He looked at Lexie with blazing eyes. "You have to do something about this, Lex."

Lexie blinked, thunderstruck. "Excuse me?"

"Keeping this baby is not an option. You understand that, right?"

"No." The anxiety Lexie had when she walked into the cafeteria was steadily morphing into something a little closer to anger. "What are you even talking about? NOT keeping the baby is not an option."

Jake leaned closer. "I already have three kids, Lexie. What the fuck would I tell my wife?"

The shock hit Lexie so hard she was dizzy; she instinctively grabbed the edge of the table keep from falling out of her chair. "You're...married?"

Jake nodded slowly.

The condescending look on his face made Lexie feel stupid. And naïve. She stared at Jake, her lip trembling. "But..."

"Look. My advice? Swing by the women's clinic down the street and get this taken care of." Jake paused for a second. Then, in the pompous voice of someone conferring a great favor upon her, he said, "Shit, I'll even pay for it. I'll swing by the bank and bring you a thousand in cash tomorrow." Another pause. "Do you think that'll cover it?"

Lexie gaped at Jake in complete disbelief. Then the rage took over. She leaned toward Jake and whispered, "Keep your fucking money." She sat up and spied her bowl of soup, now mostly cooled, on the table in front of her; she grabbed it and threw the soup in his face with everything she had.

Jake recoiled. "Fuck!" he shouted, wiping soggy noodles, carrots, and celery from his face and hair. He looked at Lexie with wide-eyed incredulity. The dining room had gone silent. "What the fuck is the matter with you?"

Lexie stood. Her voice was loud enough so that everyone could hear her. "And you, Doctor Stratton, can go straight to hell." She turned and walked calmly out the door.

Lexie couldn't help but grin; maybe she shouldn't have been so surprised when she learned he'd moved his services to a different hospital. She heard shuffling footsteps down the hall. Ava, hair tousled and rubbing her eyes, emerged.

"Good morning babydoll." She held her arms out wide.

Ava shuffled to Lexie and leaned against her. "Hi Mommy."

Lexie wrapped her arms around Ava and kissed her head. "How did you sleep?"

"Good." Ava yawned.

"Are you hungry?" Lexie asked.

Ava nodded against Lexie's robe.

"I still don't have any food in the house, so let's run to McDonald's. After that, do you want to take a bath in our new bathtub?"

"But Mommy," Ava said. "I don't have any shampoo or booty wash, remember?"

"Body wash. Okay, we'll go pick some up after breakfast. There's a drugstore just a few blocks away. Let's get dressed and we'll go, okay?"

"OKAY!" Ava bellowed and took off running for her room.

The fire in Lexie's belly extinguished itself as soon as she and Ava stepped out into the cool summer morning. She drove the mile or so to a local fast food restaurant, where she devoured a breakfast sandwich and hashbrown, and Ava ate an entire pancake breakfast. *The girl loves her pancakes,* Lexie thought as she fondly watched Ava eat.

Bellies full and fingers wiped clean of the cloying scent of maple syrup, she loaded Ava back into the truck and drove the dozen or so blocks to the pharmacy she remembered driving by on moving day. The Apothecary was housed in what looked to Lexie like a former restaurant in an old brick retail strip on the corner of 42nd and Thomas Avenues. A hair salon called Updo occupied the space right next to the Apothecary. And next to that was the quaint Cuppa coffee shop.

Lexie stopped in at Cuppa first; now that her heartburn had subsided, she was badly in need of a caffeine fix. *Coffee is just the ticket after night's sleep I had,* she thought, and opened the door for Ava to lead her inside. A bell overhead dinged. They walked into the comforting aroma of fresh-roasted coffee and breathed deeply.

An older woman stood behind the counter. She wore a black apron with a nametag that said LOUISE and half-moon glasses secured around her neck with a delicate gold chain. Her long lavender-tinted silver hair was swept up in a barrette on top of her head. An antique brass and copper espresso machine gleamed in its pride of place on the counter behind her. The woman looked up with a warm smile. "Hello," she said.

Lexie smiled back. "Hi."

"What brings you to me this morning?" Louise asked. "Need a blueberry muffin? I just pulled them out of the oven, they're still warm."

"I want a booberry muffin!" Ava declared, and did a pirouette in the middle of the seating area for emphasis.

Lexie smiled and looked at the woman. "That would be great. And a vanilla latte."

"Sure thing, hon." The woman began working her magic at the espresso machine. It whirred and whooshed and burped, and then Louise turned around with a perfectly crafted latte in her hands.

"You make that look so easy." Lexie carefully took the warm paper travel cup and sipped tentatively. The sweet, creamy bitterness made Lexie smile; her neck and shoulders relaxed instantaneously. "Mmmm," she breathed, and sipped again. "Amazing. Thank you."

"You're welcome, hon." The woman leaned over the counter and handed Ava her muffin in a waxed paper bag. "Here you go."

"Yum," Ava said as she took it. "What does your nametag say?"

"It says Louise," the woman said with another smile. "That's my name."

"I have a name too!" Ava pointed at her own chest. "It's Ava." Then she pointed at Lexie. "That's Mommy."

"Lexie," Lexie said, also pointing at her own chest.

"It's very nice to meet you both," Louise said. Her voice was at the same time strong yet frail; it sounded like honey in Lexie's ears. "Thank you for visiting me today."

Lexie paid Louise and wished her a good day, then headed two doors down to the Apothecary. Updo was deserted and dark; according to the sign on the door, it was closed on Wednesdays. Lexie made a mental note to call and make an appointment for a haircut.

She and Ava walked down to the corner and went inside the Apothecary.

A bell dinged when Lexie opened the door; one look around confirmed her suspicions: The Apothecary occupied a former Italian restaurant called Pepe's Pizza & Pasta, and rustic remnants of the old Victory neighborhood establishment could still be seen in the store's décor. The walls were painted a mild, glowing yellow. The pharmacy was set up in the former kitchen, where the old brick oven still took up the entire back wall. Lexie thought she could even still smell the ghosts of past pizzas. Her stomach rumbled – even though it was still full of breakfast. Her appetite never seemed to be completely satisfied.

It's never been a mystery why I'm fat, she thought. This was immediately followed by: *I should grab a bag of candy to keep on hand at home, while I'm here.*

The store was deserted, save for the pharmacist filling prescriptions in the back. Lexie allowed Ava to wander to the toy aisle – with a stern warning not to go anywhere else – while she stood in the personal care aisle and spent a couple minutes browsing the kids' bathing products. *So many choices,* Lexie thought. She selected a bottle of watermelon-scented shampoo/conditioner and a green apple-scented body wash, then swung by the antacids aisle to grab the biggest bottles of antacid tablets and pain medication she could find. Then she headed to the toy aisle. She found Ava there, gazing at a rack of colorful stuffed animals. Ava held up one that looked like a rainbow-colored unicorn with giant sparkly pink eyes, and gave her mother her very best puppydog look. "Can I have this one, Mommy? It's so pretty. Please?"

Lexie sighed, caving to the baby blues. "Okay, fine. But just this one thing."

"Yay!" Ava jumped up and down, clutching the unicorn stuffie to her chest.

"Come on, let's go pay for this stuff." They headed to the back of the store. Lexie grabbed a bag of red licorice from an endcap display on her way by. Just having the candy in her hands and knowing it would be going home with her filled her with an inexplicable peace. Along with the inevitable self-hatred.

"Hello," the pharmacist greeted them with a smile as they approached the counter. She pushed her coarse blonde hair, cut in a severe short bob and haphazardly curled, off her forehead. "All set?"

"Yes," Lexie said, setting her items next to the cash register. Ava reached up and dropped her stuffie on the counter next to Lexie's purchases.

The pharmacist pulled a wrapped sucker from under the counter, then leaned forward and offered it to Ava. "Hello there, dear. Would you like one?"

Ava glanced at Lexie, who nodded her approval. Ava took the sucker. "Thank you," she said. "Orange is my favorite."

The pharmacist smiled. "That's my favorite too. What's your name, love?"

Ava looked at the pharmacist without a trace of fear or shyness. "My name is Ava Jacoba Novak." She held up her right thumb, pointer, and middle fingers, like she had for Ryan. "I'm four."

Lexie and the pharmacist chuckled in unison. "What a lovely name," the pharmacist said. "My name is Joanna Elizabeth Schmitt. It's very nice to meet you, Ava."

"Hi," Ava said, then popped the sucker in her mouth and started doing ballerina twirls.

"Be careful, Ava," Lexie warned. She turned to the pharmacist and held out her hand. "I'm Lexie Novak. Ava and I just moved to the neighborhood a couple days ago."

Joanna shook Lexie's hand, grinning. "I'm sorry, what did you say your name is?"

Lexie blinked, confused, then realized what Joanna meant. She laughed. "Sorry. I'm Alexis Michelle Novak. It's nice to meet you."

Joanna leaned against the counter. "Welcome to the neighborhood, Lexie. Did you buy the house on Washburn Avenue?"

Lexie nodded. "Yep, that's us."

"Going well so far?"

"Pretty well. I haven't even started unpacking yet, and we've had a couple kind of weird things happen in the house, but overall it's been good."

Joanna's left eyebrow shot up, giving her matronly face an inquisitive look. "What kinds of weird things?"

"Well, I mean, it's nothing major. Things aren't randomly floating through the air, we're not seeing ghosts, nothing like that." *Well...sort of...*

"But still something?" Joanna pressed.

"Well. Besides the strange creaks and noises, and the fact that I can't keep family photos from ending up on the floor, I seem to always have either a headache or raging heartburn," Lexie said. Sure that Joanna would think she was a raving lunatic, she decided not to mention yesterday's incident with the knife. "It's weird because the only time I've ever had heartburn in my life was when I was pregnant with Ava. Now my stomach starts burning as soon as I walk in the door."

"Huh," Joanna intoned.

"You see that kid over there?" Lexie pointed at Ava, who had sneaked the unicorn stuffie from the counter and was now sitting on the floor next to a rack of children's books, reading *Go, Dog. Go!* to it. "She is always in a good mood. You'll never meet a happier kid. But when we're in the house, she's a cranky little nightmare. Both of us are, really." Lexie frowned slightly. "You don't look shocked."

"I'm not," Joanna said. "That house has been a topic of neighborhood gossip for years." She leaned over the counter a bit. "Many years."

"How's that?"

"Well, for the last eight years or so, until late last year, it was a halfway house for teenage girls and young women coming out of rehab. They could fit four girls in each of those main floor bedrooms, with bunk beds and such. Drug and alcohol treatment, mostly, although T'Jara Jackson, the live-in counselor there when it shut down, told me that two or three eating disorders went through there too."

This made sense to Lexie; she remembered her real estate agent telling her that the seller of her house was an investor, who had bought the house from the State of Minnesota at a discount and then remodeled and sold it for a profit.

"I contracted with the state to provide prescription medications to the house's residents. I'll bet a thousand girls went through there in ten years," Joanna continued. "And I'll tell ya, those girls were prone to violence like nothing I've ever seen."

"What do you mean?"

"Fights. Staff injuries. Self-harm. Overdoses. It was constant. Counselor turnover was incredible; T'Jara was there only nine months, and she was the longtimer. All of the counselors before her couldn't get out soon enough. I'll bet the Minneapolis Police Department visited that house at least twice a week, every week. I never felt safe when I made my deliveries; I always felt like the girls were...watching me. Waiting for an opportunity." Joanna visibly shuddered.

"An opportunity to...?" Lexie shook her head slowly, in an effort to coax more out of Joanna.

"I don't know, exactly. I kind of thought they wanted to hurt me." Joanna said. She picked up a pen and started doodling on a piece of scratch paper next to her cash register. "The state finally shut the halfway house down after one resident almost killed a young girl who had stopped by, selling cookies out of her wagon. Grabbed the poor thing by the throat, dragged her in the house, and tried to strangle her right there inside the front door. T'Jara subdued the resident, but the baby ended up in intensive care at North for a week. Thankfully she recovered."

Lexie was at a loss for words. Finally she croaked, "Who lived there before it was a halfway house?"

A shadow of sadness passed over Joanna's face, and she set her pen down. "The Dormeisters. John and Kathryn. They hadn't lived there but two months when Kath fell down the basement stairs and broke her neck. Died right there on the floor. In 2010, that was."

Lexie's hands flew to her mouth.

"Even though they hadn't lived here long, Kath's death was a big deal in the neighborhood – especially after Jim McCormick, the Hennepin County attorney at the time, brought murder charges against her husband."

"Oh my god," Lexie said. "Did he do it?"

"A jury said so," Joanna said. "But nobody in the neighborhood believed it for a minute."

"Is he in prison?"

"Yep, I believe he's still at St. Cloud, probably being a model inmate."

"What do you think happened?" Lexie asked. "Kath was helped down the stairs, but not by her husband?"

"All I'm saying is, I'm a scientist. I don't believe in coincidences." Joanna rang up Lexie's purchases and handed her a white plastic bag.

Lexie wondered what *that* meant. "Thanks," she said and took the bag. "I appreciate all the intel." She called for Ava, then waved and left the store. Her mind buzzed as she drove with all of the information Joanna had given her – and the implications.

Was she trying to tell me that my house is haunted? she wondered. Then she pushed the thought aside. *Ridiculous.* She did spend the drive home considering the fact that someone had actually died in the house; she didn't recall seeing anything about that in the real estate papers she signed. She made a mental note to call Travis Schumacher, her real estate agent. She had questions.

Lexie swung by the neighborhood market as well and picked up a few provisions to tide her and Ava over until she could get to the grocery store. Lexie drove through the alley behind the house and pulled up to the garage, then carried her bag full of snacks and soft drinks as she followed Ava through the backyard to the house. Lexie glanced to her left at the blue house next door, hoping to catch sight of Ryan and his big brown eyes. He was nowhere to be seen. *I wonder what he's heard about my house.* She made a mental note to ask him next time she saw him.

6

Ava had her bath, and then Lexie set her up at the coffee table in the living room with a shoebox full of crayons, a coloring book, her favorite DVD on the TV, and a snack of canned mandarin oranges in a bowl. She tried to ignore a headache that seemed to crouch in the back of her skull like a black cat preparing to attack its unsuspecting prey, as she unpacked and organized the kitchen. A couple aspirin helped take the edge off, but the headache waited patiently, its silky black tail whipping back and forth in anticipation. Only once or twice did she catch herself glancing toward the basement stairs and suppressing a shudder, trying not to imagine Kathryn Dormeister's fatal fall down the stairs.

Unpacking felt a little like Christmas; she'd packed these boxes five years ago as she prepared to move in with her parents, and didn't really remember exactly what she had. She was pleasantly surprised to discover she had a full set of decent pots and pans, a complete set of silverware, all the cooking utensils she could possibly need, including her set of (expensive, sharp, efficiently deadly) knives. She also unearthed a perfectly functioning toaster.

On top of the threatening headache, Lexie's heartburn had returned. Every twenty minutes or so, she found herself shaking two or three chalky tablets out onto her hand and popping them into her mouth for sweet – but temporary – relief.

By noon, Lexie had found proper homes for everything in the kitchen. She looked around with pride. *All mine, she thought. If I want to get up in the middle of the night and make myself a couple pieces of toast, I can. And my mom's not here to make me feel bad about it.*

She realized she hadn't seen or heard Ava in at least half an hour. After shaking three more antacid tablets directly into her mouth and chewing them up, she went to see why the girl was so quiet.

She rounded the corner to find Ava staring unseeingly at the TV screen, crayons strewn across the coffee table. Her show had ended, and the DVD was now stuck on its first selection screen, where happy little animated merpeople bounced around and sang the catchy theme song. Normally she would be twirling around the room and singing along. Now, though, her face was alarmingly vacant and her eyes, normally so sparkly and expressive, were dull.

Wait a minute, Lexie thought. *Something's weird about her eyes.* She took a step into the living room to get a closer look. *Are – are they –?*

Ava, sensing movement, looked at Lexie and immediately recoiled, her eyes – brown eyes – flaring like a horse's. She scrambled to the other end of the couch.

"You okay baby?" Lexie approached Ava, the acid in her stomach churning like hot lava. *I have got to get a stronger antacid.*

"NO!" Ava screamed and hopped off the couch, putting the coffee table between herself and her mother.

"Ava!" Lexie said, surprised and more than a little hurt. Her headache began creeping forward, pupils dilated and tail flicking. "It's me."

"GET AWAY FROM ME MAMA!" Ava picked up a red crayon from the coffee table and chucked it as hard as she could at Lexie. Her little hands flew over the surface of the table, searching blindly for ammo. She threw a green crayon, then yellow, then another red, then blue, furiously at her mother.

Lexie ducked and dodged, crayons raining down on her like a hail of bullets. "Ava! You stop that. Right. NOW!" she shouted. The force of her shout, combined with the acid that bubbled gaily into her throat, caused her to cough violently. She sounded like a barking seal. Her headache pounced, and her entire head lit up with pain.

"I HATE YOU!" More crayons flew; they bounced off the walls around the front door, leaving colorful marks. "MAMAS ARE BAD!"

Lexie shielded her face and took small steps toward the table. Rage – fueled by the unbearable burning in her gut and the bright pain in her head – overtook her self-control like a tidal wave. "You ungrateful little BITCH!" she shrieked.

Out of crayons, Ava picked up the fork that she had used to eat her mandarin oranges and threw it at her mother with the strength and precision of an axe-thrower.

Lexie watched the fork fly in slow motion, lazily turning end over end as it sailed through the air. The tines pierced her left forearm, driving deep enough into the muscle that the fork stood straight out from her arm at a 90-degree angle. The pain was instant and enormous, dwarfing even her massive headache. She screamed. Blood seeped out around the lodged tines, pooling and then dripping to the floor. She grabbed the fork and yanked it out, leaving a perfect line of four bloody little holes in the fleshy part of her forearm. Blood welled up from those holes like tiny mountain springs and dripped down her arm toward her fingers. She looked at her daughter with wild, pain-filled eyes. "YOU LITTLE –"

Lexie didn't have the chance to finish her sentence. "I'M-A KILL YOU!" Ava screeched, and grabbed for whatever ammunition was left on the coffee table. She picked up the softball-sized solid etched glass globe that Jane had given Lexie as the lamest housewarming gift ever and wound up like a baseball pitcher.

The mental picture of the heavy glass orb bouncing off her skull and knocking her unconscious was just enough to break through Lexie's pain and rage. Moving entirely on raw instinct, she ran to Ava and hooked her arms under the girl's armpits. She dragged the girl, who thrashed and screamed incoherent words, to the front door. As soon as Lexie set foot outside, a powerful

ZAP inside her brain collapsed her right there on the front stoop. Ava fell silent and passed out.

Lexie sat on the concrete steps and stared at the empty street; a powerful sense of déjà vu came over her. She'd sat in this exact spot, in almost the exact same position, just two days ago. She didn't know what to do, so she just sat there in the early afternoon sunshine.

A door creaked open somewhere close by. She blinked when Ryan came into view, jogging toward her from the sidewalk. He wore black shorts and a blue t-shirt, no shoes and no hat. His dark hair, hairline almost completely receded, was shaved close to his head.

He ran to Lexie. "I heard screaming. What happened?" He bent over to inspect Ava, who still lay unconscious in Lexie's arms.

She looked at him, eyes wide and confused. "I – um, I'm not sure."

He brought his face up so it was level with Lexie's. His big brown eyes were full of concern. "Is she hurt? Are you hurt?"

Lexie shook her head; some of the fog in her brain cleared. "I'm not hurt. Uh..." She had no idea how to describe what had just happened.

Ryan carefully removed a limp and snoring Ava from Lexie's arms and carried her like an oversized watermelon to the grass, where he gently laid her down on her back. *Geez, my kid can't even be normal when she's sleeping,* Lexie thought wryly. Ryan checked out Ava's head and neck, her arms and legs, and looked her over for injuries. Satisfied that she was not hurt, he stepped over her and sat next to Lexie on the front stoop. He leaned forward over his knees so he could get a better look at her face.

"She seems okay. You want to tell me what happened?"

Lexie looked down at her intertwined fingers; half of them were caked in her dried blood. "You'll never believe it."

"I'm a teacher. I've seen everything. Try me."

Lexie took a deep breath and told him everything that had just happened. When she mentioned the thrown fork, Ryan took hold of her bleeding arm and held it up so he could see better. His touch was warm.

"Holy shit," he said. "All this blood from those tiny little holes."

Lexie nodded. "Crazy, right?"

"What do you think caused her weird behavior?"

"I don't know. The pharmacist at The Apothecary seems to have this crazy notion that maybe my house is haunted."

Ryan made a noncommittal noise. "Mind if I step inside and take a look around?"

Lexie shrugged. "Sure. Just watch out for crayons on the floor, and don't mind the mess. I'm still unpacking."

"Don't worry," he said, standing up. "I won't be long. You stay here and keep an eye on Ava."

Lexie watched Ava sleep on the grass while she waited for Ryan to come back. She hoped she hadn't left a box of tampons sitting in plain sight. Or her bag of licorice. The idea that he might see evidence of her eating habits, more than of her status as a menstruating woman, made her neck feel hot.

Ryan came back through the front door and sat down next to Lexie again. "Well, I don't see anything that seemed out of the ordinary."

"I figured you wouldn't," Lexie said.

"But I'm still concerned. This isn't the first time I've heard about strange things happening in this house."

Lexie looked at him. "What do you mean?"

"I told you, I've lived next door for six years. This place was still a halfway house when I moved into my house. I assume Joanna told you about the incident with the girl selling cookies?"

Lexie nodded slowly, still staring at Ryan's face.

"I was right here at home when that happened."

"Is it true, what she said? That there were a lot of fights between the residents and injuries to staff?"

Ryan nodded. "MPD was here literally all the time. If we went one week without the police showing up, it was a good week." He ran his hand back and forth over the stubble on top of his head. "The state finally shut down the halfway house last year. The lady who ran this place was a straight up saint, you know? She dealt with a lot of bad stuff from the girls who came through here."

Ava, still sprawled in the grass, finally stirred. Lexie and Ryan went to her and squatted on either side of her. Her eyes, blue again – much to Lexie's relief – widened as they moved between Lexie's face and Ryan's face. "Mommy?"

Lexie smiled and touched Ava's forehead. "How you doing, babydoll?"

Ava blinked several times. "My head hurts a little."

Mine too, Lexie thought, although the pain had faded considerably. The inky black headache had retreated to its lair – for now.

"Feel like sitting up?" Ryan extended a hand. Ava took it, and he pulled her up.

"Do you remember what happened, pumpkin?" Lexie looked at Ava's face anxiously, watching for any changes in her mannerisms or her behavior.

Ava frowned, which crinkled her forehead adorably. Her hair blew around her face in the gentle breeze. She didn't seem to notice. "No."

"What's the last thing you remember?" Ryan asked.

"I..." Ava paused, thinking. "I was watching the TV while Mommy was in the kitchen. I ate baby oranges."

"Was your show over yet?" Lexie asked.

"No," Ava shook her head. "Gil was at the grocery store to buy a box of Bubble Puppy Bites."

Lexie, who had seen the same DVD roughly seven dozen times herself, knew exactly what Ava was talking about. "That's the last episode on the DVD. When I found her staring blankly at the TV, all the episodes were over and the disc was playing that first screen."

Ryan nodded. "So, maybe five, ten minutes?"

"That would be my guess." Lexie turned back to her daughter. "Do you remember anything else?"

Ava's eyes widened again. "My head was all smoky. I heard a little girl, but I didn't see her. She said that mamas are bad." Her little lips trembled. "I tried to tell her that my mommy is good. Then I guess I went to sleep."

Lexie sat in the grass, gathered Ava into her lap, and hugged her. "It's okay, babydoll."

Ryan stood and stretched his legs.

"Do you know about the couple who lived here before it was a halfway house?" Lexie asked.

"No," Ryan said.

"Joanna said a husband and wife lived here for a couple months in 2010, and then the wife fell down the stairs and broke her neck and died." Lexie said.

Ryan stared fixedly at Lexie. "Are you serious?"

"Joanna seemed dead serious. Said the husband went to prison, but she's convinced he's innocent."

Ryan started pacing a tight circle in the lawn with his bare feet. "I think I remember hearing about from one of my buddies who's a cop." He stopped pacing for a moment, thinking. "Yeah." He resumed, lost in thought. "He said it was the saddest scene he'd ever been to. The wife was lying at the bottom of the stairs, her head all crooked on her neck. The husband was frantic. The medical examiner said later that her skull had completely separated from her spine, and he'd never seen that in his fifteen years on the job."

Lexie gaped, horrified.

"What does that mean, Mommy?" Ava lifted her head from Lexie's chest and looked up at her with wide eyes.

"It just means that she had a really big ouchie on her neck, baby," Lexie said.

"Oh." Ava leaned into Lexie's chest again. Lexie unconsciously rocked back and forth, an action that both she and her daughter found comforting.

"Strange things certainly are afoot on Washburn Avenue," he said.

"Don't tell me you believe Joanna's haunted house nonsense," Lexie rolled her eyes.

"I don't know about that, but come on. You can't tell me you don't believe something is going on."

Lexie considered this, but did not reply. She watched Ryan pace, his tight circle now more of a long, skinny rectangle. She thought he looked like a man who had devoted his life to being a teacher and coach. His brown eyes were sharp, always assessing. The several days' worth of facial hair growth helped to hide deep lines around his eyes and mouth, as if they were carved by every bad thing he'd ever seen in his job: kids with tough family lives, kids struggling with addiction and homelessness, kids fighting with each other and with him. She guessed he was in his early forties.

Finally Lexie's back could take no more. "Can you take her? I have to stand up."

Ryan gently lifted Ava out of Lexie's arms. She stood up and stretched, her back muscles thanking her. She held out her arms, smiling. "I can take her back," she said. "Clearly it's naptime."

Ryan stepped closer to Lexie and carefully transferred Ava to her arms. His warm hands brushed her bare forearms as he let go and stepped back, leaving trails of fire behind them. Lexie smiled nervously. Ryan held her eyes and smiled back.

"Uh. Thanks," Lexie said lamely. Then she laughed at her lameness.

A genuine grin stretched across Ryan's face, lighting his eyes up as if an inner spotlight had been turned on. "You're welcome, neighbor." He then turned with a small wave and walked back to his own yard.

Lexie watched him go, feeling lucky that she had him as her neighbor.

She hoped she'd see more of him.

7

It was dark. Lexie didn't know where she was or how she got here. Black shapes that were only vaguely outlined against the charcoal darkness surrounded her.

It was cold. Lexie crossed her arms over her chest and shivered. She looked down to discover she was wearing a lavender nightgown that covered everything but her bare hands and feet. They felt like icicles.

It was quiet. Lexie listened carefully, but the only sound was the complete silence that roared in her ears.

She tried walking, slowly, one foot in front of the other, arms extended in front of her. No matter which way she turned, there was nothing but darkness. Her path was unobstructed. The vague black shapes moved on either side of her like old-timey paper backgrounds on reels.

Lexie instinctively understood that the only thing that mattered was that she keep walking. Eventually, after what felt like an eternity moving through the realm of death, she thought she could see thin lines of light, joined together at the ends to form a rectangle, directly in front of her. A door?

She couldn't help herself; she ran.

It was indeed a door. Lexie ran up to it at full speed, stopped herself with her hands, and grabbed the doorknob. She turned it, yanked open the door in a panic – and immediately threw up an arm to shade her eyes. She had grown accustomed to the dark; the sudden blinding light felt like daggers in her eyeballs. She stood in the doorway and blinked a few times, giving her eyes time to adjust –

A disembodied hand, cold and dry, shot out from somewhere within the light and grabbed Lexie's throat. Shocked, her hands instinctively flew up and tried to pry the hand off. Its grip was incredible; all of her scratching and yanking proved fruitless. Her lungs, straining with the effort to breathe against her blocked airway, burst into flame.

Somehow Lexie understood that this was a dream – but also that if she lost consciousness, she might never wake up. This knowledge only added to her growing panic as she tried and failed to draw breath. She realized her body was moving, but not under her own power. Lexie tried to plant her feet and pull away, but to no avail; the hand was effortlessly dragging her farther into the light. Her eyes bulged from their sockets, and she pulled and clawed desperately at the hand on her throat.

A face came into view: a woman with tangled brown hair, and empty brown eyes – eyes which sanity had vacated a long time ago. The woman's narrow white face split into a hideous grin as she pulled Lexie closer and squeezed her throat harder.

"WHY. WON'T. YOU. DIE," the woman croaked. The insanity that swirled in her eyes threatened to swallow Lexie whole.

Lexie opened her mouth and –

Her own scream woke her. Gasping, sweating, heart racing, Lexie sat up. She took deep, gulping breaths, feeling like she could not get enough air. Her head swiveled back and forth as she looked around the room. Her panic started to subside when she realized she was at home, in her own bed. She pushed her hair off her face and looked at the clock: 2:12 a.m. She took another deep breath, and her heartbeat steadied.

That was the worst one yet, Lexie thought. There would be no more sleep. She carefully slid out of bed and made her way to the bathroom. She peed for what felt like fifteen minutes, then inspected her face in the mirror. Her cheeks were puffy and the dark circles etched themselves ever deeper into the skin under her eyes; the nightly bad dreams and lack of sleep were taking a toll. She knew it would be most of the day before she would completely shake the bad vibe that clung to her like slime after this latest dream.

Lexie pulled her dark hair up in a bun on top of her head before making her way downstairs. The kitchen was dark and quiet. She opted not to turn on a light; instead she felt her way through the process of making coffee. She remembered Joanna Schmitt's story about the unfortunate cookie-selling girl and decided that the nightmare she'd just had was her brain's way of processing that information. The brain certainly does work in mysterious ways, she thought, shaking her head. And then she thought about the phone call she'd received yesterday after she put Ava down for a nap and resumed unpacking.

Lexie finally found the oversized bottle of antacid tablets in the cabinet under the bathroom sink – she did not remember putting it there, but she supposed anything was possible while unpacking after a move – and popped four or five of the chalky tablets in her mouth. The sour burning in her stomach settled somewhat. She decided to take it out to the kitchen, where it would be much easier to keep track of.

She was on her way there when her phone rang. "JANE" flashed on the screen, and Lexie briefly considered declining the call and making up an excuse later.

"Hi Mom," she said instead.

"Hello Alexis," her mother's tone was cool and detached, as it always was. Lexie never knew if Jane was happy to hear from her, suffering from indigestion, paying bills, or opening a Christmas present.

"What's up? I'm in the middle of unpacking."

"Oh, Alexis," Jane admonished. "You haven't finished unpacking yet?"

Lexie rolled her eyes. "I've been here three days, Mom. And I worked one of those days." She did not mention her confrontation with Jake; she knew that would spark an argument that Lexie was not interested in having with her mother again. Jane, who could never fully accept that her daughter was an unwed mother, had been pressuring Lexie for years to reconcile with and marry Ava's father – and she stubbornly refused to accept the fact that Ava's father wanted nothing to do with either of them. After their last big fight – which only ended when Paul stepped in after Jane accused Lexie of freeloading and Lexie called her mother a cold, heartless witch – Lexie began her search for her own house. She could not get out of her parents' basement soon enough.

Cool silence on the other end of the line. Then: "Your father and I would like to come for dinner. See Ava. See your house."

The very idea horrified Lexie. "It's not a good time, Mom. The house is a disaster –"

"Oh, honey. We don't care about that. We miss you two."

Lexie knew better. Her mother wanted to see Lexie and Ava's new environment and judge Lexie's house, lifestyle, choices, and her life in general. *Must be hard to do now that I'm not there, Mom,* she thought but did not say.

"Fine," Lexie said, walking into the kitchen and setting the Tums bottle on the counter next to the coffeemaker. *No way I'll forget where it is now,* she thought. "You guys can come over tomorrow night."

"Tomorrow's Thursday, we can watch reality TV. Your dad can grill hamburgers or steaks or something, and we can throw together a potato salad." With Jane it was never "I," always "we."

Lexie's heartburn flared suddenly like someone had thrown gas on a campfire; Lexie smiled through clenched teeth and reached for the Tums again. "Perfect. I'll make sure the grill has propane. See you tomorrow."

Her heartburn ratcheted up a few notches while she rushed to finish unpacking and bring her house under some semblance of control, and never stopped until she and Ava went to bed.

Lexie stirred sugar into her cup of coffee – and suddenly realized she hadn't yet cleaned or shopped or anything in preparation for her parent's visit. She took her coffee into the living room and sat. The fog started to build in her mind, but this time it was a little different. It seized on and amplified her anxiety over her parents' visit, causing her heart to thump and her hands to tremble. She stared at the black front window, her mind racing with everything that needed to get done between now and dinnertime.

I have to clean. Dear god, I swear if my mother makes one comment about dust or a dish in the sink, my head will fucking explode. Her heart pounded in her chest. *And Jesus Christ, I have to be at work in less than four hours. Not enough time. Have to get started. Now.*

Lexie set her coffee on the end table and went to the broom closet. From there she pulled out a scrub brush and a spray bottle of bleach cleaner. *Might as well do the whole kitchen with this stuff, make sure it's good and sanitized.*

That's where Ava found her two hours later – on her hands and knees, still scrubbing the tile kitchen floor, taking care to get into every grout line. Her hair was falling out of her bun in chunks, and sweat ran down her face.

"Mommy? What are you doing?" Ava stood in the dining room off the kitchen, several unpacked boxes piled neatly in the corner behind her, rubbing the sleep from her eyes.

"What does it look like I'm doing?" Lexie snapped.

Ava's face crumpled. The anxious fog still obfuscated Lexie's conscious mind, suppressing her normal emotions and leaving only absolute apathy. Her singular focus was on scrubbing the kitchen floor, and she was annoyed that the little bitch had interrupted her. She clenched her teeth and continued with her work.

"Can I watch TV, Mommy?"

Lexie's vision flashed bright red at the second interruption, and before she quite knew what she was doing, she stood and rushed at Ava. A surprised screech escaped the girl as Lexie wrapped her tightly in her arms, lifted her easily, and walked back through the kitchen toward the back door – and the basement stairs.

"Mommy!" Ava wailed. She squirmed mightily and, upon realizing she was completely immobilized, started to cry.

Jaw set, teeth clenched, Lexie stared straight ahead and kept moving. A tiny voice managed to pierce the thick fog in her brain and cry *What the hell is going on?* before a strange force in her mind silenced it. She reached the landing at the top of the basement stairs and paused. Another voice, louder but somehow foreign – the same voice that had invaded her mind as she unpacked her kitchen knives on Tuesday: *If I do it quickly, she won't feel a thing.*

Still holding Ava in a bear hug, Lexie stopped inside the back door and took a few seconds to gaze down into the darkness of the basement. A memory that didn't seem to be hers slid into view behind her eyes: a woman, a *mama*, with long blonde hair and green eyes, taking her last trip down these very stairs. The sound her neck had made when she landed – a distinct *snap* – sent a smile of satisfaction across Lexie's lips. She planted her feet firmly and started twisting at the waist, prepared to send this child on that very same trip.

Because mamas are bad. Mamas do bad things. Lexie didn't realize she was whispering these words over and over.

"No, Mommy."

Ava's calm and steady voice stopped Lexie in the middle of her wind-up. She turned her head and looked directly into Ava's earnest, wide-eyed, tear-streaked face.

"You're *my* mama, and you're a *good* mama."

Something shifted in Lexie's head; she closed her eyes against the strange sensation. The fog began to lift, and little by little she opened her eyes again. She looked around, realized where she was and what she had been about to do.

"Oh my god." She set Ava down and jerkily sat at the top of the landing, then covered her face with her hands and sobbed. "Oh my god oh my god what was I doing?" she wailed. "What the fuck is wrong with me?" She couldn't articulate any more words; great heaving sobs seemed to bubble up from some pit inside her. She felt like she might actually be going crazy.

Ava wrapped her arms around Lexie's neck and laid her head against Lexie's head. This made Lexie cry even harder. *I was about to throw her down the damn stairs, and she still loves me.* They sat like that for nearly half an hour, until Lexie was sure she didn't have a single tear left to cry.

She pulled Ava into her lap and held her tight. "I'm so sorry, babygirl," she whispered into Ava's tousled sleep-hair.

"I know it wasn't you, Mommy."

Lexie raised her head and sniffed to clear her nose. "What do you mean?

"It was the little girl."

Lexie blinked, and just as she opened her mouth to ask a clarifying question, the alarm on her watch started beeping.

"Oh my god." She stood and hustled Ava back into the kitchen. "Get your shit together, we gotta go!"

Ava's eyes widened, and she recoiled a bit. "Why?"

The fog was trying to drift back into her head and shroud her consciousness again. She shook her head hard in a fruitless effort to clear it. Her mood soured. "Because I'm going to be late for work. Now let's go! Double time!" Lexie shouted.

Ava gave a terrified screech and ran to her bedroom, and in record time came out dressed in butterfly leggings and a unicorn sweatshirt that utterly clashed with each other. Clutching the unicorn stuffie she'd gotten from the Apothecary, she pulled her shoes on and ran outside, desperate to get away from this crazy version of her mother.

Utterly unaware that she was still wearing her bathrobe over her pajamas, Lexie left her scrub brush and spray cleaner where they lay on the kitchen floor, grabbed her purse and Ava's daycare bag, and stomped after her. As soon as she stepped out the door, the strange static electricity sensation shot through her entire body. Her fingers tingled and her knees buckled. She grabbed the cast iron handrail that lined each side of the steps in order to keep from collapsing. She must have made a noise, because Ava turned around – and came running when she saw her mother half standing, half sitting on the back stoop in the dawnlight, holding on to the railing for dear life.

"Mommy! Are you okay?" Ava stood in front of Lexie, unsure what to do.

Lexie nodded and slowly made her way down the steps, still holding tightly to the handrail. She spied a neglected chaise longue in the shade of an old oak tree. Leaving her bags and mug on the stoop, she crawled to it and laid down, curled into a fetal position, and immediately fell asleep.

"Lexie?"

The voice and the hand shaking her shoulder roused her from unconsciousness. "Huh? Wha?"

"Lexie. Wake up."

She turned onto her back and opened her eyes. Ryan's head hovered above her, framed by a morning sun so bright she had to squint to make out his worried face. Her brain felt...scrambled.

"Ryan? What's happening? Where's Ava?" She scrambled up to a sitting position.

"Relax, she's right here." Ryan gestured next to him; Ava stood there, still clutching her unicorn stuffie, tears rolling down her cheeks.

The morning air was chilly; Lexie pulled her bathrobe tighter around her and held her arms out. "Come here, babygirl." Ava scurried behind Ryan's legs, clad in green plaid flannel pants, and hid her face with her stuffie.

Lexie looked at Ryan, confused. "What's going on?"

Ryan shook his head. "I'm not sure." He coaxed Ava out from behind him. "Come on, Ava. There you go." He squatted so his face was even with Ava's. "Can you tell your mom and me what happened?"

Ava burst into tears. "The little girl took over Muh-Mommy. Then she yelled at me really l-l-loud. She scared me. And-and-and then she died!" This last word came out more as a wail, and the girl disintegrated into sobs.

Horrified, Lexie slid to the end of the chaise and looked levelly at her daughter. "I'm sorry, sweetpea. I'm so sorry. I don't know what came over me." Which was the truth; her last clear memory was of making coffee. After that, she saw only solid gray.

"I told you, it's the little girl." Skeptical blue eyes searched Lexie's face. "You're not mad at me anymore?"

"No. No, baby, I'm not mad at you. I love you. And I'm really sorry."

Still clutching her stuffie, Ava threw her arms around Lexie's neck and hugged her hard. "I love you too, Mommy."

Lexie hugged Ava and looked up at Ryan with wide eyes that said *What is going on?*

He shrugged.

Lexie stood, holding her bathrobe closed in order to spare Ryan the sight of her lumpy body. "Come on, babydoll. Let me go change, and then I'll take you to Cindy's."

"YAY!" Ava bugled, and beelined for the car.

"Are you sure you're all right?" Ryan asked.

"Yes. Thanks. And thanks for helping Ava so early in the morning. I hope she didn't wake you."

Ryan dipped his head. "It's fine. I'm glad she came to me."

Lexie smiled. "Me too."

8

Lexie made it through her full twelve-hour shift, then picked Ava up, went to the grocery store and the liquor store, put away the cleaning supplies from this morning, did one more quick dusting around the living room, and was ready for her parents by the time dinnertime rolled around. She hoped they wouldn't stay too long; it had already been an eventful day and she was exhausted.

When Paul and Jane Novak arrived at 7:00 sharp, Lexie got a perfunctory cheek-to-cheek hug and a thorough up-and-down visual examination from her mother.

"Are you feeling all right, Alexis?" Jane asked. Her mother was the only person who still called her by her full name all the time. "It's the name we gave you," Jane had said stubbornly once, after Lexie asked her why she insisted on using Alexis instead of Lexie. "You look tired."

"I'm fine, Mom."

Jane set her designer purse on the floor behind one of the living room chairs, then used her bony fingertips to carefully make sure that every espresso-colored hair in her perfectly coiffed inverted bob was in its proper place. She was a slight woman, standing just over five feet tall and weighing in at less than ninety pounds. Lexie rarely saw her mother actually consume food, and suspected that she too suffered from disordered eating. Jane's perverted relationship with food had trickled down to Lexie, where it manifested itself differently – but just as strongly.

Lexie went to Paul and hugged him. "Hi Daddy."

"Hi sweetheart," Paul said, wrapping his arm around her neck and kissing the top of her head. "How's my beautiful girl?" Paul was a little grayer, a little shaggier, and a lot taller than his wife, with a careworn face and a basset hound smile. He had recently retired as the chief medical officer at Children's Hospital of Minnesota, and Lexie knew that he was looking forward to a long and quiet retirement. He'd started as a general practice pediatrician fresh out of medical school, then moved into pediatric emergency medicine before switching to administration and rising up the ranks. He'd seen a lot in his forty-year career, and watching him interact with his young patients and hearing stories of the lives he saved and the families he comforted inspired Lexie to follow him into medicine. As a nurse, she could only hope to impact even half as many lives as her father had.

"Come on in," Lexie said. She scanned every room as she led them to the kitchen; aside from the few unpacked boxes piled in the corner of the dining room, everything gleamed and there wasn't a speck of dust in sight.

Paul pulled a beer out of the fridge and loped out the back door. Lexie presumed he wanted to light the grill and say hi to Ava, who was outside playing her latest game, Spaceman Princess. Jane briefly inspected the pile of Yukon gold potatoes on the counter, then took a seat on one of the breakfast bar stools. She crossed her legs at the knee so that her sparkly new designer sandals were on full display, and gave Lexie a frank look. "You know, Alexis, your dad has to say that you're beautiful because he's your father. Wouldn't it be nice if you weren't quite so big, and he could actually mean it?"

Lexie had been hearing this comment and many variations of it since she was eight years old. Some girls responded to such passive-aggressive criticism by restricting food; Lexie had gone the other way, using food to try and fill the emotional hole her mother's comments had slowly but steadily dug over the years. It never seemed to work, but it was the only way Lexie knew to cope with the small voice in her head that often chanted *I'm fat. I'm ugly. I'm worthless.*

She decided to let this latest comment slide and tried to ignore the small pit that had opened in her gut.

Jane was completely oblivious to Lexie's hurt silence. "How are you really feeling, Alexis?"

Lexie sighed. "I'm okay, I guess. I've been having a lot of bad dreams, so I haven't been sleeping that great. And I've had terrible heartburn. There is not enough antacid in the world right now."

"Stress," Jane declared. "The move is making your body go all out of whack." She paused and blinked her expertly made-up eyes. "I mean, that's what I hear. None of that ever happened to me."

Lexie had long ago learned that challenging her mother over this behavior was pointless, even when she knew Jane wasn't telling the complete truth. So she just nodded and wondered *Why do I bother sharing anything with her?*

Jane made a show of looking around. "So this is it."

Lexie sighed again. "Yes, this is it." She knew what her mother was thinking: why would Lexie want to live in a tiny old house in the city when she grew up in a large, beautiful new house in an affluent suburb?

"Cute," Jane said, carefully noncommittal.

Lexie watched her mother massage her temples. "Is something wrong?"

Jane took a dramatic deep breath. "I have a bit of a headache all of a sudden."

Lexie didn't say anything; instead she went to the stove, turned the burner on under a large pot full of salted water, and asked, "Think you can help me cut some potatoes for the potato salad?"

"Sure," Jane said in a tone that suggested she was about to go out of her way to do Lexie a huge favor. Lexie set cutting boards and knives out on the counter, next to the pile of potatoes.

They sliced and diced the yellow-skinned potatoes in silence for a few minutes. Lexie's heartburn was raging again; burning acid licked the back of her throat. She tried to remember where she had put her bottle of antacid tablets.

"So. You think you're ready to live on your own?" Jane asked, her voice controlled but tight. Her knife easily cleaved a potato in half.

Lexie put a bit more muscle into cutting her potato than she'd intended; after the two halves fell away from each other, she found that her own knife was stuck in the wooden cutting board. She carefully wrenched it free. "I lived by myself for years before Ava was born."

Jane set her own knife down and rubbed the sides of her head, wincing but trying not to show it. "Well. You've never had to take care of Ava by yourself. I'm just not sure you can...handle it."

And there it is, Lexie thought, chuckling humorlessly. Her burning stomach churned. "Let me get this straight. You accuse me of freeloading off you and Dad, but when I move out into my own place, you don't think I can handle it. Make up your damn mind." Another *thack* as her knife sliced through a fleshy potato.

An equally loud *thack* came from Jane's cutting board. "Aren't you worried about your safety? Living in this...neighborhood?"

"As a matter of fact, no. I'm not worried at all." *Thack*.

"You look like you've gained a few pounds since you moved here," Jane said. "I wish you would take better care of yourself, Alexis." *Thack*.

Exasperated, Lexie let go of her knife. It clattered noisily on the cutting board. She glared at her mother, eyes (and stomach) burning. "In four days? Jesus Christ, Mom. Enough."

Jane calmly continued cutting potatoes, a bit more slowly than before. A deep vertical line had appeared between her perfectly-shaped black eyebrows. Without looking up, she said, "I raised you better than this." *Thack.*

Lexie knew this comment was about more than just her weight, and it was the last straw. "Raised me better than what, exactly? This house in the city? My out-of-wedlock pregnancy? My less-than-perfect body?"

Jane stopped cutting and stared evenly at her daughter. "Yes. You can do so much better."

Pure red ringed Lexie's vision and lava boiled in her stomach. "So I'm a disappointment. Is that what I'm hearing?" She didn't give her mother a chance to reply. "I choose not to live your highbrow suburban life, and now I've somehow failed as your daughter? Because, as usual, it's fucking all about you. Well, guess what. I love my kid, I love this house, and I'm proud of the life Ava and I are building together. She is going to have the best life, surrounded by love and authentic people, and she's going to have a taste of all the good and bad things." Lexie held her mother's gaze. "And I'm done with your asshole comments about my weight. You think I don't know? You think I don't think about my weight every minute of every day? Get it through your thick skull, Mom – I'm never going to be the perfect daughter you always wanted." Lexie paused for emphasis. "And I don't need your shitty comments. Back off."

Her hands shook a bit as she reached across the counter to grab the last potato. Her left thumb passed over the outside edge of Jane's cutting board. Lexie felt a tiny wisp of air and heard a loud THACK. It took a second or two for her conscious mind to catch up to her senses – and she saw Jane's knife deeply embedded in the cutting board, the deadly smoothness of the blade nearly touching the tip of Lexie's thumb. Jane had come within a millimeter of slicing it like it was just another potato.

Lexie snatched her hand back. "What the hell, Mom?" she shouted, incredulous.

Jane said nothing, and rested her head in her hands.

The back door opened and Paul appeared. "The grill is ready, where are those steaks?" He stopped midstride on his way to the refrigerator, taking in the pile of cut potatoes and sensing that something was happening between his wife and daughter. "What's going on?"

Lexie gave her mother one last mistrustful look, then started gathering the cut potatoes to transfer them to the pot of boiling water on the stove. "Nothing. We were just cutting up the potatoes for the potato salad."

The look on Paul's face made it clear that he understood something was going on, but wasn't sure he really wanted to know what. "Okay. How long for the potato salad?" He opened the refrigerator.

"Give me thirty minutes," Lexie said. She ducked under her father's arms and pulled out the sauce ingredients and the fresh dill.

Paul laid the steaks on a plate and took them outside, casting a doubtful glance over his shoulder.

Jane sat at the breakfast bar, one veiny hand on top of the other in front of her, dully watching Lexie assemble the potato salad. Lexie's heart pounded as she worked, the near miss between her thumb and her mother's knife playing over and over again in her mind. The nearly imperceptible poof of air she'd felt as the razor-sharp knife blade just barely missed her thumb was what really stuck in her mind. Her stomach roiled; she swallowed hard in an effort to keep the burning acid at bay. *Where is my goddamn antacid?*

The back door opened again and Paul stuck his head in. "Steaks are done," he announced. "Bring the potato salad out here, it's a perfect day to eat outside."

Lexie gathered plates and forks and the large bowl of potato salad. "Come on, Mom." She walked outside – the usual zing in her head barely noticeable – and headed for the picnic table, which sat under the other old oak tree in the back yard. It really was a beautiful evening; the temperature hovered around eighty degrees, and there was just enough breeze to keep the worst of the flies away. She reflexively drew a deep breath and realized her heartburn had finally subsided.

She was just setting the large bowl on the table when she heard Ava say "Gramma? Are you sick?" Lexie whipped around just in time to see Jane collapse at the bottom of the back stoop. Paul was there before Lexie could take a step; he lifted his unconscious wife effortlessly and carried her to the chaise longue. Ava followed him, wide-eyed.

Lexie went to them. "What happened?"

Paul shook his head. "I don't know. She just passed out." He examined Jane head to toe. Apparently satisfied that she was not sick or seriously injured, he touched her face. "She's out cold, but otherwise seems all right. I wonder why she just fainted like that."

Lexie debated how much she should tell her dad. *Oh, it's no big deal, Dad. This happens regularly to Ava and me. I mean, sure, it's true we don't know why this happens, but hey – at least it doesn't kill you.*

Ava decided for her. "Mommy fell down before. I thought she died but Ryan said she was just taking a nap. And I had a nap in the front yard yesterday," she said. "Just like Gramma. Is she gonna be okay, Grampa?" Her little face was strained with worry.

Paul pulled Ava to him and kissed the top of her head. "She'll be fine, Cutes. I promise." Then he turned to Lexie. "Is she saying this has happened before?"

She opened her mouth and tried to buy time to decide how she was going to explain this to her father by making a drawn-out a-a-a-a-a-a-a sound before lamely finishing with a simple "Yes."

Paul regarded his daughter for a moment. "Okay. What causes someone to randomly collapse at your house?"

Lexie shrugged. "I honestly don't know. I feel a strange zap in my brain when I leave my house. Remember when I was seven and I stuck a penny in an electrical outlet?" Paul nodded. "I got a shock then, and the zap in my head feels just like that. Only inside my brain. Sometimes I feel it all over my body too, like static electricity. Sometimes it's so strong it knocks me unconscious, other times I barely feel it."

Paul turned to Ava. "Do you feel weird things in your head too, Cutes?"

Ava nodded. "Yeah. And my arms and legs too."

"But only when you go from inside to outside the house."

"Right," Lexie said.

"Why?"

"Yeah, that's what I don't know."

Paul frowned, making his careworn face look less like a basset hound and more like a bloodhound. "How long has this been going on?"

Lexie drew in a deep breath and blinked rapidly, again trying to buy a few seconds before she had to answer, then exhaled and said "Since we moved in."

Paul stood and went to the back door. He opened it and stepped inside, then stepped outside. He did this twice more while Lexie and Ava watched. He returned and kneeled next to his unconscious wife again. "I didn't feel anything."

Lexie nodded. "My neighbor Ryan didn't either."

"Are you taking any new medications? Or did you stop any abruptly?"

Lexie rolled her eyes. "No changes in medications, Dad. Besides, if it was that, Ava wouldn't have experienced it too."

Paul frowned again and looked at the house. "Maybe there's something going on with the electrical system."

"The house just passed an inspection a month ago. Don't you think that would have caught electrical issues?"

Paul sighed and looked at his wife. Jane stirred and her eyelids fluttered. "Maybe you should come home with us. I'll call Pat and have him check the house over." Paul's old high school buddy Pat Carbone owned a construction company. "I should have done that before you bought the place. It might not be safe."

Lexie shook her head. "No," she said firmly. "We're fine here."

Paul gestured at Jane, who was now conscious and looking around uncertainly. "You call this fine?"

Lexie scowled and set her jaw. "We're fine."

Jane sat up abruptly. "What happened? Why am I outside?" Her hands patted her hair.

Paul held out his hands. "How do you feel, hon?"

"My head hurts." She batted Paul's hands away. "I want to go home. Go inside and get my purse, I set it in the living room."

Paul loped to the back door and disappeared.

Jane stood and looked at her daughter, chin raised and more than a little defiant. "Your dad and I won't be visiting you here again."

"It's probably better that way." Lexie's voice was absolutely emotionless.

Paul reappeared and handed Jane her purse. He kissed Lexie's and Ava's heads. "I'll talk to you girls soon, okay?" Then he followed his wife around the house, and they were gone.

Ava's tiny hand slipped into Lexie's. "Are we gonna be okay, Mommy?"

What Lexie thought: *I don't know. I hope so.*

What Lexie said: "Of course we are, babydoll. Come on, help me take this stuff inside."

9

Another night in her new house, another dream.

She stared at a large framed photo that hung on a blank, anonymous wall in a silent, foggy, gray room. She blinked, then squinted, trying to see the image in the photograph through the swirling mist.

It was a dark, vaguely human-shaped blob. Its edges slowly sharpened, it gradually changed from charcoal to color, and its features became more defined as it came into focus. She blinked again, and could finally see what the blob was.

It was the little girl from her dreams. Her other dreams. The tot, who couldn't have been more than four years old, stood in the front yard of the house on Washburn Avenue. Her straight blonde hair was cut in a perfect blunt bowl that, along with the photo's distinctly orange tint, suggested it had been taken sometime in the late 1970s or early 1980s. The girl wore a white dress with cherries scattered across it and white Mary Jane shoes. She held a small stuffed doll by its long orange yarn hair. A red tricycle sat next to her; it had been overturned, and Lexie imagined the larger front wheel with its white pedals spinning lazily.

The camera had captured a distant look on the girl's chubby little face. But if Lexie squinted a bit harder and leaned a little closer to the photo, she swore she could see anger, and maybe a touch of fear, lurking in those big brown eyes.

Then the eyes moved.

The little girl in the photo stared right at Lexie. Rage emanated from the child like heat from summer asphalt. Lexie recoiled –

Her eyes snapped open. She was panting and covered in a sheen of sweat; her tank top and boxer shorts stuck to her skin. She closed her eyes, covered them with her hands, and took a deep breath, willing her heart to slow its jerky pace. *What the fuck was that?* Another headache drifted behind her eyes like a cold morning's fog.

"Mama."

Startled, Lexie jerked her hands from her face and peered up, trying to blink her eyes into focus in the nearly dark room. Eventually she could make out Ava standing next to her bed, staring at her with an intensity that Lexie had never seen from Ava before. The little girl's face was slack, completely devoid of any expression – except her eyes. Ava's eyes churned with absolute rage.

She slowly sat up, blinking through intensifying pain behind her eyes. "Ava? What's wrong, baby?"

"You said we were having a picnic, Mama," Ava said.

Lexie's fear was momentarily replaced by complete confusion. Her head felt cloudy. Slow. "I – what?"

Ava's face went from expressionless to contorted with rage in a fraction of a second. "WE'RE HAVING A PICNIC! YOU PROMISED!" she screamed.

Lexie stared at Ava, who kept on screaming at top volume. Her little arms waved and slammed to her sides, and her feet stomped for good measure. She was having a full-on temper tantrum. "I WANNA HAVE A PICNIC, MAMA! MICHAEL HAS TO COME TOO!"

Something about this seemed familiar somehow. Not Ava's behavior; this was so completely out of character for her that the child might as well have been someone else's. No. It was the words Ava spoke that tickled some forgotten memory in Lexie's brain. Try as she might, she could not call the memory up through the increasingly heavy fog in her head.

Ava continued to jerk violently around the room, nonsensical noises still pouring from her – then she suddenly stopped, facing the knee-high wall to the right of Lexie's bed. Lexie watched apprehensively, waiting for whatever might come next. She didn't dare speak or even move, for fear of setting Ava off again.

Then, suddenly, Ava whirled around to face her mother. The look on her face was a perfect mixture of intense hate and pure evil -- not a look that was particularly at home on the girl's normally sweet little face. Lexie froze. *Dear God, her eyes.* Even in the dimness of her room, with its one nightlight (placed so Ava could easily get to her in the middle of the night), she could see the girl's eyes were a deep brown and not their usual pale blue. The same eyes as the girl in her dream.

Her subconscious – or maybe it was sheer panic – sliced through her foggy pain and took over from there. Lexie shot out of bed, swept her daughter up in her arms, and ran toward the stairs. Ava began thrashing and screaming about a picnic again as Lexie thundered down the stairs two at a time, in the dark, nearly going ass over teakettle when she hit the floor at the bottom unexpectedly while running at full speed. She recovered, somehow still holding her flailing daughter, and headed for the front door. For one panicky second her fingers slipped off the deadbolt as she tried to disengage it. Ava's constant squirming wasn't helping. Finally she got a grip, threw the front door open, and ran into the cool summer night.

Lexie's head zapped and her headache disappeared as she stepped through the door; Ava went silent and limp in her arms. She ran down her front walk and didn't stop until she reached the curb. Her heart galloped in her chest as she drew in great gasping lungsful of air; she hadn't run like that since she went through the haunted house at the Minnesota State Fair in the eighth grade and one of the monsters – a mummy, if Lexie recalled correctly – reached out and touched her.

She turned and looked at her house. The orange glow of the streetlight on one side cast the other side in deep, menacing shadow. For the first time, Lexie saw her house not as her safe place, the home to complete the life she was building for herself and her daughter, but as a scary, maybe even dangerous, place. Like the haunted house. Terrified tears welled in her eyes and spilled down her cheeks, and fear clamped around her chest. She couldn't get enough air, no matter how hard she tried.

A light popped on inside the front window of Ryan's house, followed by the outside light. Lexie heard the familiar creak as Ryan opened the door, then saw his silhouette. "Lexie?" he called out. "What's going on?"

"Ryan!" Lexie ran to him through damp grass, sobbing, still carrying Ava. Her back and shoulder muscles burned. Ryan, rumpled from sleep and also wearing a tank top and boxer shorts, stepped outside and lifted Ava from her arms. Her lips moved and her tongue tried to form words, but her lungs were too busy trying to breathe. Every inhale was a high-pitched squeal.

"Come on." Ryan settled Ava on his left arm, laying her head against his shoulder, and gently took Lexie's elbow with his right hand. "You're safe." He guided Lexie inside, to a couch in the dimly lit living room; he carefully laid Ava at one end of the sofa and pointed Lexie to the other. "Sit down."

Lexie sat, still struggling to breathe.

"Relax, take deep breaths, and I'll make you a cup of tea." He disappeared, and Lexie heard water running into a teapot and the comforting rattle of ceramic mugs. Her panic attack finally started to subside. The clamp around her chest eased; she filled her lungs and then blew the air out between pursed lips. A glance at Ava, curled in a ball and sleeping soundly with a decorative pillow under her head, calmed her mind even further. She felt vulnerable and basically naked in her tank top and boxers; she spied a red cashmere blanket draped over the back of the sofa, pulled it down, and covered herself and Ava with it. *There*, she thought, satisfied that the evidence of her preference for potato chips over broccoli was less obvious now.

She listened to Ryan's activity in the kitchen and looked around his living room as she worked to calm her breathing. His house was identical to hers in its layout, but the difference in ambience was stark. Lexie's house was a bright and sterile flip; this was a bona fide bachelor pad – and it appeared to have money behind it. The walls were painted a rich, warm gray. The black leather tufted sofa she and Ava currently occupied sat along the wall, facing the picture window. Two matching cube-shaped lounge chairs on wooden legs sat next to each other at a ninety degree angle to the couch, facing a fireplace with a handcrafted slate surround. A heavy-looking cast iron and barnwood console table sat directly in front of the window; upon it sat a variety of framed photos and small bronze table lamp with a stained glass shade (Lexie came from affluence herself and recognized a vintage Tiffany dragonfly shade when she saw one; her mother had one just like it – bigger, of course) that cast the room in a dim but comforting glow. An antique grandfather clock stood sentry in the hallway between the front entry and the stairs leading to the half-story above.

The room had an air of luxury and pretentiousness that its resident did not. *How does he afford this stuff on a teacher's salary?* she wondered.

The teacher in question reappeared with two steaming mugs in his hands; much to Lexie's disappointment, he had wrapped himself in a plaid flannel robe. He handed one mug to Lexie, who took it gingerly, then sat in the chair closest to her. She took a tiny sip of the steaming herbal tea. *Mmm, eucalyptus.* The tension melted from her shoulders and neck.

Ryan sipped his own tea and looked frankly at Lexie. "If I were a betting man, I'd guess you were looking around this room and admiring my impeccable taste in interior decorating." A wry smile crossed his lips. Lexie realized that this must be what he'd looked like as a kid: impish, yet serious.

Her cheeks heated up like a burner on a stove. "Well, I did notice the vintage Tiffany lamp," she admitted. "My mom has one like it. I guess I didn't realize you had such..."

"...expensive taste?"

Lexie drew in a long, deep breath, stalling for time as she tried to find the right words. Finally she blew the air out and said, rather lamely, "Yeah, pretty much." Her entire face burned now, a fact she tried to hide by dropping her eyes and taking another sip of the soothing tea.

"Don't be embarrassed. I'm a teacher. I notice pretty much everything," he said, and touched her bare arm.

Gooseflesh coursed across Lexie's skin. She looked up and directly into his eyes, and a strange, almost forgotten sensation started in her chest and made its way down her spine, settling in her belly. She swallowed, tried to smile, then looked away and hastily took another sip of tea. *God, I suck at being around attractive men,* she thought. *How did I ever manage to get one interested enough in me to get pregnant?*

"I inherited some of it," Ryan said. He turned and gazed fondly at the grandfather clock at the base of the stairs. "My grandparents owned a high-end antique shop in St. Paul. They kept a few of the more valuable pieces when they sold the place and retired, and passed them to me when they died."

"Oh." Lexie suddenly saw the entire room differently. Where she had first seen extravagance, she now saw precious heirlooms. What she had mistaken for flamboyance turned out to be a deep appreciation for the craftsmanship of bygone generations. She remembered the garden trowel he held in a gloved hand on the day they met and wondered why his appreciation of the finer things should surprise her. Clearly there was more to him than just his job. *I guess he's not just a macho football coach*, she thought.

"The rest I saved up for, piece by piece. It's pretty easy to do when you're chronically single and all you do is work." He looked at Lexie levelly. "I mean, except during the summer. This summer, anyway; usually I pick up a summer school class or two, but this year I thought I'd give myself a break, see how the other half live."

Lexie nodded. Her tea was cooling in her hand, but she was too engrossed in Ryan's deep brown eyes to notice. After a few beats, he grinned and she blinked. "Oh. Sorry. Um, how are things going with your hostas?"

Ryan let out a surprised laugh, and a delicate snore burst from Ava just as he opened his mouth to reply. She mumbled something unintelligible, turned over to her other side, and stilled.

Ryan set his tea on the side table next to his chair. "Oh, they're fine. The biggest problem with those is that I have way too many." He chuckled again and shook his head, running a hand over the dark stubble on the rear forty of his scalp. "You know, it's funny. Growing up I always thought I'd be a cop."

"Yeah?" Lexie said, and took another sip of her tea.

"Yeah. I wanted to be a cop because I wanted to help people. I know it sounds cliché, but it's true." He sipped from his own tea. "You know my grandparents' antique shop? When I was nine years old, I had a day off school and my mom dropped me off at the shop so she could go to work. I was in the back moving some stuff around for my grandpa when I heard my grandma give this godawful scream from the show floor. The sound scared the bejesus out of me, and I still hear it in my dreams sometimes." He shuddered.

"I snuck out to the front of the store and hid behind this huge armoire. I was just in time to watch my grandpa finish filling a paper bag with what little cash they had and hand it to a crazy-looking guy who was pointing a gun at my grandma's face. He took the bag and ran for the door, but he stopped just long enough to fire a round into the ceiling. I remember I jumped and covered my ears. I'd never heard a noise so loud before."

"Did he – were they –?" Lexie had so many words she wanted to say, and none of them would come out.

"No, he didn't shoot my grandparents, and they were okay. Although they were shook up pretty bad. They called the police right away, and within just a few minutes two officers arrived. I remember they seemed so big and strong in their police uniforms with the cool hats and the guns on their hips, and it seemed like them just being there was enough to calm my grandma and grandpa down. I know I felt safer with them there." He sighed. "That was the exact moment I knew that's what I wanted to do. Help people during some of the hardest times in their lives."

"Did they catch the guy?"

"Yes, they sure did. I got a good look at the guy from my hiding spot, so I was able to give the officers a description. Within the hour they found the strung-out cokehead wandering down University Avenue, holding his ancient .22 caliber revolver in one hand and the bag of money in the other hand, and babbling about how the aliens were watching his every move." He laughed out loud. "He made it easy for them."

Lexie set her mug on the mahogany coffee table and took his hand in hers. "What made you decide to become a teacher?

"I took a lousy tackle during a game my senior year of high school and blew every ligament in my left knee," Ryan said, gently squeezing her hand. His warmth gave her a bit of comfort after a rough week. "The surgeons put it back together, and I did six months' worth of rehab, but it'll never be the same. I couldn't chase a suspect on foot or carry an incapacitated adult without likely reinjuring my knee, so that meant the end of my law enforcement career before it even began." He sighed. "Luckily I had a decent Plan B; I was a hell of a running back, and I had already committed to the University of Minnesota when I was injured. So I decided to translate my passion for football into a career – and I majored in both education and kinesiology so I could teach physical education."

Lexie was impressed. "Wow."

They sat in silence for a few moments. Ryan stared at their joined hands, and Lexie stared at Ryan. Then his smooth, deep voice broke her reverie.

"Hmmm?" She hadn't heard a single word he'd said. She was too focused on how holding his hand made her feel more at peace than she had since the day she moved in.

Ryan smiled. "I said, what happened at your house just now?"

She blinked and let go of Ryan's hand. "The strangest thing," she said, and pulled the blanket up over her shoulders and crossed her arms under it to ward off a sudden chill. "I woke up from a nightmare to find Ava standing next to my bed, staring at me. The look on her face..." She shuddered. "I swear to god she meant to hurt me."

"Why?" Ryan asked.

Lexie shrugged. "I don't know. Although..."

"Although what?"

"Never mind. It's too weird. I must have imagined it."

"Tell me."

Lexie gazed at Ryan's face, trying to decide if she could trust him not to laugh. She sighed. "Ava's eyes were brown."

A frown creased Ryan's forehead. "What do you mean?"

"I mean, Ava has blue eyes. But I have a nightlight in my bedroom and even in that dim light I could see that she was looking at me with brown eyes. Very *angry* brown eyes."

Ryan sat back into his chair and regarded Lexie with a carefully passive expression. *Great. He's trying not to laugh right in my face,* she thought. She picked up her mug again and sipped her tea, then said, "She went into an absolute rage over a picnic I'd apparently promised her, and screamed that Michael had to come too. And she called me 'Mama' – that's a new one, she always calls me 'Mommy.'" Lexie pulled the blanket tighter around herself. "All I could think to do was grab her and just run."

"Did she pass out as soon as you stepped outside? Like those other times?"

Lexie nodded.

Ryan was silent for a moment, then: "You know what I think?"

"What's that?"

Ryan leaned forward again. "I think Joanna Schmitt might be on to something."

It was Lexie's turn to frown. "What do you mean?"

"Didn't you tell me you thought she was trying to tell you your house is haunted? Without actually saying your house is haunted?"

Lexie nodded, slowly at first, and then faster as she recalled her conversation with the pharmacist on Wednesday. It seemed like an eternity ago. "That's right. She implied that people get violent and kill and die in my house." She chuckled. "Seemed like a crazy idea at the time."

"Does it seem that way now? After all the strange stuff that's been going on the last few days?"

"Not so much anymore, no."

"Let's think about why she would say that," Ryan said. He opened a drawer in the side table and pulled out a blue Bic pen and yellow legal pad. He noticed the look on Lexie's face and smiled. "I'm a teacher. I keep these everywhere. Just because I teach phy ed doesn't mean I don't need a notebook occasionally."

Lexie took a deep breath while Ryan turned to a clean page in his legal pad. "Okay." She thought for a second. "Joanna said that before me, an investor bought my house from the State of Minnesota and flipped it within a month or so."

Ryan nodded as he wrote in his notebook. "That's affirmative. Nice guy. His name was Jason. Borrowed a tool or two from me."

"Before that, Joanna said the state owned the house for I want to say eight years, ran a halfway house for teenage girls coming out of treatment."

"Yes. That's who was in the house when I bought mine six years ago. Lots of police calls. One very close call for one unfortunate girl." His pen scratched against the paper as he wrote furiously.

"Before that…" Lexie struggled to recall. A veil of exhaustion settled over her brain; she'd gotten maybe a couple hours of sleep, and she had to work in – she glanced at her watch – four short hours. *It's going to be a very long Friday.*

"The lady who fell down the basement stairs." Ryan looked up from his pad.

Lexie remembered. "Yes. Kathryn Dormeister. Joanna called her Kath. Her husband went to prison for her murder, but Joanna seems pretty convinced he's innocent." Kathryn's name triggered the memory of herself nearly throwing Ava down those same stairs the day before; Lexie pushed it away. *He'll have me arrested for sure if I mention that.*

"Got it. What else?"

Lexie shook her head. "That's as far as we got. We had to leave before Ava talked me into buying every sparkly-eyed stuffed animal in the store." She looked affectionately at Ava, sleeping soundly under her end of the blanket.

"What if we looked it up?" He stood and walked into the kitchen, then came back holding a black-cased tablet. He sat next to Lexie on the couch, careful not to disturb Ava. "Let's do a search for your address, see what we come up with."

He powered up the tablet, opened a search engine, and typed in Lexie's address. Search results popped up immediately. Ryan scrolled past two pages' worth of real estate listings from when Lexie's house was for sale, then:

www.startribune.com: **Minneapolis group home resident arrested for attempted murder.** February 24, 2018.

There were a number of these, documenting the entire case. Ryan kept scrolling until:

www.startribune.com: **Dormeister guilty in wife's Minneapolis murder.** March 2, 2012.

They skimmed a few of the articles about Kathryn Dormeister's murder case, which underscored everything Joanna had told Lexie. John Dormeister had fierce advocates in his neighbors and an attorney who tried everything to get a not guilty verdict for his client, even going so far as to accuse Hennepin County Attorney James McCormick, who personally tried the case, of suffering from tunnel vision and cherry-picking evidence to fit his theory. In the end, despite the defense's best efforts, the jury sent John Dormeister to prison for life.

Lexie studied a photograph of Dormeister being led out of the courtroom after the verdict. He was tall, skinny, dark-haired, and wore khaki pants, a white collared shirt, and a striped tie. Glasses with narrow rectangular lenses sat on his long nose. *He looks more like an accountant than a wife-killer,* Lexie thought.

There was nothing beyond the Dormeisters until, roughly a dozen pages into the search, one obscure result caught Ryan's eye:

www.newspapers.com: **Gilmartin, Lucy.** October 21, 1981.

He clicked the link and immediately encountered a paywall. He typed in a username and password, and an obituary scanned from an old newspaper appeared on the screen. He grinned proudly at Lexie. "I'm a bit of an amateur genealogist as well as an antiques collector. This subscription does come in handy."

Lexie chuckled and shook her head. "You continue to surprise me. A handsome teacher and coach with a soft side and refined tastes? Who knew such a thing existed?"

Ryan nudged her with his shoulder. "Right. And a pretty nurse with an adorable kid who may have accidentally purchased a haunted house? That's a new one for me."

She smiled and nudged him back with her own shoulder. At the exact moment her face was closest to his, he leaned in and kissed her. Surprised, Lexie pulled air in through her nose. His lips were warm and soft, and tasted like eucalyptus tea. Her hand found the back of his head and pulled him closer; their kiss deepened, became more urgent, and their tongues intertwined. Lexie sensed in him the same loneliness that she lived with every day; being a full-time single parent with a career didn't leave much extra time for a life. He'd used the words "chronically single;" she could completely relate.

Familiar and unwelcome thoughts cruised across her mind: *How can he stand to touch me? Doesn't he see how fat I am?* She squinched her eyes closed even more tightly and tried to ignore them, focusing instead on the warmth of his lips and the pleasant scratchiness of his whiskers against her cheeks. Her heart leapt in her chest.

Finally they disengaged and pulled back. Lexie caught Ryan's wide chocolate eyes and held them for one electric moment. "Um. Wow."

"I've been wanting to do that for a long time," he whispered. "Ever since Ava invited me over for dinner and you offered me one of your chicken wings."

That made Lexie laugh, which in turn made Ryan laugh. Quietly, so as not to wake Ava, who was snoring again. Ryan said, "Let's see what Lucy here is about, shall we?"

I'd rather kiss some more, Lexie thought. But the moment had passed, and they turned their attention back to the screen.

Gilmartin, Lucy

Lucy Gilmartin, nee Madden, age 26 of 4741 Washburn Avenue North, Minneapolis, passed away at home on October 14. Mrs. Gilmartin took her own life less than two years after the untimely death of her husband, George.

Mrs. Gilmartin is survived by her son, Michael. She is predeceased by her beloved husband, George and her parents, Lee and Joyce Madden. Services have been held.

"Well. That might be the most depressing death notice I've ever read," Lexie remarked.

Ryan bookmarked Lucy's obituary in his browser. "No kidding. Let's see if we can find George's obituary. Maybe we can find out what kind of freak accident he had." Ryan typed George Gilmartin's name into a search engine, and the first result was:

www.newspapers.com: **Gilmartin, George**. January 15, 1980.

Ryan clicked the link, and another obituary appeared.

Gilmartin, George

Funeral services for George LeRoy Gilmartin, age 27 of 4741 Washburn Avenue North, Minneapolis, were held January 14 at Church of Saint Austin.

George passed away unexpectedly as a result of a workplace accident on January 10. He spent all of his life in Minneapolis, and was the proprietor of the Gilmartin's Garage on Washington Avenue. He was a lifelong member of St. Austin Church, a skilled mechanic, a kind father, and a loving husband.

George is survived by his wife Lucy and twin children Michael and Melissa Ann. He was preceded in death by his parents Frederick and Susan, and his infant brother Frank.

"Those kids lost both of their parents in the span of about eighteen months. Poor things." Lexie yawned.

"Wait a second," Ryan murmured. He pulled Lucy's obituary up in a second browser window and placed it next to George's on the screen, then pointed. "Look at this. According to George's obituary, he had two kids, Michael and Melissa Ann. But Lucy's obituary only mentions Michael."

Lexie, who'd been having limited success with keeping her heavy eyelids open, remembered something and suddenly sat up straight. "Hold on. Ava said the name Michael during her picnic tantrum." She looked at Ryan, wide-eyed. *And...I've heard the name Michael somewhere before.* The memory remained tantalizingly out of reach, however, so she didn't mention it.

He looked back at her with equally wide eyes. "So what happened to Melissa Ann?"

10

A steady, maddening high-pitched beep slowly drew Lexie out of the deep darkness of a sound sleep. She tried to ignore it and dive back down into unconsciousness. She almost succeeded, too, until her favorite little voice whispered, "Mommy, it's time to get up. Your Alabama is going off."

Lexie cracked one eye open, and there was Ava's sweet face just inches from her own. The girl had lines carved into her left cheek from the decorative pillow she'd slept on, and her curly blonde hair was a tangled mess, but she broke into a thousand-watt smile as soon as Lexie opened her eyes. She and Ava were cuddled on Ryan's couch under the cashmere blanket. Even though she'd only slept for a few hours, it was the best sleep she'd had all week.

"I think you mean my alarm," Lexie said. She silenced her watch and looked at the time: 5:00 a.m. *I must have fallen asleep while Ryan was searching for Michael Gilmartin,* she thought. *I wonder if he found him.*

"Where are we, Mommy?" Ava asked. She'd sat up and was looking around the room. "Is this Ryan's house?"

"Yep," Lexie said, then stretched and yawned.

"Did we have a sleepover?"

"Kind of," Lexie said. "You and I both had bad dreams last night, so Ryan said we could stay here."

"Oh," Ava said. The sky outside Ryan's picture window was starting to brighten.

A plan for the day formed in Lexie's head: she would run home to quickly get ready for work and pack a bag for Ava, then take her to Cindy's. After work she'd take Ava to her parents' house to stay. *Better get moving, or I'll be late for work.*

"You stay here, babygirl. Mommy's going to run home and get ready for work quick. After Cindy's you're going to Grandma and Grandpa's house for a little while."

"YAY!" Ava shouted, and bounced on the sofa.

Lexie shushed her. "Ryan's still sleeping babydoll, we have to be quiet. And don't jump on his couch please. Sit."

Ava sat.

"Don't move. I'll be right back." Lexie slipped out the front door and jogged through the dawnlight to her house. The front door was still ajar, but otherwise the house looked exactly as it had when she went to bed last night. Except now, alone in the house for the first time, Lexie could sense an actual presence – an unseen energy that she swore was trying to force its way into her brain. The foggy headache was creeping back. She gritted her teeth against the invisible pressure and moved quickly, changing into clean scrubs and her athletic shoes, pulling her hair into a messy bun on top of her head, and throwing a bag together for herself and Ava.

At the last second she remembered to grab her Kum & Go cup from the dishwasher, and her purse, then beelined out the front door. She barely registered the zap in her head. Then she closed the door and locked it behind her. *There. Neither of us will sleep in this house again until I know what the hell is going on.*

She carried her tote bag, Ava's tiny rolling unicorn suitcase, her purse, and her empty coffee mug over to Ryan's, where she found the two of them sitting in the dining room, at a 1950s-style chrome and laminate table with matching vinyl chairs, eating breakfast and watching a cartoon on a small TV. The retro dinette set should have looked out of place in Ryan's otherwise luxurious home, but oddly enough, it didn't. Morning sunlight streamed through a sliding glass door and fell on the retro black and white tile floor. A large framed poster print of a palm tree adorned the blue wall. The checkered floor extended into the kitchen, where white cabinets and multicolored granite countertops gleamed. She could smell coffee brewing.

Ryan, wearing the same flannel robe as last night, glanced up from the pink milk in his bowl. "Everything go all right?"

"I guess so," Lexie said, collapsing into the chair next to Ava, who ignored her.

Ryan finished his cereal, then stood and said, "Ava, your mom and I are going to go in the living room for a minute, okay?"

"Okay." Ava shoveled a spoonful of cereal into her mouth, never moving her eyes away from the TV.

Ryan led Lexie into the living room, where they sat side by side on the couch. Lexie flashed back to the night before, when they sat in this exact spot and shared a wonderful kiss. That intense sensation fired up in her belly again. She didn't really hear what he was saying because she couldn't stop staring at his lips while he talked.

"Lex?"

She blinked. "Huh?"

He grinned. "Did you hear a word I said?"

She briefly considered trying to fake it, but then realized he probably already knew what was on her mind. "Not really. I'm sorry. I was distracted..."

"Thinking about that kiss? Me too," he whispered. He touched her chin, forcing her to look him in the eye, then leaned in and pressed his lips to hers. Her eyes closed and she savored him – his warmth, his personal scent that reminded her of aged vanilla, his warm lips. She touched his stubbled cheek with her hand. She wanted more of this man. Much more.

And then the self-doubt crashed in again. Panicked thoughts tumbled over themselves in her mind like balls in a revolving bingo basket. *He's so handsome and fit, why would he kiss me when he could have his pick of any pretty woman out there? Is this some kind of trick? Why would he do this?* She couldn't ignore them this time and pulled back abruptly.

Ryan opened his eyes and frowned. "What's wrong?

"I – I don't want to be late for work," she said. She couldn't quite meet his gaze.

He gazed at her for a moment, confusion clear on his face. "Okay. So what's next?"

Lexie pulled her hair tie out and ran her hands through her hair. "I have to figure out what the hell is going on with my house. I'm going to take Ava over to my parents' after work, then I thought I'd swing by The Apothecary and have another chat with Joanna. I was thinking the library might be a good resource too, I could swing in there..."

Ryan took her hand and shushed her. "Lexie. Let me help you."

"No, I can't ask you to do that, Ryan. You have enough on your mind. This is my problem to solve."

"You don't have to do this alone, Lex. I have nothing but time, and I want to help you. I want to know what's going on as much as you do."

Lexie stared at Ryan, unsure of what to think. Lexie had been doing everything herself for so long. Oh, sure, her parents helped with Ava, but her mother always made sure she knew there were strings attached. Beyond that, Lexie was a one-woman show, and it never really occurred to her to ask for help.

"Let me help you. Please?" he said again.

She finally relented. "Okay. Thank you."

He smiled. "Great. While you're at work today I'll call over to The Apothecary and ask Joanna if she can meet with us this evening. I'll also spend some more time looking online to see if I can find anything on Michael Gilmartin. That must be the same Michael we keep hearing about. Has to be."

"You didn't find anything last night?" Lexie asked.

"I fell asleep about ninety seconds after you did. Woke up an hour later, just enough to cover you and Ava up and take myself to bed."

Lexie pulled her hair back up into its customary messy bun. "Okay. Keep me posted."

She started to stand up, but Ryan took hold of her arm and pulled her back down. "You understand that you can't go back to your house, right?"

"Yes. We won't be spending one more night there until I – I mean, we – figure this out."

"Where will you stay?"

"My parents' house, I guess." She shrugged and tried to hide her disdain; she did not want to go crawling back to Mom and Dad, but she didn't see any other options. "I'm taking Ava there tonight after work."

"Drop her off there and come back here."

Lexie blinked. "Come back...here?"

Ryan was still holding her arm. "This will be much easier if you stay close, and Ava will be safe with your parents."

"Um, okay," Lexie stammered. *Oh god oh god oh god, don't be awkward.*

Ryan grinned. "Don't worry, you won't have to sleep on the couch again. I'll make up the guest bed for you."

Lexie relaxed and returned his smile. "Sounds like a plan." This time Ryan didn't stop her as she got to her feet. "I really do have to go. See you later."

"Have a good day."

Lexie collected her bags and Ava, who had finished her cereal, and dropped her off at Cindy's. Then she called her parents on her way to the hospital, hoping she wouldn't wake them considering the early hour. She braced herself for her mother; they hadn't spoken since yesterday's incident. As luck would have it, her father answered the phone, already halfway into his second cup of coffee. *I suppose it's hard to stop living on a doctor's schedule, even after retirement.* She explained what she needed, and prayed he wouldn't ask too many questions.

"Yes. Of course Ava can stay here," Paul said immediately. "What's going on?"

"Well, you know how Mom randomly passed out when you guys were over for dinner yesterday?"

"I do. I have a message in with Pat to come take a look at your electrical system, just waiting on a callback."

Lexie rolled her eyes. "The electrical system is the least of my worries, Dad."

"But there's *something* wrong with the house," Paul said. "Your mom won't tell me what happened, but she's adamant that she won't go back there. Not even to see Ava."

"Yes. It's become clear that there is something going on with the house. But I'm not sure exactly what yet, and I need Ava to be in a safe place while I figure it out."

"Okay, and what about you?"

"My next door neighbor has offered to let me crash in his guest room. He has some time on his hands, so he's going to help me research."

A few seconds of silence from Paul, then: "This is the Ryan Ava has talked about?"

The sound of Ryan's name made Lexie's heart skip a beat. "Yeah."

"All right, we'll see you when you get here," Paul said. "Will you want some dinner? I have steaks in the freezer."

"I'll take a raincheck," Lexie said. "I have appointments to talk to people tonight, so I'll just drop her and head out." Lexie paused. "I'm glad you answered the phone instead of Mom. I don't know if I could have had this conversation with her. Thanks, Dad."

"Of course, Cutes. And don't worry about your mom. She'll come around. You and Ava moving out has been harder on her than she admits; it'll help to have Ava back here for a few days."

Lexie blinked, more than a little surprised. It had never once occurred to her that her mother might be sad that she'd moved into a place of her own. Jane so carefully cultivated an aloof façade that Lexie tended to forget that she had actual feelings like everyone else. Hot shame crawled up her neck as she remembered some of the things she'd said yesterday – *Get it through your thick skull – I'm never going to be the perfect daughter you always wanted.* and *I don't need your shitty comments. Back off.* in particular stuck out.

"See you later, Dad." She ended the call feeling like a complete jerk.

Lexie slogged through another uneventful day at work, assisting with a gastric bypass procedure on the largest man she'd ever seen and a knee replacement on an older man who was also grossly overweight. Lexie imagined that the fate of the latter awaited the former if he didn't get his weight under control. Then she thought, *Someday I could end up where they are now if I don't stop eating like an asshole.*

She dropped Ava off at her parents' with a promise that she would call as soon as she had an update, then headed back to Minneapolis and the Cuppa coffee shop, where Ryan was already sitting with Louise and Joanna.

11

Ryan's first stop on his investigative journey was actually the Apothecary.

"Ryan!' Joanna said warmly as he approached the pharmacy counter in the back of the store. "Long time no see! How are ya, doll?"

"Doing all right," he replied. "Listen, Joanna, I was wondering if I could ask you a few questions. About Lexie's house."

Joanna's lined face softened. "Things keep happening, don't they?"

"Yeah," Ryan nodded. "And it's getting worse. I want to help her do some research on the history of her house. You've been in the neighborhood for a long time, I figure you're as good a place to start as any."

"Let's go grab a cup of coffee," Joanna said, removing her pharmacist's lab coat. "I'll be back in an hour," she told her assistant, Kate, who nodded and waved.

Joanna led Ryan down the block and into Cuppa. The bell dinged when she opened the door. "Hi, Lou."

Louise, in the middle of taking inventory, looked up from her clipboard. Her lavender-tinted silver hair cascaded to her shoulders, and her glasses were perched on the end of her thin, straight nose. The shop was deserted and smelled pleasantly of roasted coffee. "Judging by your expressions, I'd better get a couple of lattes going, stat."

"That would be great, Lou. Make one for yourself too." Joanna pointed Ryan to a table in the corner, away from the windows and near the antique espresso machine. "Have a seat."

Ryan, who had been raised to respect his elders, especially the women, obediently sat. Joanna took the chair next to him. "So what's going on, doll?"

Ryan ran a hand over the dark stubble on his head and face in one smooth motion. He struggled with where to start. "Lexie hasn't been in her house a week yet, and strange things keep happening to her and Ava. It's like she cannot catch a break."

Joanna nodded. "Lexie told me about some of it, when she came in on – what was it? – oh, it was Wednesday."

"Twice now I've found them outside, one or both passed out cold. I know Lexie's been having nightmares too; she had a doozy last night and they both ended up sleeping on my couch," Ryan said.

The bell dinged and Lexie walked into the shop, still in her scrubs. The bags under her eyes could have told the entire story of her week all on their own.

"Vanilla latte coming up," Louise called over the whirring and whooshing of her espresso machine.

"Thanks Louise," Lexie said, and sat in a chair that Joanna had pulled over. "What did I miss?"

"I was just telling Joanna about our impromptu sleepover last night." Ryan winked.

Lexie chuckled, then sobered and looked at Joanna. "You would not believe what happened."

"I bet I would," Joanna said, and leaned forward.

Lexie described the dream that woke her and Ava's bizarre behavior. "I swear she meant to hurt me. Her eyes...they were someone else's." She shuddered. Ryan laid his warm hand over hers and gave it a comforting squeeze.

Louise brought two steaming mugs over and set them in front of Ryan and Joanna. "Yours is next, hon," she said to Lexie. On her way back to the machine she called over her shoulder, "It sounds to me like Ava was under some kind of...influence. Something that makes her behave strangely."

Lexie made a connection. "That happened to me too! I was feeling anxious about my parents visiting, and I think some...some unseen force seized on my anxiety to turn me into a completely different person." She turned to Ryan. "That was yesterday. When you found me passed out on the chaise in my backyard."

"It sounds to me like whatever that influence is loses its power when the person being influenced leaves the house," Louise remarked. She set Lexie's coffee in front of her and sat in her own chair.

Joanna was silent, her gaze focused on the contents of her ceramic mug. Then she said, "In the early 1990s, a mother and daughter – I think their name was Krueger – were found dead in the house. The mother stabbed the daughter and then shot herself with her husband's rifle."

Thunderstruck, Lexie gaped at Joanna. "Excuse me?"

Louise nodded. "Maybe ten years before that, a mother drowned both of her daughters in the bathtub and then hanged herself in a closet. Their name escapes me – Lundquist? One of those Swedish names, anyway."

Lexie turned her shocked attention to Louise.

"There have been people who have lived there with no problems," Joanna offered. "Larry Lekvold was a bachelor, no kids, and he lasted fifteen years without a problem. That was right before the state took over the house."

"So you're saying that Kathryn Dormeister isn't the only person who lived in my house that died."

Louise shook her head. "I've lived and worked in the Victory neighborhood most of my life," she said. "Your house has had a reputation for almost as long as I can remember. It's seen more than its fair share of deaths."

Lexie blinked disbelievingly, then remembered the latte cooling on the table in front of her and took a sip. Louise's coffee, sourced from a small roaster across town and usually so smooth, tasted like cigarette ash.

"Seems like it's the women who have the most trouble," Joanna said.

"What do you mean?" Ryan asked.

"Well, think about the Kruegers and the Lundquists; the fathers and sons survived. Kath Dormeister didn't have any kids, but she was a woman. Larry Lekvold lived there happily for a couple decades." Joanna paused for emphasis. "And...look at what's happened with Lexie and Ava so far."

"Holy shit," Lexie breathed, gooseflesh running up and down her arms. She sat back in her chair.

"Just a minute," Louise stood and stepped behind the counter, emerging with a yellow legal pad and a pen. She sat. "Let's write down everything we know for Lexie and Ryan here." She transcribed in perfect elementary school teacher penmanship as they discussed:

2018: Assault on girl at group home (Ashley Lee) "Even though nobody died, we should include it," Joanna said.

2010 (November?): Kathryn Dormeister, fall down stairs. Husband John in prison for murder "A real miscarriage of justice, if you ask me," Joanna said. Louise nodded in agreement.

1992?-2009: Larry Lekvold There was some debate about exactly which year Lekvold moved in, but both Joanna and Louise agreed it was sometime in the early nineties. "I'll never forget that boat of a car he drove. 1985 Oldsmobile Toronado, I think it was," Louise said. "He was so proud. I swear the hood was twice as long as the boot." She smiled fondly at the memory.

1990?: Mom & daughter Krueger, murder/suicide Joanna and Louise agreed that the incident had happened two or three years before Lekvold moved in. Neither woman had trouble remembering the details, even after nearly three decades. "They moved out shortly afterward, let the house go back to the bank," Louise said sadly.

1982 or 83? Mom & 2 daughters Lundquist?
Double murder/suicide Louise realized she'd gotten the name wrong. "It wasn't Lundquist, it was Gustafson. Hans and Lillie. How could I forget something like that?" She shook her head and corrected her notes, scratching out *Lundquist* and writing GUSTAFSON next to it. "I knew it was one of those Swedish names. Hans was tall and had a red beard. And great big square glasses." She frowned. "We have a gap in our timeline."

They all leaned in to peer at Louise's legal pad. "Where?" Joanna asked.

Louise's chewed pen tapped the paper between GUSTAFSON and *Krueger*. "Who lived in the house between 1983 and roughly 1990?" She looked up at Joanna. "Do you remember?"

Joanna sat back in her chair and sighed. "I don't recall hearing of any tragic deaths between the Gustafsons and the Kruegers. Probably that means some childless person or couple lived there...but to be honest, I'm drawing a blank."

The bell on the door tinkled, and Beth Ripley, proprietor of the salon next door and also a lifelong Victory resident, walked in. She was in her mid-thirties, and her frosted brunette pixie cut had been gelled into carefully sculpted spikes. She wore a black nylon apron with the name of her salon – Updo – stitched in white on the chest over black pants and a white collared shirt. "Hi Lou," she called. "My back is killing me and I don't have any appointments right now, so I thought I'd take a quick coffee break..." she trailed off when her eyes fell on Louise, Joanna, Lexie, and Ryan huddled around a corner table in deep discussion. "Um, am I interrupting something?"

Louise abruptly sat up. "Hi hon," she said. "Not interrupting, we're just giving Lexie here some background on her house. She lives in the old Lekvold place. I'll make your Americano." She stood and stepped back behind the counter.

"The house on Washburn?" Beth slid into Louise's chair and inspected the list scribbled on Louise's legal pad.

Geez, does everyone know about my house but me? Lexie wondered. She reminded herself to give Travis Schumacher, her real estate agent, a call. She had more questions.

Beth pointed to the Krueger entry on the list. "I remember when this happened. Abby Krueger was my best friend in the fifth grade." She fell silent for a moment. "When my mom told me she had died, I think I cried for two days straight."

Louise returned with Beth's Americano. "If you were in the fifth grade, then she must have died in 1990 or 1991." She pulled up another chair, sat, and corrected her notes.

Beth's forehead crinkled and she pointed at the list again. "The Betz family lived there before the Kruegers. They had one son, he was I want to say two grades ahead of me at school." The lines on her forehead deepened in concentration. "His name was...Jason? No, Justin. Yeah, Justin Betz."

Louise noted this on the list.

Lexie just sat there, numb. Her coffee had gone cold on the table in front of her with only a single sip taken.

Joanna's warm hand covered hers. "You okay, doll?"

She looked up. "I just...I can't believe it." She turned to Louise. "You weren't kidding when you said my house has seen more than its fair share of deaths."

"Where can we go to find out more about these incidents?" Ryan asked.

"The Kruegers and the Gustafsons were all over the news; you could go to the history center in St. Paul and find Strib articles from when those incidents happened," Louise said. "If there were incidents prior to the early eighties, you should be able to find those too."

"You could track down the families," Joanna offered. "Ashley Lee's family moved to the suburbs about six years ago – Brooklyn Park, I think? – and John Dormeister can be found at the St. Cloud prison. I think I heard that Don Krueger is in a nursing home in St. Louis Park; you could go talk to him and maybe his son Eric too."

"I saw online a while back that Justin Betz lives in Eagan or Eden Prairie. One of those cities that starts with E," Beth said, sipping her Americano.

"I haven't heard where Hans ended up. But isn't the internet a wonderful thing?" Louise jotted Don & Eric Krueger and Hans Gustafson on the list, added St. Cloud prison next to John Dormeister's name and Eagan/Eden Prairie next to Justin, and drank from her latte.

They all looked up when the bell on the door jingled again. A young couple strode in; their dog, a large mixed-breed with friendly eyes, laid on the sidewalk outside the plate glass window.

Louise got up and tended to her customers; Ryan tore the list off the legal pad, folded it, and stuck it in the pocket of his shorts. "Thank you all. You have no idea how helpful this conversation has been."

Joanna and Beth both downed the last of their coffee and stood. "I should get back too," Joanna said. "Glad we could help, doll."

They waved to Louise and parted ways outside the shop; Joanna insisted on giving Ryan a hug. "You take care of that girl," she said. "Don't let her anywhere near that house."

Ryan nodded. He and Lexie waved, then headed toward their cars parked on the street a block away. Ryan's hand slipped into Lexie's, causing her heart to flutter and the flame in her belly to reignite. The summer sun was starting to take on a muted evening hue; she glanced at the watch on the wrist of her free hand; it was just past 8:00. She could feel every hour of this long day in her bones, and wished she could take a long, hot bath and crawl into her own bed. Then she glanced at Ryan and realized that he was staring at her intensely, a small smile on his face.

Lexie smiled uncertainly, eyebrows raised. "What?"

"You. I've had more excitement in the past week than I've had in years." He stopped next to his pickup truck and pulled Lexie to him so that they were nearly nose to nose. "The most exciting thing about my house is that the occasional mouse finds a way in and feasts on my cookies. But you?" His face moved closer; his lips hovered within a fraction of an inch of hers. His breath caressed her face; it smelled of hazelnut and coffee. "You move in next door, and now we have a haunted house and a mystery to investigate."

Lexie couldn't help but grin. "Yeah. I'm a regular Nancy Drew, ready to solve The Case of the House on Washburn Avenue."

Ryan's lips finally connected with hers, and the flame in her belly burst into fireworks. He held her tightly against him as his lips carefully explored her lips, her face, her neck. She responded in kind.

Finally they pulled apart, both breathing heavily and staring at each other with a new and different kind of intensity. A more primal energy lurked in Ryan's deep brown eyes. Lexie recognized it as the same energy that coursed through her own body and understood that it would reign supreme, not allowing either of them to concentrate on anything else, until it was satisfied.

"Come on," Ryan said, opening the passenger door of his truck and motioning for her to get in. "We'll come back for your car."

The six-minute drive to Ryan's house felt like an eternity. Neither said much, their entwined hands rested on the center console. It was almost like they didn't dare let each other go or say anything that might ruin the mood.

Lexie didn't give her own house a second glance as Ryan pulled into his garage; she was singularly focused on one thing. One person. He led her through the back yard and unlocked the door. Once inside, Lexie turned toward the kitchen to head for Ryan's bedroom; he grabbed her hand and pulled her back, then kissed her deeply right there inside the door, on the landing at the top of the basement stairs.

Lexie melted into his embrace, heart racing. Ryan pulled away long enough to lead her down the stairs, fumbling for a light switch as he went. At the bottom, deep chocolate eyes blazing, he guided her backward, step by step, across the linoleum floor. He stopped only when she bumped up against a cold wall. The basement, which had not yet seen the benefits of Ryan's yearslong renovations, had that vintage musty smell that always seemed to settle into the bones of old houses.

Lexie held Ryan's fierce gaze as she stepped out of her pants and kicked them into the corner. While she did that, Ryan pushed his own shorts down. Breathing heavily but evenly, he pressed his entire body against her. Her usual self-doubt tried to crowd her mind with thoughts like *How can his face even reach mine with my giant belly between us* and *Oh my god I think I'm jiggling.* She closed her eyes and instead focused on the pleasing contrast of the cold wall on her back and his hot body against her front. It had been a long time, and she wanted this man. More than anything.

Lexie placed her hands on his shoulders for balance, wrapped one leg around him, and moaned as he slid easily into her. They stood joined, nose to nose, for at least sixty seconds, breathing in unison, neither of them moving.

Slowly at first, Ryan moved back and forth, in and out, grunting softly. He increased the frequency of his thrusts gradually, as if he didn't want to get to the end too soon. Lexie focused all of her energy on their intimate connection, tears prickling behind her eyelids.

Ryan finally passed the point of no return. He propped himself against the wall with one muscled arm and squeezed Lexie close to his body with the other. He thrust deeply one, two, three times; on the third thrust he threw his head back, cried out, and exploded inside her.

Breathing hard, they stayed in position for a few more seconds. Ryan's face was flushed and covered with sweat; Lexie gently kissed his eyes, forehead and whiskered cheeks and chin. He kissed her again. "Come on," he whispered. "Let's go to my room and lay down for a bit."

Yes. Lay down for a bit. That sounded heavenly to Lexie. She followed him up the stairs and to his bedroom. When she got there, she was astonished to discover that he had removed the wall between the two main floor bedrooms to create one large master suite. It was tastefully decorated in the same high end masculine chic as his living room. His king-sized bed with its tufted leather headboard sat between two heavily curtained windows. Piled with a flannel-backed plaid comforter and numerous pillows and blankets, it beckoned to her. Ryan turned out the lights, and crawling in next to him felt like crawling into a cloud of warmth and serenity.

They laid next to each other, saying nothing, for several minutes. Lexie was just drifting off when Ryan's deep, disembodied voice said: "That was the first time I've made love in eight or nine years."

Lexie sighed through her nose. "Yeah...it's been at least five years for me. But...you were married, weren't you?"

"Yeah, I was married. But not happily."

Lexie adjusted her position so she was lying on her side, staring at a black space where she thought his face must be. "What happened?"

Ryan sighed. "It's a long story."

"I have time," she said. Her hand searched for his under the cover, and found it lying on his fuzzy chest. She entwined her fingers with his, and could feel his heartbeat quicken.

Another sigh. "Nobody told me that there was more to marriage than just the wedding."

12

Nobody told him how much work it would be.

Nobody told him how badly it would hurt when it ended.

Ryan and Jenny were high school sweethearts, the "it" couple at Minneapolis Southwest High School. He played football, made captain his senior year. She was a cheerleader. They took the crowns at homecoming every year, led every pep fest, and were the envy of their classmates.

It just seemed like they should get married. Ryan didn't realize that there were any other options. When he broached the subject with his dad one day while helping him change the oil in the old International Scout, Steven was nothing but supportive.

"You might as well do it now, before she gets pregnant," Steven's muffled voice wafted from underneath the truck, as if Jenny getting pregnant sooner rather than later was a foregone conclusion.

They stood in front of friends and family and said "I do" a few months after he graduated from college with two shiny new Bachelor's degrees. They spent the next nine miserable years living in a dumpy apartment in Dinkytown on Ryan's meager salary as a new public school teacher, paying on his student loans, and just generally struggling. They never seemed to be able to get ahead.

*Jenny's aversion to working didn't help; she was always
"looking," rarely gainfully employed. Her habit of running up
credit card balances on things they couldn't afford was the primary
source of conflict in their marriage; they fought constantly about
money. Other fights were typically about the one thing Ryan's dad
had assumed would happen sooner rather than later. Jenny was the
first of her cheerleader friends to get married, and wanted to be the
first to have a baby – as if a child were some sort of trophy that told
the world she had "made it." Ryan, understanding their
precarious financial situation, steadfastly refused. He faithfully
wore a condom every time they had sex.*

*And then Ryan received a midnight message that changed
everything.*

Hi Ryan –

You don't know me and this may be absolutely inappropriate
but my husband Brock has been having an affair with your wife for
the past three and a half months. I may be grasping at straws here
and if you don't feel inclined to respond at all I understand. I'm in
the dark on a lot of things as you can imagine. My husband and I
are still together however he is still carrying on with your wife.
Again I understand that this may be absolutely inappropriate but
I'm just trying to get some answers. This whole mess started when
your wife came to our office for a series of chiropractic
appointments, and despite my suspicions which Brock kept
assuring me were ridiculous, continued right under my nose the
entire time. He doesn't have any plans from what I see to end his
relationship with your wife, and to make matters worse, Brock told
me yesterday that your wife is now pregnant with his child. I'm
curious if you are aware of this. If you feel anywhere close to the

same way I feel I'm sure your pain is unbearable. I apologize if this is catching you off guard. I'm just trying to find some answers amidst all the lying and deceit. Thank you for anything you feel inclined to share.

The note was a sucker-punch to the gut – but suddenly a lot of her behavior lately made sense. He laid in the dark next to his sleeping (soon to be ex) wife and thought about the recent changes he'd noticed in Jenny, but hadn't thought much about until now.

The twice-weekly chiropractor appointments. Jenny had sought relief for her lower back pain and apparently received so much more.

The "girls' weekend" to Duluth last month; Ryan never saw a single online post or photo of the trip from her or any of her selfie-loving girlfriends.

The time he found her wedding ring in the washing machine. She'd claimed she slipped it into her pocket before washing dishes, and simply forgot to put it back on before tossing her jeans in the laundry.

How she never left her phone unattended, even taking it with her into the bathroom while she showered. In fact, it lay right next to her head right now.

He stared into the dark. He took deep breaths but still felt like he was suffocating, and his head pounded in time with his broken heart; he didn't think he'd ever known such pain. Yet there was a tiny glimmer of hope that maybe none of this was true. It was plausible that a (decidedly shitty) friend was playing a prank on him, and he was blowing everything out of proportion. He clung to that hope.

He couldn't take it anymore; he needed answers. As if moved by some puppeteer's invisible strings, he jerkily sat up in bed and turned on the lamp next to him. Jenny didn't stir until he took hold of her shoulder and shook her.

She snorted and turned from her side to her back. "Wha –?" she mumbled. Her blonde hair was a jumbled nest around her head.

"Wake up."

She came fully awake and looked at Ryan, sleepy confusion in her green eyes. "What time is it?"

"Doesn't matter," he said. Her face, once so familiar, looked different to him now. Foreign somehow.

"What's wrong?" she asked, struggling to sit up in bed.

"We need to talk," he said. He couldn't stop his voice from trembling.

Sensing that something was not quite right, Jenny's eyes were wary. "Right now? About what?"

"I hear you've been...busy," he said.

Her eyes widened. "What do you mean by that?"

"Don't bother lying," he said. Unable to sit still any longer, Ryan swung his legs over the side of the bed and stood. He walked to the bedroom window and looked out over the deserted street. "I know all about it."

"I don't know what you're talking about," Jenny said defiantly, brushing a tangled chunk of hair back from her face.

Ryan turned from the window and faced her. "You've been cheating on me!" he shouted. "With your fucking chiropractor!"

Jenny recoiled.

Ryan's heart shattered into a billion tiny shards. "So it is true." His voice cracked.

Jenny didn't say anything at first, preferring instead to closely inspect her neatly manicured fingernails. Then, slowly: "Brock and I have been...close."

"'Close?' What the fuck does that mean?"

"There have been...um...feelings." Now she was picking at the edge of the bed comforter. She still wouldn't look at him.

"I know you've been fucking him, Jen."

Silence.

"How long did you think you could keep this a secret?"

"I was going to tell you..." she trailed off.

"Yeah? Was that going to be before or after your baby bump started showing?" Ryan was shouting again. He couldn't help it; his emotions kept whipsawing between intense anger and unbearable sadness.

Jenny burst into tears. "I...I didn't know how to bring it up," she sobbed. "I didn't want to h-h-hurt you."

He looked at her dispassionately as she swiped tears off her cheeks. "Do you want to know how I know all this?"

She nodded slowly.

"His wife – a lady named Susan who seems quite lovely, actually; I gather she works in his chiropractic office – just sent me a message. She knows all about it too, Jen. He told her."

She froze, eyes wet and wide, red blotches climbing up her neck and face. He took a little satisfaction in the fact that he had clearly just rocked her world; perhaps this little fairy tale wouldn't be ending the way she wanted it to.

"How the fuck is that better?!" he shouted, still standing next to the window. "I had to find out my wife is cheating on me from her lover's goddamn wife in the middle of the night because you – the one who told me 'till death do us part' – didn't have the guts to tell me!" Something occurred to him and he paused. "Is this because of the baby thing? Did you step out on me because I wasn't ready to start a family?"

Silence from the bed. Her head hung. Ryan watched a tear swell at the tip of her nose, then drop into her lap. He took no answer as an answer; his chest felt as if it might break wide open. "Oh, god." He sat on the edge of the bed and covered his face with his hands.

"I'm sorry," Jenny whispered after a few beats.

Ryan didn't say anything at first; his head spun as he tried to see what his future was going to look like after tonight. His American dream of a house in the suburbs (perhaps Apple Valley or Woodbury if he could land a job in one of their high schools), two cars, 2.5 kids, and white picket fence was dying in front of his eyes, right here in this crappy one-bedroom apartment just off the University of Minnesota campus. His future was darkness, and he was afraid of the dark.

He let go of his head and stared at the floor. "Get out."

"What?" Her voice was small.

"Get the fuck out," he said, his voice much more level than he felt.

"I can't leave!" Jenny started crying again. "Where am I going to go at two o'clock in the morning?"

"I don't give a fuck," Ryan said. "Go to your mom's, go to your sister's, go to – what's his name? Oh, right, Brock – go to Brock's house for all I care," he said. "Gather up your shit and leave. Now. Take the car if you have to."

"But what about all my other stuff?" she wailed as she struggled out of bed.

"The stuff you spent money we didn't have on? Don't worry, you'll get it. I sure as hell don't want it."

He watched her collect a couple outfits, her makeup case, her shower supplies, and a pair of running shoes, and stuff them into a distinctive red, white and black reusable bag. The activewear she'd brought home in that bag had cost over $150, triggering one of their bigger money fights; he was glad to see that stupid bag taking useless expensive crap out of his apartment. He went out to the living room while she stayed in the bedroom and made some calls. He sat on the threadbare couch, turned on the TV, and flipped through channels full of nothing but late-night infomercials, trying to ignore the sobs, whines, and wails drifting from the bedroom.

After roughly half an hour – enough time for Ryan to seriously consider purchasing a "nutrition extractor" (blender) and the "world's most versatile lawn machine" (trimmer) – Jenny emerged, wearing her pajama t-shirt, a pair of old yoga pants, and her old flip-flops. She carried the bag, a pillow, and her favorite quilt. Her curly blonde hair had been thrown up into a messy ponytail. Her eyes were red and puffy, her face blotchy. She clutched her phone and her wallet-on-a-$50-lanyard. "Uh. My mom's on her way to pick me up."

Ryan's eyes slid from the TV screen to Jenny's face, and then slid back again. His face remained absolutely expressionless. "Fine," he said.

"Listen –"

He put up a hand to stop her. "I don't want to hear it, and I don't want to look at your face anymore. Go wait for your mom outside."

Her face crumpled and a sob escaped her as she walked to the door. Then she was gone.

Ryan never did have to see Jenny's face again. He made sure he wasn't there when she came to pick up her belongings, and their divorce was conducted entirely by mail. On the day he pulled the executed divorce decree out of the mailbox, Ryan swore that he would never marry again. His heart couldn't handle it.

He lived in the crappy Dinkytown apartment for another couple of years, diligently paying down debt and saving for a down payment on a house. He was determined to have his American dream – just maybe not in the suburbs, and probably without the smiling wife and the 2.5 kids.

When the time came to start house shopping, it didn't take him long to find the perfect fixer-upper in the Victory neighborhood of north Minneapolis. By then he had moved to Patrick Henry High School to teach physical education and run the football program – his personal version of "making it" – so the location was ideal. Max Luedtke, his real estate agent, was less than impressed with the battered midcentury story-and-a-half, watching Ryan enthusiastically check out every nook and cranny with a bemused expression on his face.

"Dude. This place is a shithole," he'd remarked. "My nonprofessional opinion, of course." He consulted a stapled packet of papers in his leather folder. "I mean, it's been a rental for years. Tenants are hard on houses. And " – he flipped to a second page of disclosures – "do you really want to live next door to a halfway house?"

"It's not pretty," Ryan admitted, running his hand over a hole someone had clearly punched in a bedroom wall. "But it's got good bones."

"I hope you have a pile of money stashed away," Max said, running the toe of his cowboy boot over a large gash in the wood floor. "You're going to need it if you buy this house, man. Come on, let me show you another one that's in better shape. It's just a couple blocks away, and not next to a halfway house."

"Nah. I want this one," Ryan said. Where Max saw a money pit, Ryan saw potential. He knew in his heart that he could turn this tired old house into something awesome. Max rolled his eyes but didn't argue. He never argued with a 4% commission.

The house became his, and Ryan spent the next six years renovating it in his spare time. He would go to work during the day, then come home to his latest project in the evening – except during football season; then he could only work on the house on *weekends. He would fall into bed after midnight, rise with his alarm at 4:00 a.m., and start all over again.*

He did everything himself: repairing drywall, tearing out carpet and refinishing wood floors, replacing the entire HVAC system (with help from his dad), upgrading the entire electrical system (with help from his brother Tyler) and plumbing system (with help from his brother Sam), replacing windows, replacing the roof and siding, spraying ceilings, painting, landscaping.

He found the work to be therapeutic. The highly physical labor allowed him the mindspace to work through the emotional effects of his failed marriage. Looking back, it was clear that he and Jenny were never going to work; in fact, Ryan realized they shouldn't have gotten married in the first place. We didn't really love each other – we just knew we looked as if we belonged together. Turns out "because I think I should" is not a real good reason to get married, he thought as he patched the hole in the bedroom wall.

"I didn't pay much attention when Max mentioned the halfway house next door, but it wasn't long until I became aware of it." Ryan's bedroom room was pitch black and still, save for Lexie's deep, steady breathing. "I lost count of the number of times I had to call 911 to break up fights between residents and resident attacks on staff. It got to the point where I was on a first-name basis with the dispatchers and pretty much all of the officers at the Fourth Precinct."

He chuckled quietly. "I'm not sure this neighborhood went one full week without a visit from the MPD. I remember one time, I called 911 after a nasty fight spilled into the front yard. The screams were crazy. They didn't sound human. One of the girls – fifteen years old, maybe? – lost an eye." He shuddered. "Rick Thomes, an officer who's been here so many times that we're now close personal friends, said that the MPD was called to the house next door something like three times more often than any other address in the entire city. And that is saying something in Minneapolis." He laid in silence for a moment, staring into the blackness. He didn't know if Lexie was still awake. But he kept on talking; it was nice to have someone there, even if she wasn't listening to him. "The state finally shut down the halfway house last year. The lady who ran the place as a live-in counselor or whatever was an absolute saint, you know? The bad behavior she dealt with from the girls who came through here was unreal."

He laid in silence for a moment, then said, "Lex?"

She made a sound through her nose, and he could feel her head move ever so slightly as she burrowed even deeper next to him under the covers. Then she stilled. He kissed the top of her head. "Thanks for listening." Then he closed his eyes and drifted away.

13

"Lex."

Lexie resisted the deep, sexy voice that was trying to pull her up from a deep dark well of blessed unconsciousness.

"Lex." A warm hand took hold of her shoulder and shook.

"Mmmm-whaaaa...." she whined, squinching her eyes shut tighter and turning over on her other side. "Leemee lone."

"It's seven o'clock."

Her eyelids popped open like spring-loaded shades, and she scrambled to a sitting position. "What?"

"I didn't hear an alarm, and I wasn't sure if you had to work today, so I thought I'd better wake you up." Ryan gazed at her with the bright eyes of someone who'd had the kind of sleep that usually followed a round of headbusting sex.

"Shit. Shit shit shit." Lexie flailed around in the blankets, searching for her phone. She was way past late; her shift started an hour ago, and she would be in deep trouble for not calling in ahead of time to let the supervising nurse know she wouldn't be there. Lynn was probably on the phone, frantically alternating between calling her and calling every available sub in the floater pool. *I just postponed someone's emergency procedure,* Lexie thought glumly; there were no scheduled surgeries in the OR on Saturdays.

Finally she realized that her phone was in her purse, probably still sitting on the floor inside the back door, where she'd dropped it the night before. She scrambled out of bed, yanked her scrub shirt back over her naked body (*quick, before Ryan sees the fat rolls,* she thought) and ran out of the room, through the house, and into the kitchen. She picked up her purse and rummaged until her fingers wrapped around the familiar shape of her cell phone. One glance confirmed her suspicion: five missed calls and two voicemails awaited her. She walked slowly back through the kitchen and sat at the dinette, staring apprehensively at her phone; the tiny voice mail symbol in the top left corner of the screen seemed to mock her. She didn't hear Ryan tiptoe into the kitchen.

After several minutes of stalling, and with a cup of fresh coffee cooling in front of her, Lexie decided to skip listening to the voicemails and just call Lynn. She braced herself for a tirade from the perpetually-stressed nurse supervisor. Lynn answered her call on the first ring.

"This is Lynn." Her tone was frosty; she'd recognized Lexie's phone number.

"Hi Lynn, it's Lexie."

"Yeah, and where the hell are you? Your shift started over an hour ago."

"I know. I –"

"Do you have any idea the bullshit I'm dealing with right now? Sam's on vacation and Kelly called in sick, so now I literally have no OR nurses on staff here this morning!" As Lynn's volume steadily increased, Lexie held her phone farther and farther from her ear to protect her eardrum. "And good luck finding a floater on such short notice. You'd better be sick or dead, Lexie. There's literally no other excuse I will accept for leaving me high and dry on a fucking Saturday."

"So I guess 'my alarm didn't go off so I overslept' falls in the unacceptable excuses category?" As soon as the words were out of her mouth Lexie knew her attempt at humor was a mistake. She gritted her teeth.

"Are you serious?" Lynn's voice was at maximum volume now. Lexie winced and held the phone as far from her head as she could. "You'd better hope I find a sub before Dr. Stratton has to reassemble the hip of a 96-year-old lady who fell at home yesterday. That's not a procedure we can really reschedule, is it?"

Jesus, I would have had to work with Jake today. Lexie shuddered, but said, "Do you want me to come in and finish my shift?"

"No. No, I do not. In fact, I don't want to see your face around here for two weeks."

""You're suspending me?" Lexie was incredulous. "Over one mistake?"

"A no-call-no-show is a pretty big mistake that has serious downstream impacts. This was Lesson Numero Uno during your new hire orientation, if you'll recall. Two weeks with pay, then we'll regroup and decide on next steps."

"But –"

"If you'll excuse me, Lexie, I have to go now and find someone to do your job before Stratton's procedure." Lynn hung up.

Lexie set her phone on the table and her head in her hands. Tears welled in her eyes, and self-pity came knocking. *Great. I can't live in my own house, my kid is staying with my parents, and now I can't even go to work.* She blinked, and two tears landed in perfect tiny puddles on the laminate top of Ryan's vintage kitchen table.

Something soft draped over her shoulders, and she looked up to see Ryan's smiling face. "I thought you might be cold," he said. "What with the skimpy outfit and all."

Lexie looked down at her bare legs and realized she was wearing nothing but her scrub shirt from yesterday. No pants, no underwear, nothing else. She chuckled in spite of herself and wrapped the blanket around her.

"The call with your boss went about as well as could be expected, I'm guessing," he said.

Lexie sighed. "Yeah. She suspended me with pay for two weeks. There isn't a single disciplinary action on my record, and I've worked at North nearly ten years. I've never been even five minutes late for a shift. A two-week suspension seems kind of extreme." She noticed the coffee on the table in front of her and took a sip. It was good and strong; the bitterness and sweet, sweet caffeine lifted her spirits.

Ryan shrugged. "Maybe this is a good thing."

"What do you mean?" Lexie asked, skeptical.

"Well, now you don't have to worry about trying to juggle your job and your house. You'll be free to do the kind of research we need to do."

Considering, Lexie took another sip of the rich, dark coffee. *Damn, this is almost as good as Cuppa*, she thought. "This is a very good point. Although we haven't really talked about the research we need to do. Maybe we should make a plan."

Ryan pulled a folded piece of lined yellow paper from the pocket of his plaid bathrobe. "You read my mind." He unfolded the paper and spread it flat on the table. "Here's everything we talked about last night at Cuppa. I thought we could divide and conquer."

Lexie examined the notes:

2018: Assault on girl at group home (Ashley Lee) Bklyn Pk?

2010 (November?): Kathryn Dormeister, fall down stairs. Husband John in prison for murder (St. Cloud)

1992?-2009: Larry Lekvold

1990? 1991: Mom & daughter Krueger, murder/suicide — Don & Eric, St. Louis Pk?

1983-1990: ??? Betz — Justin Eagan/Eden Prairie

1982? Lillie & 2 daughters ~~Lundquist?~~ GUSTAFSON Double murder/suicide

"Joanna suggested checking out the Star Tribune's archives; we've actually already started doing that," Ryan said. He went to the kitchen and dug around in a drawer until he found a pen; he sat again and added to Louise's list:

George Gilmartin d. 1980, survived by wife Lucy, twins Michael & Melissa Ann

Lucy Gilmartin d. 1981, survived by son Michael

Ryan's words from the night before rolled around in Lexie's head: *What happened to Melissa Ann?* She tapped the paper and said, "I wonder if it all starts here. The parents dying so close to each other and the apparent disappearance of one of their kids in between seems a little too coincidental to me." Then, borrowing a line from Joanna, she said, "I'm a nurse, I don't believe in coincidences."

Ryan nodded, but more in acknowledgment than agreement. "Who knows, maybe whatever happened to the Gilmartins is part of it. Maybe there's something bigger at work here. We won't know for sure until we go all the way back to when the house was built in 1955."

"That's true, we don't know anything prior to 1980," Lexie admitted. "I'm guessing we'll have to go to Hennepin County or even the Minnesota History Center for records going back that far."

"Which is why I think we need to divide and conquer," Ryan said. "We need to get this figured out quickly so you can decide what to do with the house you just bought."

Overcome with a sudden chill, Lexie sat back in her chair and pulled the blanket back up around her shoulders. "I think the first step is we search my house."

"You're kidding, right?"

"I'm dead serious," she said. "Maybe there's something hidden in a nook or cranny I haven't discovered yet."

"It's a sixty-five-year-old house that's probably seen a couple dozen families," Ryan pointed out. "I can't imagine what you think we might find. No. It's a terrible idea."

"Let me put it this way," Lexie said with a mildness that barely disguised her rising temper. "I'm going to look around my house. You're welcome to join me if you want to."

Their gazes locked for a couple beats; Lexie held steady until Ryan blinked and looked back down at the paper. "All right, if that's what you want to do."

Lexie was more than a little surprised by Ryan's quick reticence; Jake's reaction would have been...not that. "Yes. It's what I want to do. Then what's the next step?"

"Well, we have a few people we can possibly visit. Let's split those up and focus on them over the next few days. After that we'll hit the books and try to fill in any gaps we have left," Ryan said. He wouldn't quite meet her gaze, and went back to staring at the paper. A pit opened in Lexie's gut. *I messed up,* she thought.

"Where do you get your coffee?"

"Huh?" Ryan's head jerked up. The befuddled look on his face made her smile.

"I said, where do you get your coffee? It's delicious."

"Oh. Uh, I buy beans in bulk from Louise every week."

"I knew it," Lexie declared before taking another sip. "I thought it tasted like it came from Cuppa."

Ryan's brow creased.

Lexie offered a weak smile; she felt terrible that she'd let her temper get the best of her. "Whenever Ava and I have a disagreement and she's so mad she won't talk to me or look at me, I ask her a completely random question like that. It usually throws her off balance just enough that she forgets she's not talking to me." Lexie shrugged. "It's a technique I learned in Toddler Class when she was not quite two years old. Keeps the lines of communication open, even during conflict."

"I don't know what –"

Lexie held a hand up. "I made you feel bad with how I chose to express my frustration with you not wanting to go back to my house. And I'm sorry; I could have handled that differently. You're probably right, now might not be the right time. Let's talk to the people first."

Ryan blinked. Then blinked again.

"Are you all right?" Lexie asked, wondering if something short-circuited in his brain.

"Um. Yes. I'm fine. It's just that I've never been with a woman who actually makes an effort to communicate." He shook his head. "My ex-wife let her credit cards do all the talking, you know?"

"If my dad taught me one thing, it's that the only way to say something is to just say it. My mom is the exact opposite; she never says what she really means. She expects you to pick up on her subtle hints and somehow read her mind." Lexie drained the last of the delicious coffee from her mug. "I picked up some of her bad habits, but I gave up on being opaque and passive-aggressive around the time I got pregnant with Ava and her narcissist asshole father abandoned us."

"I wondered what the story was," Ryan said, "but I didn't want to pry."

"Oh, it's a tawdry tale," Lexie said. "But not all that complicated. I walked right into the trap of a self-centered two-timing creep, completely fell for every single one of his stupid lines, slept with him a couple times, and got pregnant." She shivered again under the cashmere blanket. "He tried to convince me to get an abortion, and when that didn't work he just disappeared. I saw him at work the other day, for the first time since I told him I was pregnant. I should have pretended he wasn't there, but I had to tell him about Ava. Frankly, I kind of hoped hearing about his daughter might make him come around." She shook her head. "No such luck. He wants nothing to do with either of us." As she talked, Lexie realized that talking about Jake wasn't quite so painful anymore.

"What is wrong with this guy?" Ryan asked. "Seriously."

Lexie shrugged. "Like I said, he's a two-timing creep. He cheated on his wife with me, and rather than give her a reason to leave him he just pretends we don't exist."

Ryan shook his head. "It's his loss," he said. "And my gain." He smiled.

Lexie smiled back, heat rising up her neck and face.

Ryan turned his attention back to the paper. "Okay, so we have Ashley Lee, who is around eleven years old now, and possibly living with her family in Brooklyn Park. We might also track down Destiny House's – that was the name of the halfway house – last live-in counselor. An amazing woman named T'Jara Jackson." He wrote this on the list, then stuck the pen between his teeth and thought for a moment. Lexie found the gesture completely endearing. "Then we have Mr. John Dormeister, resident of the St. Cloud Correctional Facility. Don Krueger may be in a nursing home in St. Louis Park, and he has a son named Eric we should probably talk to. Justin Betz is probably in either Eagan or Eden Prairie. And finally, Larry Lekvold and Hans Gustafson – but nobody knows where they are, so we'll have to do some internet sleuthing to find them." He looked at Lexie. "How should we split these folks up?

"Well, you already know T'Jara Jackson, so you should be the one to talk to her." Ryan carefully wrote his name next to T'Jara's on the list. "I can try talking to Ashley Lee; being a mom of a four-year-old might help with her." Ryan marked the list. "Beyond that, I don't think it really matters." Lexie shrugged.

"Then you take Dormeister and I'll take Krueger and Betz. Ever visited a prison?"

"Um, no. Never had the pleasure."

"Me neither." He gazed at her with a mischievous twinkle in his eyes.

A confused half-smile crossed Lexie's face. "What? What are you staring at?"

"You." Ryan scooted his chair closer to hers; the worn floor protectors at the ends of the tubular aluminum chair legs screeched across the linoleum. "I'm wondering what you've got on under that blanket."

Lexie laughed. "Pretty sure you know I'm wearing basically nothing. You're the one who covered me up!"

"My mistake." Ryan's arms snaked around Lexie, pulling her closer to him so that they both sat on the very edges of their chairs. His warm lips touched her neck and his soft whiskers brushed against her skin, sending gooseflesh across her entire body. She closed her eyes, smiled, and leaned into him.

"What do you say we go to my room?" He whispered between kisses, his warm breath caressing her skin. "It's just around the corner, and I can help you remove the rest of those pesky clothes."

Lexie wrapped her arms around his neck. "Mmmm." She kissed him. "As tempting as that is, I'm afraid it'll have to wait. We have entirely too much work to do, and now that I'm on hiatus from my job, I'd like to get started as soon as possible."

Ryan buried his face in her neck and growled. "Damn."

She pulled his face up and kissed him again. "I'm going to get dressed." Then she disappeared around the corner toward Ryan's room.

Ryan went to the kitchen and began cooking up his famous broccoli and cheddar frittata. After a hearty breakfast, they got started.

PART TWO:
LEXIE & RYAN

14

Lexie spent the weekend hanging with Ava and her parents during the day, and strategizing – among other things – with Ryan at night. Nearly all of their free time over the following week was spent researching the history of Lexie's house. Lexie decided to pick up a scrapbook to hold and organize whatever information they might pick up along the way. She found one on clearance at the craft store on Sunday; its cover was gray, the phrase "So this happened" scrawled across it in fancy black script. It was completely absurd – yet somehow completely appropriate – considering the task at hand, but it was cheap and more paper could be added if needed. She grabbed a few packets of plain white filler paper and several rolls of Scotch tape as well.

As it turned out, a lot of things happened.

15

T'Jara Jackson had no regrets. She wouldn't change a damn thing, even if that crazy white-haired doctor showed up with his time machine car and told her to hop in, he was gonna take her back to 1991. After the kindness and tough love of a counselor had helped her break her own cycle of drug use and prostitution and finally get off the streets, T'Jara dedicated herself to paying it back. She made it her personal mission over the past twenty years to help young girls during the hardest times in their lives, just as Ray Howard had helped her.

Every time she thought of Ray, she sent a little prayer up for his soul. *Bless you, Ray. Bless you,* she thought. She still missed him, nine years after he was murdered on a troubled north Minneapolis street corner in broad daylight by a teenage boy he'd been trying to counsel. The kid had been wrecked on crack and two forty-ouncers of cheap beer, and shot Ray right through the heart with a stolen 9mm Glock hidden in his waistband.

A least he didn't suffer, T'Jara often thought. It was a small comfort.

She had spent the latter half of 2017 and early 2018 as a live-in facility supervisor and counselor at Destiny House, a small sober living house for teenage girls in Minneapolis' Victory neighborhood. The house was owned by the State of Minnesota and run by T'Jara's employer, Transformation Services Treatment Program. It was nothing to write home to Mama about, in T'Jara's opinion; it looked like every other house in the neighborhood, and only had two bedrooms. T'Jara had to sleep on a bed in the creepy-ass attic. Destiny House could house up to eight girls at a time, and was where the state of Minnesota sent its most troubled charges.

Destiny House had a problem management had hoped T'Jara could solve: the state had performed an audit and discovered the program wasn't working as intended. Girls stayed in Destiny House's 90-day program an average of 59 days. Its residents relapsed at a nearly 100% rate (the ones who died didn't count as relapses). The rate of violence against staff and other residents was astronomical. TSTP had one year to turn Destiny House around, or face closure and possible revocation of their license.

She didn't make it the full year. The state promptly closed Destiny House after Lisa Hardwick tried to kill that poor little girl.

"Ashley. Yeah, that was her name." T'Jara muttered as she folded what seemed like the thirteenth pair of billowy light blue boxer shorts. She laid them on a growing pile on the coffee table in front of her. Monday was laundry day. She liked to sit on the couch and watch noontime soap operas while she folded clothes fresh out of the dryer.

Another reason she waited until after lunch to fold laundry: Victor. Seventy-five years old and in the throes of dementia, he spent his waking hours shuffling aimlessly around the house, picking things up and inspecting them, then dropping them and leaving them where they lay as he moved along. By T'Jara's count, he'd broken half a dozen photo frames, a golf trophy he'd won as a younger athlete, three potted plants, an antique vase that had belonged to his late wife, two lamps, and countless dishes and drinking glasses. She'd finally had to pack up all the breakables in his tiny postwar rambler and hide them away, leaving the house's interior barren – much like its owner's slowly atrophying brain. His two sons didn't want to place him in a nursing home, so they'd hired T'Jara to care for the frail old man who had once been a proud union pipefitter and was now not much more than a shell.

She'd learned to wait until Victor's naptime – right after his early lunch, usually tomato soup and applesauce that she carefully fed to him – to fold the laundry, otherwise he'd upset her neat piles and force her to refold everything. No, best that she take care of this business while he was sleeping.

Being a live-in personal care assistant for an old man with dementia wasn't such a bad gig, as far as T'Jara was concerned. Unmarried and childless, it was a perfect arrangement for her. She had a roof over her head, a stipend that was small but enough to buy an occasional lottery ticket, and the kind of responsibility she'd missed after Destiny House closed and TSTP let her go for failure to perform. She chuckled under her breath as she remembered *that* day.

"Failure to perform?!"" T'Jara stared incredulously at her supervisor Miranda, who sat on the other side of the massive desk looking exactly like an early 1980s white businesswoman, down to the perm cut short and drab but sharply tailored tan skirtsuit. "Perform what? You got no idea what I been through these last nine months!"

"Your job was to turn things around at Destiny House," Miranda said tersely. Her hands were folded on the desk in front of her, without a trace of a tremble. T'Jara suspected Miranda had this conversation often in the high-turnover world of drug treatment services. "You failed. So you're fired. I don't know how to be any clearer."

T'Jara flapped her right hand in the air. "Fine. Y'all enjoy the lawsuits." She hefted her considerable frame out of the standard-issue office guest chair and made her way to the door – but not before she sneaked one last glance at Miranda's face. T'Jara had pierced her calm veneer, and fear now gleamed in her former supervisor's eyes.

"Lawsuits?" Miranda's steely voice stopped T'Jara at the door.

She turned slowly, a small smile on her ample face. "Oh, you don't need to worry about me," she said. "I ain't gonna come after you for racial discrimination. I'm done with TSTP. But I don't think that little girl's family is gonna be as charitable as me." T'Jara's hips swung widely as she stepped out of Miranda's office and made her way to the elevator. She didn't know where she was going to go or what she would do, but at that moment she didn't care. She was free of Destiny House forever.

As she folded yet another pair of boxers – *How many times that man gotta change his drawers*, she wondered, then remembered how fortunate she was that he could still wear regular underwear and hadn't yet moved into adult diapers – her cell phone rang. She didn't recognize the number flashing on the screen, but answered anyway.

"T'Jara, it's Ryan Laughlin. I lived –"

"Next door to Destiny House," T'Jara finished for him; she'd recognized his voice instantly, and her face broke into a wide, red-lipsticked grin. Her strong white teeth were a stark contrast against her dark skin. "How you doing, honey?"

"Not bad, T – how are you? What have you been up to since you left Washburn Avenue?"

"Oh, you know me, I always land on my feet. I'm taking care of a nice old man with dementia in Crystal. He keeps me on my toes." She gave a robust chuckle that made her generous bosom jiggle.

"Good for you, T. I'm glad you found something after the craziness at Destiny House. Speaking of, I'm calling to ask a favor."

"Well, sure."

"A woman and her daughter moved into the house about a week ago, and they've been experiencing some strange things. We're trying to figure out what's behind it. Can I ask you a few questions about your time at Destiny House?"

T'Jara sat back into the couch cushions and considered. She wasn't sensitive like her mama was, but she believed in ghosts – and she always suspected there was something within the house causing trouble. And she was sure as H-E-double-hockey-sticks that whatever it was lived in the attic. "Of course, honey."

"How long were you there? Was it a full year?"

"Nine months," T'Jara confirmed. "TPTS told me I had a year to turn Destiny House around."

"What do you mean, turn it around?"

"Well, you know that Destiny House was supposed to help teenage girls transition from an inpatient drug treatment program back into society. Right?"

"Right."

"Well, it wasn't doing that. It was failing. None of the girls stayed all 90 days they were supposed to, and when they left, they were in worse shape than when they came. The ones who didn't die ended up back in treatment."

"Die?"

"Yeah." T'Jara said. "I can think of at least three girls who left and were dead of an overdose within days. One went home and refused to eat until her heart just gave out."

"Holy shit."

"I been doing this twenty years, and I can't remember when I ever broke up so many fights, stopped so many suicide attempts, took so many fists to the face, or called so many ambulances to come and take an injured resident to the hospital."

"Jesus, T. Why did you stay around?"

"Because I wanted to help," she said before she quite knew which words would fall from her mouth. "Those girls needed *help*."

"Did you ever experience anything strange yourself?"

T'Jara thought for a moment. "The girls complained about things like headaches and heartburn all the time, but I never had any of that. All I ever had was...a feeling."

"What do you mean?" Ryan's voice sounded distant, like the phone's microphone was pointed the wrong way while he furiously took down notes.

"I always felt like someone was watching me. Especially when I was in bed, trying to sleep. Lord, the bad dreams I had!" She shivered.

"Which room did you sleep in?"

"The girls shared the downstairs bedrooms, and my bed was up in the attic."

A moment of silence from Ryan. She could hear his pen scratching on paper. Then: "The state shut Destiny House down after that resident attacked the young girl, right?"

"Yeah," T'Jara said. "Are you a mind reader? I was just thinking about that right before you called."

Ryan chuckled. "Not usually, but things are so strange with Lexie's house right now that I wouldn't be surprised."

T'Jara's ears perked a bit. "Lexie? Is she the one who moved into the house?"

"Yes ma'am," Ryan said. "Can you tell me what happened with the young girl?"

"It was the damndest thing. The doorbell rang one day – it was a nice day for February, isn't it funny the things you remember? Anyway, some of the other girls told me that Lisa Hardwick was right there to answer the door. Right *there*, as if she'd been waiting for the child."

"How old was Lisa?" Ryan asked.

"Sixteen and, I found out later, eight weeks pregnant. Ashley – that was the girl's name – was standing on the front step, her red wagon full of mint cookies and those delicious caramel-and-coconut cookies right behind her. The noises that came out of Lisa were the most inhuman screeches I ever heard. I came running from the kitchen to see Ashley lying on the entry floor and Lisa leaning with her entire weight her throat." Overcome, T'Jara paused.

"You all right, T?" The concern was clear in Ryan's voice.

T'Jara took a deep breath and wiped the tears from her eyes. "It was by the grace of God that I got there when I did. If I'd been any later, that girl would have been dead."

"You saved her life, T."

"I still dream about it sometimes," T'Jara admitted.

"Thank god you were there."

T'Jara was beyond ready to change the subject. "Tell me about this Lexie."

"An investor bought the house from the state and remodeled it, and Lexie just bought it and moved in a week or so ago."

"And she's having troubles?"

"She is. Headaches, heartburn, bad dreams – her daughter's been behaving strangely too. But only when they're inside the house."

"How old is the baby?"

"She holds up three fingers and says she's four." Ryan laughed. "It's the cutest thing."

T'Jara heard in Ryan's voice something she'd never heard before: optimism. Hope. The man was all about his house and his job, but she didn't think he put much thought into his future. His voice now sounded like that had changed with this Lexie and her little girl.

"You have to help them, Ryan. That house has some *bad* juju. They could get hurt. Or worse. You gotta protect them, keep them safe."

Ryan was silent for a moment, then said, "I'm trying, T. I'm trying."

T'Jara heard Victor's bedroom door rattling in its frame, indicating that he was up from his nap and trying to figure out how to turn the doorknob. *Lord, it's like babysitting a toddler,* T'Jara thought. "Listen, honey, I gotta go. Duty calls. You take care of yourself and those girls, you hear?"

"Thanks, T. You take care too." He ended the call, leaving T'Jara still sitting on the couch, holding her phone and thinking about her newest worry: that the house on Washburn Avenue wasn't done. Done with what, exactly, she didn't know – but she knew that those girls would be next if they weren't careful. She picked up the remote and turned the TV off, then laboriously pushed herself off the couch and lumbered toward Victor's rattling door.

All she could do was hope for the best.

16

Ryan called just as Lexie's GPS was telling her to "In one thousand feet, take a right on Seventy-Ninth Avenue North." She answered his call with more irritation than usual. "This better be important." She was in an unfamiliar neighborhood and feared the interruption would cause her miss her turn and get lost.

"Sorry," Ryan said. "I was hoping we could chat about my conversation with T'Jara. I just hung up with her."

"I'm almost to Ashley's house. What do you say we discuss both conversations when we see each other tonight." Then, because she felt guilty for being so snarky when she answered the phone, she made Ryan an offer he couldn't refuse. "I'll even pick a pizza up on the way home."

"That's a deal," Ryan said. "See you soon." Then he was gone.

Lexie turned the SUV slowly and uncertainly into the suburban cul-de-sac. Brooklyn Park was loaded with these peculiar dead-end circles, and it took Lexie a while to find the right one. The houses in this neighborhood were bigger and newer than in her own, but not as big and new as the ones in her parents' neighborhood. This was primarily blue collar middle class at its finest.

She crept along the street peering at house numbers until she found the one she was looking for: a 1970s-era split entry home with two windows on the front that reminded Lexie of eyes and a two-car garage attached to the side. She parked along the curb and walked up the driveway, where she encountered a young girl with creamy, unblemished skin the color of a café latte.

17

Ashley Lee waited outside her house for the visitor her mom said was coming to talk to her today. It was a gorgeous Monday in June, so she pulled her long black hair, entirely braided into cornrows, into a hair tie at the nape of her neck, then grabbed her book and sat cross-legged on one of two lounge chairs on the concrete patio outside the front door. She was working through a wedge of juicy watermelon when an old SUV pulled up to the curb. She pushed a pair of heavy black-rimmed glasses up her nose with her free hand and watched an overweight white woman with long brown hair make her way up the driveway.

"Are you Alexis?" she asked. Her voice was raspy, like that of a lifelong chain smoker. She knew her voice did not jibe with her cherubic eleven-year-old's face. Most people did a double-take when she spoke, and this woman was no exception.

"Lexie. It's nice to meet you, Ashley. Mind if I sit down?"

Ashley gestured toward the empty lounge chair next to her. "Sure."

Lexie sat on the flat end of the lounge chair, setting her purse on the patio next to her feet. "What are you reading?"

"To Kill a Mockingbird," Ashley said, then took a bite of watermelon. A drop of pink juice landed on her denim shorts;

she ignored it. "I've read it probably fifty times. It's my favorite book." She held the book up so Lexie could see its wrinkled cover, cracked spine, and dog-eared pages.

Lexie nodded, impressed. "I read that in the eighth or maybe ninth grade. What grade are you in, Ashley?"

"I'm going into sixth grade. Middle school. This past Tuesday was my last day of elementary school." She ate the last bit of pink flesh from her watermelon and set the rind on the concrete next to her chair.

"Congratulations," Lexie said. "That's big stuff."

Ashley nodded and pushed her glasses back up her nose.

"Did your mom tell you why I'm here?"

Ashley shrugged. "You want to ask me about what happened when I was eight?"

"Yeah," Lexie said. "I live in that house now, and I'm trying to figure out why that happened to you."

"What do you mean?" Ashley asked. "That girl just went crazy and attacked me. What other reason could there be?"

"Can you tell me exactly how it went down?" Lexie asked.

Ashley shrugged again. "I was out in the neighborhood with my wagon, selling cookies. The other girls in my troop didn't want to go door-to-door, but I didn't mind because I really wanted to sell 2,500 boxes so I could get a tablet." She'd really wanted that device; she'd heard that there was an app that would let her buy and read all the books she wanted right on the tablet – a powerful motivator for a bookworm like Ashley.

Lexie nodded.

"I remember it was pretty warm that day, so I didn't have to wear my coat under my vest. I walked up to the house and rang the doorbell, just like I did with all the other houses. The door opened really fast, and this crazy-looking teenager just stood there staring at me." Ashley shuddered. "I started saying the words my troop leader made me memorize, to tell her about the kinds of cookies and how much they cost. Then..." Ashley fell silent for a moment. Her heart started skipping as she remembered what happened next.

"Then?" Lexie prompted gently.

"Then the crazy girl reached out and grabbed my neck. With both hands."

Lexie blinked. "Did she have to step outside to reach you?"

Ashley shook her head. "You know how some houses have two front doors? A screen door on the outside and, like, a heavier door on the inside?"

Lexie nodded.

"I opened the screen door after I rang the doorbell. I was holding it open with my leg."

"Got it," Lexie said. "So you were standing right in the doorway, and she could easily reach you from where she was standing on the other side of the heavier door."

"Right," Ashley said. "She didn't even take a step. She just reached her arms out and took hold of my neck. And she squeezed. And then she pulled me right through the door and into the house. That girl yanked so hard, I'm pretty sure my feet left the ground."

Lexie winced.

"She just kept on squeezing until I couldn't breathe, and my head felt like it was going to explode. I tried and tried, but I couldn't budge her hands from my neck. Not even when I dug my fingernails into the skin on her hands and made her bleed." Another shudder. "Not being able to breathe was scary. Knowing I was going to suffocate and die was scary. But you know what keeps me awake some nights? Her eyes."

"What were her eyes like?"

"They were a neverending, swirling pool of sheer *crazy*. I felt like if I looked in those eyes too long, I would go crazy too and it wouldn't matter if I was dead." Ashley shook her head and ran her fingers over the open pages of her book. "If I think about those crazy eyes, I don't sleep."

"Jesus," Lexie said.

"Then I guess just squeezing my neck with her hands wasn't working fast enough, because the girl made me lie down on my back. She put all her weight on my throat and screamed 'WHY WON'T YOU DIE?' right in my face. Something inside my neck cracked, and I thought my eyes were going to pop right out of my head." Ashley shivered despite the warm day.

Lexie sat up straight in her lounge chair as if she'd just remembered something important.

"The lady T'Jara came just as I was passing out from not getting any air," Ashley said. "She saved my life. She's my hero."

Lexie nodded. "She sure is."

Ashley looked at Lexie with a frankness that is a specialty of eleven-year-olds who are about to start middle school. "I stayed at the hospital for three weeks. I couldn't eat anything but gelatin and frozen pops for three months. My voice will sound like this forever because she broke my voice box. That's what cracked inside my neck. I sometimes have seizures because my brain is damaged from not having oxygen for so long. I didn't do anything to deserve that, you know? I was just a kid." Spoken as if she were such a worldly adult now. "I was trying to sell cookies. I thought everybody loved cookies. Until that day." She shook her head. "My parents went in front of a judge and got some money for what happened to me, and we moved away. I'm damn glad we left Minneapolis." She emphasized the cuss word, then looked around guiltily as if her mother might be hiding nearby. "If people there hurt kids like that girl hurt me, I don't ever want to go back there again."

"I'm so sorry that happened to you, Ashley. I'm glad you made it, and that you're okay. Thanks for talking with me today." Lexie pointed at the girl's book and grinned. "You keep up reading like that, and you're going to do just fine in middle school. You'll rock it." She held out a fist.

Ashley smiled and bumped Lexie's fist with her own. "Thank you."

Lexie waved at Ashley's mom Melanie, who was keeping an eye on them through the kitchen window, then walked to her car and drove away. Ashley watched her go, then settled into her lounge chair for another trip to the tired old town of Maycomb, Alabama.

18

Lexie and Ryan met back up at Ryan's house that evening; Ryan had picked up a bottle of Lexie's favorite pinot noir, and Lexie, true to her word, had picked up a large pepperoni. They discussed the events of the day while they sat on Ryan's couch, ate pizza, and sipped wine from fine crystal glasses.

"Ashley said something that gave me chills," Lexie said. "She told me that, as Lisa Hardwick was trying to strangle her to death, she screamed 'WHY WON'T YOU DIE?'. I couldn't figure out at first why that stuck with me, and then, in the car, I realized: that exact scenario happened to me in one of my nightmares."

Ryan took a giant bite of the greasy pie, then washed it down with some wine. "T'Jara said the older girl's screams didn't even sound human. If she hadn't gotten there when she did, Ashley would have died."

Lexie nodded. "That's what Ashley said too."

Ryan stood and went into his bedroom, then came out holding a short stack of clean white papers. "After I hung up with T'Jara, I went online and printed out every article I could find online about what happened at Destiny House. I figure we can put them in the scrapbook you bought, to help us keep track of everything." He handed the papers to Lexie, then he went into the kitchen to retrieve the scrapbook and tape rolls. Lexie skimmed through the articles and didn't learn anything she hadn't already gotten straight from the source. They worked together to tape the articles, as well as Ryan's handwritten notes from his conversation with T'Jara, into the scrapbook pages while chatting and drinking wine.

Ava called to say good night. "I miss you, Mommy. Can you come over to Gramma and Grampa's tomorrow?"

A pang of guilt shot through Lexie. "I miss you too, babygirl. But I don't think I can tomorrow."

"Why nooooot?" Ava whined.

"Because I'm trying to make it so you can come home to our house, love. It's a lot of work, you know?"

"Can I help?"

"Yes. You can help by keeping Gramma and Grampa company, okay?"

"But I wanna help yoooooooouuu!" Ava wailed.

Lexie heard her father's muffled voice in the background, and Ava's mood improved dramatically. "Never mind, Mommy. Grampa's gonna take me to the zoo tomorrow to see the monkeys and chandeliers! Yay!" In her mind's eye, Lexie could see Ava doing her customary ballerina twirls.

"I think you mean chimpanzees, babycakes. Have fun, okay?"

After dark – and after sharing an entire bottle of wine – they retired to Ryan's bedroom. She wasn't sure if it was the wine, or the darkness, or if she was becoming more comfortable with him, but all night long Lexie hardly worried at all about what Ryan thought about her body. She just enjoyed his touch.

19

Larry Lekvold still had that 1985 Oldsmobile Toronado. Bought it in 1992 with less than 20,000 miles on it, drove it around the brutal arctic tundra that is Minneapolis for sixteen years, and on the day after he retired, packed it up and drove it to his new home in Bonita Springs, Florida. She was a magnificent specimen of a car, too – the height of luxury when it rolled off the line in Lansing, Michigan in late 1984. It was two-door coupe with a long front end and a short trunk, with an automatic transmission, plush leather seats, power windows and locks, and a cassette player. She was painted a rich brown color, with a white vinyl roof and fancy spoked wheel rims. The car was gorgeous, she was elegant, and Larry fell in love with her on sight. He named her Brunhilda. He could not bear to part with her – no modern piece of crap on wheels could compare to her sturdiness and reliability – so he made a point to take excellent care of Hilda. She didn't have a spot of rust on her, and now that they were permanent residents of the great state of Florida, there never would be. Hilda responded to his loving care in kind; at thirty-five years old and with nearly 300,000 miles on her engine, Larry estimated she had at least five good years left in her as long as he drove her conservatively and made sure to keep up with her maintenance schedule.

Not a problem when he didn't often see a need to leave his comfortable mobile home in the lovely Bonita Terra 55+ trailer park community. He had everything he needed right within walking distance; Hilda rarely left her spot in the carport.

In fact, he had just gotten home from his Tuesday morning bridge tournament at the community room and settled into his recliner with a ham sandwich and the noontime news on the TV when the phone rang. He picked the cordless handset up from the small table next to him and answered with a gruff "Hello?"

"Hello, may I speak to Larry Lekvold?" A strange man's voice.

"Speaking."

"Mr. Lekvold, my name is Ryan Laughlin. I'm calling from Minneapolis..."

Larry's bushy white eyebrows shot up in surprise. "Did you say Minneapolis?"

"Yes, sir."

"Do I know you?"

"Um, no..."

"How do you know me?"

"I..."

"Huh. Why on earth would anybody from Minneapolis be calling me? I left there damn near ten years ago now."

"Mr. Lekvold, I live next door to your old house. On Washburn Avenue?""

"So?"

Awkward silence on the other end. Then: "Well, I was hoping..."

Orville Lekvold's son Lawrence had no patience for pussyfooting. A trait that served him well as a manufacturing supervisor for twenty-three years, but sometimes made interactions with other people rather difficult. "Well? Out with it, son."

"I'm sorry. I was hoping to ask you some questions about your time in the house. You might have some information that could help me understand some...experiences my new neighbor is having since she moved in."

Larry's eyebrows fell straight down in a scowl, nearly obscuring his eyes. "Are you trying to waste my time?"

"No, sir. I don't mean to intrude. If I could ask just one question?"

Larry grunted.

"Did anything strange ever happen to you while you lived there? Bad dreams, strange sensations in your head, anything like that?"

This time a surprised chuckle escaped Larry. "Excuse me?"

"I take it that's a no?" Ryan said.

Larry looked longingly at his ham sandwich and potato chips. "Look, son. I lived in that house seventeen years, and I never so much as saw a damn mouse in all that time. Strange sensations? What the hell, boy? I don't know what you want from me, but I can't help you."

A pause at the other end, then the young man said, "Okay, Mr. Lekvold. Thank you for your time." And then he was gone.

Larry looked at his handset for a moment, bemused, then pushed the OFF button and set it back on his side table. *Dunno what the hell that was all about.* Then he turned his attention to the Channel 7 news and bit into his sandwich.

Needs a bit more mustard, he thought.

20

"Well. That was a complete waste of time," Ryan muttered. He set the phone aside and retrieved his tablet. He spent an hour or so printing out old newspaper articles on the Krueger murder/suicide, and was even able to find and print one or two on the Gustafsons. He pasted the articles into Lexie's scrapbook. That done, he thought for a moment and started a new online search. Thirty seconds later he'd found Eric Krueger.

21

Tuesday was free fruit day at Twin Cities Auto. Not that Eric Krueger particularly cared for apples, oranges, or bananas – he was more of a fast food kind of guy – but he enjoyed getting things for free. Especially food. Free fruit was the one thing his employer did to help encourage healthy eating habits; later in the afternoon Eric would be in the breakroom, surreptitiously emptying the baskets of whatever was left (not everyone took advantage of the free fruit, which was just fine with Eric) and taking it back to his office to eat it all in one sitting. For free.

Food had been his one constant comforter since he was a kid, to the point that now, at the ripe old age of forty-two, he tipped the scales at over five hundred pounds. His knees and hips were bad, he slept with a machine that kept him breathing at night, and he wore an insulin pump to manage his Type 2 diabetes – but still he kept on eating upwards of ten thousand calories a day.

When he was bored, he ate.

When he was watching TV, he ate.

When he was happy or celebrating something positive, he ate.

When he was sad, or wanted to quell the bad feelings that came with bad memories, he ate.

The especially bad memories – like what happened to his family when he was thirteen years old – invariably triggered a delivery order from his favorite fast food restaurant. He would demolish a bucket of extra crispy chicken, mashed potatoes and gravy, mac and cheese, coleslaw, and six biscuits with butter and honey – enough food to feed six people – while sitting in front of the TV. The act of mindlessly eating salty, fatty, delicious comfort food while watching something escapist on TV always made him feel better.

Every time Eric encountered a fit person who moved around easily and never seemed out of breath, he was envious. As he lumbered from the breakroom to his office, arms loaded with what was left of the day's free fruit, his eyes fell on one of those very people standing at the customer service desk: a man in his early to mid-forties, wearing athletic shorts and tennis shoes, with close cropped brown hair (Eric guessed he shaved his head to hide his receding hairline) and a few days' worth of scruff on his face. Laurie Watson, the dealership's Director of First Impressions, pointed right at Eric and the man turned toward him.

Eric hurried down the nearest hallway, belly, butt, and chins jiggling. He stood there for a moment, sweating and panting, hoping the man wasn't looking for him.

"Eric Krueger?" The man appeared a few feet from him, a friendly smile on his handsome face.

"Oh. Uh, yeah." Eric stammered, embarrassed that he'd been caught trying to hide with his arms loaded with apples, bananas, and oranges. His cheeks, already red pretty much all the time, heated up.

"My name is Ryan Laughlin. I was wondering if I could talk to you for a few minutes." He stepped forward. "Do you need any help with that?"

"Oh. Uh, no. I got it. Um, what did you want to talk about?" Eric was strictly a back-office guy, handling the dealership's books. He did not work directly with car-buying customers, and couldn't imagine what this Ryan could possibly want to talk to him about.

"I was hoping to ask you a few questions about your family."

"My...family?"

"Yes, and what happened when you lived on Washburn Avenue in Minneapolis."

A wave of dizziness hit Eric, and he very nearly dropped his load of fruit.

"You're white as a ghost, man. Are you sure I can't help you with that fruit?" Ryan took another step toward Eric and held out his hands.

Without a word, Eric abruptly turned and made his way to his office. Ryan followed him, and closed the door while Eric dumped the fruit onto his messy desk and took an extra minute to carefully arrange it into separate piles: two oranges, two apples, four bananas. *That'll make a perfect snack*, he thought. Beefy arms finally free and breathing hard again, Eric stood up and asked, "Why in the hell do you want to talk about that? How do you even know about that? I've never met you before in my life."

Ryan stood a respectful distance away, just inside the door. "I know, and I'm sorry to spring on you like this. It's just, I live next door to your old house, and my new neighbors are having some...trouble there."

Still unsure, Eric asked, "What kind of trouble?"

Ryan gestured to one of the chairs sitting in front of Eric's desk. "Do you mind if I sit?"

"Sure." Eric decided that was a splendid idea, and lowered himself into his own chair. It wheezed under his massive weight like a dog's tortured squeaky toy.

Ryan sat and gave Eric a frank look. "Here's the deal. My neighbor Lexie and her daughter Ava have been having some strange experiences since they moved into the house. Headaches, heartburn, bad dreams, random fainting spells, and personality changes, just to name a few. We've been investigating the house's history, and there's a pattern of strange things going back many years. Including, I understand, your family in 1991. I was hoping you could help me understand what you went through so maybe we can figure out what the hell is going on with that house and stop it."

Eric frowned. "What do you mean, stop it? Stop what?"

Ryan shrugged. "Not sure yet. But since most houses don't have the kind of sordid history this one does, I gotta wonder if there's something causing all this trouble."

Eric blinked, and without realizing he was doing it, reached out and grabbed a banana. "You think it's haunted?"

"Like I said, I don't know. But I intend to find out."

Eric considered this as he peeled the banana and popped a piece into his mouth. *This would be better dipped in chocolate*, he thought as he chewed. He knew he would be venturing into dangerous territory, telling this stranger his story. He didn't even allow *himself* to think too much about his story. *I don't know, maybe it's time*, he thought. *Maybe I can help this lady and her kid, keep what happened to Mom and Abby from happening to them.* He sighed. "Okay," he said.

"Thanks, man." Ryan said. "Can't tell you how much I appreciate this."

Eric nodded, his mouth full of banana. He swallowed and said, "So what do you want to know?"

"How old were you when you lived in the house on Washburn?"

"I was thirteen. My sister Abby was eleven. We only lived there for two months." Eric tossed his banana peel into the garbage can – already full from his regular day's meals – and picked up another. "It was the craziest couple months of my life."

"How's that?"

"Well, for one thing, my mom became a completely different person. When we were little she was the perfect mom – kind, caring, and she doted on my sister and me. That all changed once we moved to Washburn. Her entire personality changed; she was so cranky all the time, constantly yelling at us kids.

Especially my sister." Eric paused, banana half-peeled in his hand. "One time, not too long before everything went to shit for the Krueger family, she hit my sister. Slapped her right across the face when she interrupted Mom's yelling to ask what the hell her problem was." Tears began to effervesce behind his eyes. "Her hand left a perfect red print on Abby's left cheek that took a good couple days to fade." Eric paused, then took a deep breath. "Abby was always way braver than I was. I just sat there and took it. She fought back."

Ryan looked at Eric with wide eyes. "Did your mom ever say what was bothering her?"

Eric shook his head. "Not really, although she did complain about having headaches a lot. Beyond that, it seemed like just having us kids around pissed her off."

"Huh," Ryan intoned. "And what about your dad?"

Eric remembered the half-peeled banana in his hand and set it aside. He didn't have much of an appetite anymore. "My dad did the best he could, but he worked. He traveled, so he wasn't home a lot of the time. When he was around, he would take Abby and me to hang out at the mall or swimming at the pool, or window shopping downtown. But when he was at work, it was just us and Mom."

"How was your sister during all this? Did she have nightmares? Sudden changes in personality? Weird electric sensations in her head when she'd leave the house?"

"How do you know about that?" Eric's shock made the question come out much harsher than he'd intended. Nobody knew about Mom's & Abby's brain zaps; Eric never mentioned them to the police, and as far as he knew his father hadn't either. It was too weird.

Ryan's eyes were intense. "Because all of that is happening to my neighbor and her daughter. I've found one or both of them passed out in their yard twice in the last week. Twice." He emphasized this last word by gently hitting his fist on Eric's desk.

All Eric could do for a moment was sit there and stare at Ryan. Finally he blinked. "You mean...you mean it wasn't just my mom and my sister?"

Ryan shook his head emphatically. "Nope. And I'd be willing to bet it's happened to others too."

Memories started popping up in Eric's mind at an alarming rate: going outside to find his mom out cold in the backyard, her purse lying on the grass next to her (that happened twice). Following Abby out the front door and having to catch her when she suddenly fainted, saving her from a tumble down the concrete front steps. Waking up in the middle of the night to find Abby out of her bed and standing next to his, staring intently at him with eyes he didn't recognize. Walking into the kitchen one morning...

He hadn't been totally truthful with Ryan.

"My mom wasn't just cranky," he admitted. "She was batshit crazy while we lived in that house." The tears were trying to come back, and they made his voice crack. "She had it out for my sister."

"You mean –"

"Yeah. My mom was actively trying to hurt my sister." The tears finally broke free of their restraints and coursed freely down Eric's meaty face. "After I caught her in the kitchen one morning sneaking up behind Abby with a knife in her hand, I promised myself I would never leave Abby alone with her ever again." A huge chunk of raw emotion broke free in his chest and overwhelmed him. "I tried, oh god I tried, and I f-f-f-failed!" That last word faded into a wail, a scream, and then nothing but violent weeping. "It's my fault, I'm so sorry Abby oh god I'm so sorry!" He covered his face with his hands and cried like he hadn't in many years.

Ryan's warm hand grasped his forearm. "I'm so sorry, Eric. So sorry."

It took a few minutes and half a box of tissues, but Eric was finally able to pull himself together. He felt...cleaner. More...whole. Like he'd finally started filling the gaping emotional hole that he'd tried all his life to fill with food. He took a deep, ragged breath, then asked, "Do you know what happened to my mom and my sister?"

"I know they both died in the house."

"About fifteen minutes before my dad was due home from work on Wednesday, August 7, 1991, my mom stabbed my sister to death in the living room, then went down to the basement and shot herself in the head with my dad's .22 caliber rifle."

"Jesus." Ryan's eyes ate up most of his face.

"I had been invited to sleep over at my best friend Derek's house. My mom encouraged me to go. She seemed to be having a good day, so I decided to let my guard down just this one time. It was the first time I'd left Abby home alone with my mom in almost two weeks." The tears were rolling again. "All my mom needed was for me to be out of the house."

"Your dad found them?"

Eric nodded, blotting his hot cheeks with another tissue. "A Minneapolis police officer picked me up from Derek's house and took me home. When I got there, my dad was sitting on the curb in front of the house, still wearing his suit and tie, in shock and not able to speak." A sob escaped Eric, and he teared up again. "It was days before he could talk. He was never the same after that. Neither of us were."

"Where's your dad now? His name was Donald, right?"

Eric nodded. "Yeah. My mom was Shirley. My dad passed away in 1997."

"Oh, I'm sorry to hear that," Ryan said soberly.

"The medical examiner said he had a heart attack in his sleep, but I know what really killed him: a broken heart. He was only forty-nine years old."

Ryan and Eric sat in silence for a moment. Then Eric said, "It feels good to talk about it." A sob. "I miss my family."

Ryan leaned over the desk and grasped Eric's forearm again. "I'm glad you're talking about it. I hope you will get some help, Eric. You need to work through this and start taking care of yourself, or you're bound to die younger than your dad did."

Eric thought about a line he'd read in a book once: *Murder injures the survivors*. He didn't recognize the truth in that statement then, but he did now. He'd carried the scars of unbearable guilt and sorrow over the deaths of his mother and sister, and later his father, for most of his life -- and they manifested themselves in his wildly out-of-control weight. Which he realized would kill him sooner than later if he didn't make some drastic changes in his life. "I know I do. And I will." He paused, then said, "Thank you."

Ryan stood. "No, Eric – thank you. The information you gave me today could save Lexie's and Ava's lives. You should feel good about that." He extended his hand.

Eric shook it. "Will you let me know what comes of all this?"

Ryan nodded. "Absolutely. You take care of yourself." And then he was gone.

The first thing Eric did after Ryan left was take the rest of the pilfered fruit back to the breakroom. Then he called his doctor and asked for a referral to a good therapist. He used to think he didn't care if he lived or died; now he realized he wasn't done with this life just yet.

He thought Abby would be proud of him – and he smiled.

22

While Eric was telling Ryan about the single worst day of his life, Lexie was on her way to the Restful Ways memory care home in the suburb of St. Louis Park. Joanna had thought it was Eric's dad Don Krueger who was a resident there, but it turned out to actually be Hans Gustafson, now in his late seventies and living with Alzheimer's disease. Lexie hoped she could get him to talk to her; she knew from personal experience that the chances he'd remember anything useful were pretty slim. *It's worth a shot,* she thought. *I just hope I don't upset him too much.*

23

Hans was Lily Cornwall's favorite patient. He was quiet, he was a good eater, he was generally okay about following her directions, and he rarely wandered or went off on rages like some of the other patients at Restful Ways. And he always called her by her correct first name.

Hans had been a resident at Restful Ways for many years. Lily didn't know his whole story, but did know that he didn't have much family left and never had visitors. She imagined that in his younger days, he was tall and slim with a beard, heavy glasses, and a booming voice. Now, though...now his voice was not much more than a whisper, his hair white, his body thin and fragile. He spent his days folded in his wheelchair, watching television or staring at the birds flitting about outside his window. She and the other nurses were his only connection to humanity, and she often wondered what was in store for the old man. Would he slowly waste away here, die alone, and be buried in a pine box in a potter's field? Lily thought so...and she worried about him.

Hans' memory seemed to be stuck somewhere in the early 1980s. He often said things like "Fuck Reagan. You ask me, any president who is anti-union is anti-American." After he'd said this three or four times, Lily, a 1992-born millennial to the core, did an online search – and that's how she learned about the air traffic controller strike of 1981. She wondered if he was one of the unfortunate ones to have no job to come back to after fighting the Federal Aviation Administration for better working conditions and pay. She tried asking him once.

"No," Hans said. "I'm not an air traffic controller. I've been at Ford fifteen years. Card-carrying union member from day one. Union brothers stick together." He raised a bony, liver-spotted fist in solidarity. "But you knew that already, Lily." He looked at her with more than a little irritation in his bleary gray eyes, magnified by the thick lenses of his glasses. The reason for that was lost on Lily; she could never figure out why Hans would expect her to know anything about his life.

Now, as Lily rolled Hans in his wheelchair to the dining room, she reminded him, "Today is Tuesday, Hans. You remember what we have for dinner on Tuesdays?"

"Turkey and mashed potatoes," he said, a small smile on his face. It was his favorite meal of the whole week.

Lily got him situated at his table. Most of the residents – the ones who could still eat independently – ate at large round tables that seated eight people. Because he needed extra help to eat safely, Hans sat at a small table next to the large windows with Lily or another nurse. They were just digging into the mashed potatoes with turkey gravy when a voice said, "Excuse me?"

Lily and Hans both looked up to see a young woman with long brown hair and large brown eyes standing next to their table, an uncertain look on her face. She looked to be five or six years older and forty pounds heavier than Lily herself. "Can I help you?" Lily asked.

"I'm looking for Hans Gustafson," the young woman said. "The nurse at the front desk said I could find him here."

Hans's eyes, usually dull and starey, brightened. "Liesl? Is that you, honey?"

Lily looked at Hans curiously. The young woman gestured toward Lily and said, "My name is Lexie. I was hoping I could ask Mr. Gustafson a few questions."

Lily frowned. "Questions? About what?"

"Why haven't you visited, Liesl? Pull up a chair and sit with your old dad." Hans' voice had brightened as well, his normally expressionless face full of wonder as he watched Lexie.

Lexie smiled at Hans, then pulled an empty chair over and sat facing him from across the table; Lily was on her right, holding a fork loaded with mashed potatoes in midair. "I live in his old house, and strange things have been happening to me and my daughter since we moved in. I know he lost his wife and daughters while he was living there, so I thought he might have some insight."

Lily sat in stunned silence for a moment. "He...what?"

"All I know is what I've read in this old newspaper story. I guess his wife Lillie and his daughters Liesl and Britta died in my house back in June of 1982." Lexie pulled a folded printout from her purse and handed it to Lily, who set her fork down and started skimming the article.

"Britta. Where is Britta?" Hans asked, looking around the nursing home's massive dining room. "Lillie and I never had any boys, you know. Only girls. I always thought we should change our last name to Gustafsdottir. Lillie thought that would be foolish." Hans chuckled.

Lily looked up from the article with wide eyes. "Lillie? That was his wife's name?" Suddenly a lot of things about Hans made sense. When he called her by her name, or expected her to already know something, he wasn't talking to her. He thought he was talking to his wife. *He really is stuck in the past*, she thought, setting the paper on the table in front of her.

Lexie turned to Hans. "Mr. Gustafson, my name is Lexie."

Hans' magnified eyes blinked, but he didn't say anything. White hairs, fine as spiderwebs, randomly sprouted from his shiny scalp.

"Do you remember when you lived at 4741 Washburn Avenue North in Minneapolis?"

Hans' dry, wrinkled lips worked for a moment while he thought, then he said, "Yes. You lived there too. You shared the second bedroom with Britta." His dinner sat forgotten on the table in front of him.

"Did we fight a lot?" Lexie asked.

"Not when you were very little," Hans said. "But when you were eight and Britta was six..." Hans trailed off, and Lily watched a cloud of sadness descend upon his wrinkled face.

"That's when we moved into the house on Washburn Avenue, wasn't it? And things changed, didn't they?" Lexie asked. Lily watched Hans closely.

Hans didn't speak for a moment, only stared out the window. Then he said, "You chased Britta all around the house with a...um..." He looked uncertainly at Lily and waved a closed fist in the air, thumb up, as if he were holding something in it.

"A hammer?" Lily said.

"Yes. A hammer." A watery sigh. "Britta had such terrible nightmares."

"What about Lillie?" Lexie asked.

"Lillie." Hans sighed again. "Your mother was the most beautiful, gentle soul. But she changed. In that house." Hans paused. "So...angry. She hid knives."

"She hid knives in the house?" Lexie asked.

Hans nodded.

"Did she ever use one of the knives to try and hurt us?"

"No, but I believe she meant to." Another pause. "She pushed you down the basement stairs. Do you remember?"

Lexie shook her head, wide-eyed.

Hans nodded. "I was down there, tinkering with the furnace. I heard every terrible thud. How you cried after you landed on the floor." Tears welled in Hans' eyes; Lily opened her mouth to stop this conversation immediately. Hans calmly held a hand up, and she closed her mouth again.

"Why did she do that?" Lexie asked. Lily saw tears in her eyes too.

"I ran to you, and Lillie was standing at the top of the stairs. She...she had a crazy look on her face. She was smiling." Tears left wet trails as they coursed down Hans' cheeks. "But she screamed like the devil when she saw you were not dead." Hans broke into full-on sobs. "Thank God, you were not dead."

Lexie, also crying, reached across the table and took Hans' frail hand in hers. "I'm so glad you were there."

"But I wasn't there later." Hans' voice trembled.

"When?" Lexie said.

"I was at work. Lillie – she was better. I thought she could be trusted with you girls. I even hid all the knives. But I never thought about the bathtub. And then – and then you were all gone." Hans dissolved into great, gusting sobs.

Lexie let go of Hans' hand and covered her face. Lily could do nothing but sit and stare out the window. It looked to be a lovely summer day outside, but right here, at Hans' special table in the Restful Ways dining room, there was no sunshine. Only darkness and unbearable pain for a man who truly didn't deserve such misery. Whose loss had been so great that his poor brain just stopped functioning.

"She killed the girls?" she whispered to Lexie.

"Yeah," Lexie whispered back, wiping tears from her cheeks. "I guess she drowned them in the bathtub, laid them in their bed, and then hanged herself. He found them all when he got home from work."

My god, I had no idea, Lily thought. *No wonder he doesn't remember what he had for dinner last night, but remembers that time period so clearly.* Her heart broke for him.

It took a few minutes, but everyone at the table finally composed themselves. Hans wiped his eyes with his shirtsleeves and looked at Lily. "I'm hungry."

Lily smiled. "Still want your turkey and mashed potatoes?"

Hans nodded, then noticed Lexie. "Who are you?"

Lexie gazed fondly at Hans for a moment, then gathered her purse from the floor next to her chair. "I'm just visiting," she said. To Lily: "Thank you. I hope he'll be okay."

Lily waved a hand in the air. "As long as he's still eating his favorite dinner, I think he's fine."

Lexie bid them both goodbye and left the dining room.

"She looked like my Liesl," Hans said.

Lily scooped mashed potatoes and gravy with the fork and moved it toward Hans' face. "Will you tell me about Liesl and Britta?"

24

When Ryan got home from his visit with Eric Krueger at Twin Cities Auto, Lexie was already there with Italian takeout for dinner. He kissed her gratefully, then collapsed into a chair at the dinette table. A plate full of spaghetti and meatballs steamed in front of him, and he dug in while they debriefed each other on the day's conversations.

"Man, Eric Krueger is one poor, messed up individual," Ryan said, shaking his head.

"Yeah," Lexie said. "Hans too. I feel so bad for him."

Ryan pointed his fork at Lexie. "Here's what gets me. These families were completely normal right up until they moved into the house. Right? Then, within just a couple months of being in the house, these families were utterly shattered. And the survivors never really recover." He took a bite of warm buttered Italian bread, thinking as he chewed. "I mean, what has that kind of power?"

Lexie shook her head. "I don't know, but I feel like we're getting closer to figuring this out. Where's that list Louise wrote for us?"

Ryan got up and retrieved their original handwritten list from the living room. He flattened it out on the table, and they both moved their plates out of the way so they could lean over and examine the list closely without fear of getting tomato sauce on their shirts.

"So far we've talked to T'Jara Jackson, Ashley Lee, Larry Lekvold, Eric Krueger, and Hans Gustafson." Lexie's finger touched each name on the list as she recited it. "What patterns do we see after learning more about their experiences in my house?"

Ryan got up again and brought a fresh legal pad and a pen back into the dining room with him. He wrote T'Jara Jackson on a sheet of paper, then pulled the scrapbook into the middle of the table and opened it to the page that had his notes from their conversation.

"Okay," he said. "T'Jara spent nine months in the house, constantly breaking up fights and trying not to get her ass kicked." He wrote 9 months next to her name.

"Did she experience any of the crazy stuff that happened to us?" Lexie asked.

Ryan shook his head. "No. She mentioned bad dreams. And feeling like she was being watched." He noted these.

Lexie thought for a moment. "Let's also add what Lisa Hardwick screamed while she was trying to strangle Ashley to death. Ashley didn't live in the house, but it seems significant because I had a dream very similar to that."

Ryan nodded and wrote Ashley/Lisa – Lexie dream – 'Why won't you die' on the next line.

"What about..." Lexie hesitated, unsure she wanted to go in this direction, then pressed on. "What about the times mothers tried to hurt their kids? Lillie Gustafson pushed Liesl Gustafson down the stairs. Shirley Krueger got caught sneaking up on Abigail Krueger with a knife. And..."

Ryan looked up, "And?"

Lexie took a deep breath. Her face heated up, but she opened her mouth anyway; she couldn't deny the truth. "And I may have found myself trying to do both of those things to Ava." She winced, and apprehensively watched Ryan's face.

It didn't change at first, but as what she'd said started to sink in, his eyes widened and searched Lexie's face for even a hint that she was kidding. Finding none, he finally blinked. "Are you serious?"

Lexie nodded, then dropped her eyes. Hot shame flooded her entire body.

"When?"

She couldn't look at him. "Um. On Friday before you found me sleeping on the chaise in my yard, something came over me and I damn near threw Ava down the basement stairs. The day we had chicken wings, I found my kitchen knives and thought seriously about slitting her throat with the chef knife. I remember thinking, both of those times, "If I do it quickly, she won't feel a thing."

Ryan blinked again, still wide-eyed, but didn't say anything. His notebook sat forgotten in his lap.

"I swear to you, Ryan, I was not in my right mind. My head was all foggy and pounding with pain. It was almost like...like something else was controlling me."

"What stopped you?"

"Ava," Lexie said, still speaking to her hands, folded in her lap. "Both times she said something that broke my trance." Lexie frowned, hearing Ava's ghost-voice in her head. "More than once after the stairs incident she said, 'It was the little girl.'"

Ryan sat silent for a moment, reading over Louise's list and his notes, and thinking. Lexie watched him anxiously, convinced that she'd just given him his out – he wouldn't be around much longer. She'd be back to doing everything on her own. *Just like Jake*, she thought.

Instead of jumping up in horror and demanding that Lexie leave his house immediately, Ryan calmly said. "Couple things. First, all the mothers on this list, excluding you but just barely, did actually kill their kids. Their *daughters*. Second, both Eric and Hans mentioned that the mother was always angry, and neither could be trusted alone with the daughters." Ryan paused, thinking. "Again with the mothers and daughters." He started doodling on his legal pad, trying to fit all the information they had into a flowchart that made sense.

"Kathryn Dormeister didn't have kids," Lexie pointed out. "How does she fit with the mother/daughter theory?"

Ryan set his pen down. "She doesn't."

Something occurred to Lexie. "My mom tried to attack me with a knife."

Ryan's eyes moved from staring at his paper to staring at her face. "What?"

"My parents came over after work the evening of the stairs incident, and my mom helped me cut potatoes for a potato salad. I said something she didn't like, and her knife – her very sharp butcher knife – came within a cat's whisker of lopping my thumb off." Lexie shuddered at the memory of the barely perceptible *fwip* sound the knife made as it sliced through the air mere nanometers from the tip of her thumb.

"Holy shit, Lex," Ryan said. "Your mom doesn't even live in the house. Only been there the one time. Does that mean that anyone who comes in could be affected by this?"

Lexie shrugged. "It must. I mean, look at what T'Jara said about Destiny House."

Lord, the nightmares I had. Ryan nodded.

"And here's the other thing. What about this Michael? If it's only mothers and daughters, where is he?"

"Hey, it was Joanna who first said anything about the women being the most affected. Although you're right, it seems that theory has some holes in it," Ryan said.

Lexie referred again to Louise's original list. "We still have John Dormeister and Justin Betz to talk to." She touched their names as she recited them, as she had before.

"You looking forward to visiting St. Cloud prison?" Ryan asked, grinning.

Lexie smirked at him. "Oh, yeah. Bucket list item for sure."

"Just be sure to abide by the bright yellow signs along the highway that say DO NOT PICK UP HITCHHIKERS. They're there for a reason." He burst out laughing at the look on

Lexie's face. He reached over the corner of the table, took hold of her shirt, and gently pulled her closer to him until they were nose to nose. "I'm kidding. You, my sheltered suburban girl, will be just fine. I promise."

"Okay," Lexie whispered. It was all she could manage; waiting for him to kiss her already was making her crazy. *Probably he knows that,* she thought.

Ryan closed his eyes and pressed his lips firmly against hers. The butterflies in Lexie's belly awakened and started fluttering. After several seconds he slowly pulled away and smiled, deepening the laugh lines around his eyes.

"I dug that," he said softly.

"Me too," she whispered, unsure whether her actual voice still worked.

"And I dig you." He touched her forehead with his. "You and your cute kid and your crazy house saved me, I think."

"Saved you from what?" She closed her eyes and breathed in his scent. She felt...safe. Appreciated. Like she mattered. Jake had never, ever made her feel this way. *Jake who?*

"Saved me from a life of loneliness."

Lexie's eyes popped open, and she moved her head backward so she could see his entire face. "What are you saying?"

Ryan laughed and sat back in his chair. "I'm saying that I'm crazy about you and I want you and Ava to be part my life. You know, like maybe we could be boyfriend and girlfriend."

Lexie blinked. "But...why?"

"Why what?"

"Why do you want to be with me? I'm teetering on the brink of complete lunacy with my house; I came this close to hurting my kid twice, and yet still you sit here, not being mad at me. Not to mention the fact that you're athletic and fit, and I'm so...so fat. I can barely look at myself in a mirror. I don't know how you can stand to touch me."

The amusement on Ryan's face swiftly morphed into complete disbelief.

"I have a kid who is the result of a torrid affair with a surgeon I work with. I live in the city and not across the street from my parents in the suburbs." Lexie took a breath and looked directly at Ryan with no emotion, just pure conviction. "I'm my mother's only child and easily the biggest disappointment of her entire life."

By now Ryan had crossed his arms over his chest and was regarding Lexie levelly. "I'm going to go out on a limb here and guess that's your mom talking."

Lexie frowned.

"Everything you just said sounds exactly like what an insecure mother might say to her beautiful and ambitious daughter to keep her in line. Below the line, actually...an insecure mother simply cannot have her kid competing with her for attention."

Lexie's eyebrows shot up. "I don't –"

Ryan leaned forward and took Lexie's hand. "I see it all the time at school. Parents tend to fall in four categories. First are parents who absolutely pressure their kid to perform.

Athletically, academically, in every way, they expect perfection –
because my god, what would the neighbors think? The second
group of parents are the truly supportive and loving parents who
do everything they can to raise happy, well-rounded humans.
There are far fewer of those than you'd think, sadly. The third
type of parents ignore and/or abuse their kid; don't give them the
tools and skills they need to function in life, then wonder why the
kid turns to drugs or gangs just to cope. The fourth group of
parents are selfish. They hold back their kids who have a ton of
potential because they're scared people will pay more attention to
the kid than to them." Ryan shook his head. "I've been a teacher
in city schools for twenty years now, and I've seen it all. I'm sure
she has no awareness, and she thinks she means well, but your
mom could be the president of that last group of parents."

Lexie just sat and stared; it was like Ryan had taken a giant
flashlight and shone it on her relationship with Jane. Suddenly
everything made sense.

"You know what I see?" Ryan asked.

Still struck dumb, Lexie slowly shook her head.

"I see a strong, independent woman who learns from her
mistakes and loves fiercely. You're a fantastic mom. You take care
of yourself and your daughter so well. You're brave enough to
forge your own path in life. To be honest, I don't even see your
extra pounds." He lifted Lexie's hand to his lips and kissed her
knuckles. "I see your beautiful heart. You are an absolutely
beautiful person, inside and out."

Lexie didn't know she was going to cry until the tears were already running down her face. She clamped her hands over her mouth, afraid she might start weeping and never stop. Ryan stood and pulled her up with him, then wrapped her in a tight hug. Lexie allowed herself to disintegrate, sobbing against his chest. *Is this what it feels like to have someone supporting and loving you no matter what?* she wondered. It was a completely foreign feeling...yet one she thought she might be able to get used to.

25

One could forgive John Dormeister for being bitter. A decade or so in prison did that to a man. An *innocent* man.

After the Minnesota Supreme Court denied his last attempt at a new trial in 2017, he gave up and accepted his fate: he would be a resident of the Minnesota Correctional Facility – St. Cloud for the rest of his life.

Being incarcerated for a horrific crime he did not commit did something to a man. Being forced to grieve the loss of the love of his life while wrongfully incarcerated for her murder was a double-whammy that gradually sucked the life out of him, turned him into little more than a shade of his former self. He carried constant anger in his heart: anger at a criminal justice system that would put an innocent man in prison for the rest of his life, anger at the prosecutor who somehow invented a case against him and made it stick, anger at Kathryn for leaving him. But the lion's share of his anger was directed at God. He'd been raised Lutheran, taught in Sunday School that God is good and kind. Upon his arrival at St. Cloud, he read the Bible cover-to-cover; nowhere in the "great book" was there an explanation of how a God who is so great and good could allow such an injustice as what had happened to him.

He spent a lot of time thinking about that, and invariably came to the same conclusion: there couldn't possibly be a God. Entire religions were built on a goddamn fairy tale. It was the only explanation that made sense. But the Sunday School lessons were deeply ingrained, and he could never completely let go of the idea of God. So the anger stayed in his heart, churning and boiling his blood. He threw the Bible in the trash, shaved his dark curls off, and watched as new lines carved themselves into the skin around his eyes and mouth with every miserable year.

As prisons went, John supposed St. Cloud wasn't so bad. Built in the 1880s from gray St. Cloud granite with inmate labor, the prison's four-story Victorian main building and tower, three-story cell wings, and perimeter wall – one of the longest granite walls in the world – had felt imposing to John when he first arrived. It looked like every creepy haunted Gothic building in every Scooby Doo episode.

Inside the buildings were bright and sterile, walls painted white and lit by powerful halogen overhead lights. He endured the intake process, then was taken to his six-foot by ten-foot single cell in B House, the oldest cell block at the prison. That he wouldn't have to deal with a cellmate was as close to good news as he could imagine at that low point in his life.

He got settled and learned the prison routine, but he never smiled, never laughed, rarely talked. He had stopped living long ago, and simply existed through each day. He went where they told him to go, did what they told him to do, and spent every free minute alone in his cell, reading a book from the prison library or writing furiously in the spiral-bound notebook that served as his journal. He had dozens of these notebooks piled on the tiny desk in his cell. The forty hours he spent every week working in the shop that manufactured Minnesota license plates paid him just enough to buy those notebooks and pens, and the occasional candy bar and can of pop, from the commissary.

Visitors had always been a rarity for him, and after his mother died of leukemia in 2015, the slow trickle stopped entirely. So when he received word that someone wanted him to add them to his visitor list, he was perplexed – and curious. He obliged, then waited to hear when the mysterious Alexis Novak would be visiting him.

He only had to wait a couple of days. "Brutus," his nickname for a prison guard who looked more like an NFL linebacker, arrived at the shop just before ten o'clock on Wednesday morning to take him to meet his visitor. "Let's go, Dormeister. She's waiting for you," he rumbled through a handlebar mustache that made Brutus' face look much older than his actual age of thirty. His uniform stretched so tightly across his muscular arms and chest that he squeaked when he walked.

After glancing at the supervising guard, also adorned with a handlebar mustache, and receiving a curt nod of approval, John left his position on the manufacturing line and followed Brutus from the shop to the prison's main building. John knew that because this Alexis was neither friend, family, nor attorney, theirs would be a non-contact visit under the close watch of yet another prison guard. He would only be able to see her through the reinforced glass window of a prison visiting booth, and talk to her through a black handset like those used in old phone booths.

Brutus led John through a heavy steel door that had opened with a loud buzz and into a long and narrow room where visitation booths lined up like soldiers against the wall. Brutus pointed him to Booth #1, reminded him of the sixty-minute time limit, then left; the heavy steel door slammed with a clank behind him.

He sat in a molded plastic chair and regarded his visitor. He guessed she was in her mid-thirties, with long, straight brown hair pulled back into a ponytail and pretty doe-like brown eyes. She carried more than a few extra pounds, but John guessed she carried them well, with the ease of someone who has spent her whole life battling her weight and learned how to function in spite of it. She looked at him nervously, unsure what to do next.

He reached for his handset. She did the same, and pressed it to her ear.

"So," he said into the phone. "Finally I meet the mysterious Alexis."

She smiled nervously. "Call me Lexie. Please."

He looked at her for another couple beats without saying anything. She didn't seem sure of what to say next, so he said, "And you want to talk about my wife?"

She nodded. "Yes. I live in your house now."

"Really. The house on Washburn Avenue." He hadn't thought about the house in a while. A pit started to open in his gut.

"My four-year-old daughter and I moved in about a week and a half ago, and we've had nothing but strange and scary experiences ever since." Her free hand found the zipper on her hoodie sweatshirt and started fiddling with it. "The only time either of us feels even remotely normal is when we are outside the house."

Old memories – memories he'd spent the last decade trying to forget – started bubbling to the surface. Kathryn, complaining of headaches and eating Tums like candy. Kathryn losing her legs and sitting on the steps sometimes when she walked out the door. "Headaches? Heartburn? Nightmares? Weird zings in the head?"

Relief visibly washed like a wave over Lexie's face. She put her hands on the stainless steel counter in front of her to steady herself. "Yes!"

John nodded. "Kath had all those same symptoms. We only lived in the house for a couple of months, but I don't think there was a single day that Kath felt normal in the house. 'I have a bit of a headache all of a sudden' became her catchphrase of sorts. That, and 'I think I need to lie down for a minute.'"

"Did she have nightmares?"

John nodded. "The nightmares were incredible; she would toss and turn and thrash until all the covers ended up on the floor. Every night."

"Did you and Kathryn have kids?"

John wasn't prepared for this question. Long-forgotten emotion bubbled up from the pit in his gut, and the sadness was almost more than he could bear. He didn't answer for a long time.

Lexie looked stricken, like she wished she could snatch the words out of the air and pretend she never said them. "You don't have to answer that, John. I'm sorry if I crossed a line."

He was too caught up in memories of Kathryn to hear her. "Kath and I didn't have kids together," he said. "But we were trying. Then something happened the day before Kath died that changed everything for us. She left her phone out on the kitchen counter while she was in the shower, and I saw the notification light blinking." He paused; sometimes he dreamed about that blinking red light. Then: "I wasn't the kind of husband who monitors his wife's phone, but for some reason I felt absolutely compelled to see what the notification was. She didn't password-protect her Blackberry, so it was easy to do." He propped his head in his free hand and stared down at his own stainless steel counter, still ashamed of his actions over a decade ago.

Lexie waited a few beats, then tentatively asked, "What was the message?"

"It was a message from a young lady named Isabella. I told myself I didn't need to read it. I even set the phone back on the counter and left the kitchen. But I couldn't ignore it. It was like that blinking red light was mocking me. And damn it, I was curious. You see what I'm saying? I needed. to. know." His pointer finger tapped the counter with each of those last three words. "I went right back into the kitchen, and I read the message."

"What did it say?"

It took effort, but John tore his eyes from the counter and looked at Lexie through the glass. "Isabella was eighteen years old, lived in Oakdale, and had it on good authority that Kathryn was her birth mother."

Lexie's eyes widened.

"She looked just like Kathryn. Same blonde hair, same green eyes. There was no denying it."

"You didn't know?"

John shook his head. "I had no idea. I was absolutely gobsmacked. And so pissed that she would keep a secret like that from me."

Lexie winced. "What happened?"

"Kath came out of the bathroom, hair still wet and wearing her old terrycloth robe, and of course I immediately confronted her with Isabella's message. At first she was angry too, demanding to know what I thought I was doing, looking at her phone while she was in the shower. I kept pushing – hard – and eventually she backed down and told me everything. How she'd lost her virginity when she was a sophomore in high school and got pregnant from that one time. She had the baby during the summer between her sophomore and junior years, gave it up for adoption, and went back to school in September as if nothing had happened. She cried, telling me that giving the baby up was the hardest thing she'd ever done and all she wanted to do was forget. Isabella was never supposed to find her." John couldn't keep the tremble out of his voice. "She begged me to forgive her. I told her I didn't think I could, and then I left the house. I'd never been so – so *angry* in my entire life. I felt betrayed, like my entire marriage was a lie.

"I drove around aimlessly all night. When I got home the next morning, ready to talk this out and find a path forward, I found Kathryn lying at the bottom of the basement stairs." John looked directly at Lexie now; he felt like his actual soul was on fire. "She was dead. Broken neck. But I did not kill her. I didn't kill my wife."

Lexie blinked.

"Jim McCormick, the Hennepin County attorney, built an entire case around convincing the jury that I never actually left my house, because nobody saw me leave or heard my gas/electric hybrid car drive away. That, because there was no evidence of an intruder, I was the only person on planet Earth who could have killed Kathryn. My motive was my anger over finding out Kathryn had had a baby by another man and didn't tell me." He paused for a moment, trying to swallow back the tears that now threatened.

"My entire life ceased to mean anything after Kathryn died. I didn't care what McCormick said about me, I didn't care that I ended up here. I actually felt like I deserved to be here. McCormick was right about one thing: I was a shitty husband. But he was wrong about what made me a shitty husband. I didn't kill her. What I did do was leave her in anger, and she died believing I hated her." The tears he'd tried to stop now came in full force, spilling over his lower eyelashes and running down his scruffy cheeks. He angrily palmed them away.

"I'm so sorry, John."

He took a moment to compose himself, then said, "But you didn't come here to listen to my sob story, did you?"

Lexie shrugged. "I'm here to listen to whatever you have to say. Who knows, maybe it'll help me figure out what the hell is going on with my house." Then: "How did Kathryn end up at the bottom of the basement stairs? Do you know?"

John sat back in his chair. "Well, McCormick would tell you I lured her to the back door and then pushed her so hard that she sailed down to the basement without actually touching any of the steps, and she landed just right on the concrete floor so that her skull actually separated from her spine. They were supposedly able to recreate such a bullshit scenario, and then pinned it on me with some pretty sketchy circumstantial evidence. I mean, of course my fingerprints were on the wall inside the back door and on the railing going downstairs. It was my house, for God's sake."

Lexie nodded.

John leaned forward again and draped himself over his stainless steel counter. "But that isn't what happened. I wasn't there, so I don't know how she ended up at the bottom of the stairs. We were big-time planning for our future, so suicide never seemed likely to me. I suppose it could have been an accident, but I don't think so. The closest Kathryn ever got to those stairs was to leave the house by the back door, and within a couple weeks of moving in she was using the front door exclusively. She hated the basement almost as much as she hated the attic. She said she didn't like the vibe." He sighed. "We started talking about selling as soon as we moved in. I guess we just didn't get our shit together in time."

"So the question is, if you didn't push her and she didn't accidentally fall, how did she die?" Lexie said.

"Exactly. I will tell you, with all the other strange shit that happened to her in the house, I always wondered if it was all related somehow."

Lexie frowned. "Related?"

"Yeah. Like, maybe there's something in the house that's causing all this trouble."

"And killing people?"

John shrugged. "I know, it sounds crazy."

A thought flashed across Lexie's face; John wished he could know what it was.

Lexie didn't have many more questions, and John didn't have much else to offer, so he signaled to the camera hanging from the ceiling in the corner that the visit was over. Brutus arrived to take John back to his station in the license plate shop, and a female guard came to escort Lexie back to the outside world. Before hanging up his handset, John asked, "Will you write to me and let me know what you find out about the house?"

"Definitely," Lexie said. "Thanks for meeting with me."

John nodded and hung up, and then Lexie was gone. He followed Brutus back to the mundanity and routine of his prison life.

26

Back at Ryan's house, Lexie was barely in the door before she was babbling. She couldn't get the words out fast enough.

"Whoa. Slow down," Ryan said from the stove, where he was frying up a couple of eggs for a late lunch before heading over to the hospital to meet with Justin Betz.

Lexie took a deep breath and tried again. "I learned something new today."

"What's that?"

"Kathryn Dormeister had a baby girl when she was a teenager, and gave it up for adoption. The girl, Isabella, reached out to her the day before she died."

Ryan blinked. "Holy shit. Seriously?"

"Yeah. Which really plugs some of those holes you thought you had in your theory that mothers and daughters are the most affected in my house. Turns out Kathryn actually fits!"

"I'll be damned." Ryan slid the eggs out of the pan and onto his plate, buttered the toast that had just popped from the toaster, and sat at the table with a big glass of chocolate milk. "None of the newspaper articles mentioned that." To be fair, he hadn't read them all word for word. He'd spent an hour printing out the huge number of articles reporting Kathryn's death and

John's arrest, indictment, trial, conviction, and sentence. Then he'd spent another half an hour carefully placing them in the scrapbook, in chronological order. There were so many that he'd had to add paper to the scrapbook itself.

Lexie sat at the table with him. "The county attorney knew all about it. It was part of the case they built against John. They said that was why he killed her."

"How convinced are you that John killed Kathryn?" Ryan asked, mopping up egg yolk with a piece of toast.

Lexie thought for a moment, then said, "Before I met him, I didn't think there was any reason to think he didn't kill her. If a jury could find him guilty, then it must be true, even if Joanna and Louise don't believe it. Now, though?" She shook her head. "I met him, I talked with him, and I am one hundred percent convinced that he's innocent."

"So how do you think she ended up at the bottom of the stairs?" Ryan gulped down the rest of his chocolate milk, which left a totally endearing brown mustache on his newly-shaven upper lip.

Lexie grinned and wiped it off with a napkin. "Well, considering what has happened to me and Ava in that house, and the fact that everyone's stories are just like mine, let me be the first to say out loud that I'm pretty sure my house is haunted by an evil, murderous ghost."

"And our mission is, and really has been all along, to figure out who this ghost is." Ryan said, smiling. "That sound about right?"

"Yeah. It's just been hard to admit until now."

"I get it." Ryan stood. "I'm heading down to Abbott Northwestern to see if I can catch Justin Betz. Why don't you come with me?"

"Aw. Our very first date," Lexie said, and grinned.

27

As far as the American Dream went, Justin Betz had it. He had the career (leading acute rehabilitation physical therapy for a large local health system), the family (wife Sarah, daughter Sydney and son Cooper), the house (5 bedrooms, 3 baths in suburban Eden Prairie), the dog (a crazy blue-eyed Australian Shepherd named Lulu)...he even had the literal white picket fence. He spent summer evenings and Saturdays coaching Cooper's baseball team. He spent summer Sundays mowing and trimming his massive green lawn to perfection, then sitting in front of a Major League Baseball game on TV with a local craft-brewed beer.

Monday through Friday, regardless of the season, he was at Abbott Northwestern Hospital in Minneapolis, overseeing a team of twelve physical therapists in the hospital's large rehabilitation program. He loved his job; he was making a difference people's lives, helping them learn how to work their bodies again after a serious injury or prolonged illness. There was no better gig than that.

On this summer Wednesday afternoon, he was in his windowless office, reviewing his therapists' notes in patient records on his computer. He'd left the door open so he could see out into the large physical therapy room, where two therapists were helping a young man, who had broken his back in a snowmobiling accident just before Christmas, gingerly navigate a treadmill. He was proud of the progress Parker had made; when he first came to them he was completely wheelchair bound and convinced he'd never walk again. Now, nearly six months later, he was standing upright, boldly taking more and more steps, and hoping to run cross country for his senior year in high school, Justin had no doubt he could do it, too; it took a while, but once Parker found that fire in his belly, he started fighting and didn't intend to stop.

"But no more snowmobiles, right?" Justin had asked once, holding out his fist.

"Damn right," Parker replied, bumping Justin's fist with his own.

Justin shook his head, smiling at the memory, then turned his attention back to his computer. Within a few minutes the phone on his desk rang, interrupting his concentration. He picked up the handset. "Betz."

"Hi Justin, it's Mary." Mary Gibbs was the rehab center's receptionist. "I have two people here to see you."

Justin frowned; he wasn't expecting anybody today. "Who is it, Mary?"

"An Alexis Novak and a Ryan Laughlin. They say they urgently need to speak with you."

Justin sighed, then checked his calendar; he was free for the next hour. Paperwork could wait for a bit. Truth was, he was curious to know who these people were and what was so urgent. "All right, please have one of the assistants show them to my office."

They were there within a couple minutes: a woman about his age with long brown hair pulled back in a ponytail and frank brown eyes, and a slightly older man in a baseball cap, athletic wear, and running shoes.

"Hi, are you Justin Betz?" the woman asked.

Justin stood and extended his hand. "I am. And you must be Alexis."

She shook his hand. "Lexie."

"Hello, Lexie," Justin said, then held his hand out to the man. "And you're Ryan?"

"Yes, sir," Ryan said, and shook Justin's hand. "Thanks for taking some time to meet with us on such short notice."

Justin gestured at the two chairs in front of his desk; they each took a chair, and then he followed suit. "No problem. What can I do for you?"

"Well, this is going to sound kind of strange, but I'm hoping you might have information about my house," Lexie said.

Justin frowned again. "Your...house?"

"Yes. I recently purchased 4741 –"

Justin knew. Immediately. "—Washburn Avenue North," he finished for her. The memory floodgates had opened, and suddenly in his mind's eye he saw the small postwar home where he had spent a large chunk of his childhood.

"Yes," Lexie said. "My four-year-old daughter and I moved in about ten days ago, and we've been experiencing some really weird stuff. Did your family have any troubles when you lived there?"

Justin thought for a moment, slowly shaking his head. "Not that I remember. It was just me and my mom and dad, and honestly I had a pretty normal childhood."

'How long did your family live there?" Ryan asked.

"My parents bought it in 1983, when I was three years old, and we moved to Bloomington in 1990, when I was ten." He looked at Lexie with raised eyebrows. "What kinds of weird things have you and your daughter seen there?"

Lexie took a breath. "It seems like just being inside the house does strange things to us. If I don't have a massive headache, I have raging heartburn. Both Ava – that's my daughter – and I have tried to hurt each other. Sometimes when we walk out the front or back door, we get this strong electrical sensation is our heads; we call them brain zaps." She shrugged. "I'm digging into the history of my house to see if I can figure out what's causing all this." A pause. "The more I talk to people, the more convinced I am that maybe the house is, in fact, haunted."

Justin didn't hear most of this; another memory had popped up behind his eyes. "I found something in the attic."

Lexie and Ryan in unison: "You did?"

"It was super cold outside that day, and I was bored. So while my dad was at work and my mom was in the kitchen, I snuck upstairs to explore. I was maybe six or seven years old.

"There was really nothing up there besides a bunch of dust and spiderwebs, and a few boxes that my parents hadn't unpacked yet. The attic wasn't finished; there was exposed insulation in the walls, and the floor was old, creaky plywood. There was one light fixture at the top of the stairs, a plain hanging bulb with a pull-chain. I remember it was cold up there, which seems strange now." Lost in the memory, he shivered. "I was going to go back downstairs where it was warm, but then I saw it – the one thing that no small boy could resist: a tiny door."

Neither Lexie nor Ryan said anything, just watched him with wide eyes and listened.

"It was maybe twenty-eight by twenty-eight inches, set in a short insulated wall that ran the length of the house. Now, with the wisdom that comes with age, I know this is very common in story-and-a-half houses like that one and usually the area behind that wall, in the eaves of the roof, is used for storage. But back then I was pretty sure that door led to somewhere magical. I had to see what was behind it. It took a couple minutes, but I was able to turn the rusty old knob and pull the door open enough to fit through."

Lexie's eyes widened even further, and she covered her mouth and nose with her hands. "What was in there?"

"Not much. Just more insulation. An old wood chest. Tons of dust, spiderwebs, and mouse poop. And..."

"And?" Ryan could not handle the suspense.

"And a doll."

Lexie leaned forward, placed her elbows on Justin's desk, and set her chin on her hands. Her eyes were wider than ever. "A doll?"

"Yeah, one of those rag dolls. It had long orange yarn for hair, and it was missing one of its black button eyes. It was lying on the floor, covered in dust."

"What did you do with it?" Ryan asked.

"I picked it up and brushed the dust off of it. I could tell it was very well-loved by someone once, and I felt bad that it had been abandoned in the gross, dusty attic. So I decided to take it back downstairs with me." Justin paused as yet another memory popped up. "I carefully closed the tiny door so my parents wouldn't know I'd been in there, and I headed back to the stairs. I passed by that area that juts out to the side; do you know where I mean?"

Lexie nodded. "That's my master bathroom now."

"On my way by there, something else caught my eye. I walked over and found a photograph lying on the floor. It was in the middle of a square shape outlined in the dust; I realize now it must have been hidden under a box of framing nails or something that probably my dad recently moved."

"What was in the photo?" Lexie's hands were covering her mouth and nose again, and her eyes were eating up her face.

"It was a photo of a little girl with a tricycle. She –"

Lexie's gasp interrupted Justin. Then she said, "Was the little girl blonde and wearing a white dress and white shoes? Did the dress have cherries on it?"

It was Justin's turn to blink. "How did you know that?"

"Oh, God." Lexie buried her face in her hands. "That photo showed up in one of my nightmares."

Ryan: "Are you all right?"

Lexie raised her face and nodded. "Yes. Go on, Justin. Please."

He shrugged. "There isn't much to go on about. I took the doll and the picture downstairs with me. For some reason it felt extremely important that my parents not know I had these things, so I hid them in my secret hiding spot. For all I know they're still there."

"What's the secret hiding spot?" Ryan asked.

"I found a loose floorboard inside my closet shortly after we moved in. Again, curious little boy here." Justin smiled.

Lexie: "Which room was yours?"

"I had the room on the right at the end of the hall. Next to the bathroom. My parents were in the other one, on the left."

"That's Ava's room. I'll definitely be checking the floorboards in her closet," Lexie said.

Justin leaned back in his chair; another memory had popped up. "There was something else."

"Good lord, what else could there possibly be?" Lexie sat back in the chair and feigned exhaustion.

"A boy," Justin said.

Ryan frowned. "A boy? What do you mean?"

"Not too long before my parents sold the house and we moved to Bloomington – so I must have been nine years old or so

– I was riding my bike on the sidewalk out front. A boy with bright, messy blond hair, maybe two or three years older than me, turned the corner at the end of the block and walked toward me. He stopped in front of my house and just stood there on the sidewalk, staring at it."

"Whoa," Lexie breathed.

"I rode back and forth past him a few times, trying to figure out what he was doing. Finally my curiosity got the best of me, so I stopped next to him and said hi. He didn't say anything, just turned his head and looked at me with these big brown eyes for a minute, then looked back my house."

"What did you do?"

"I asked him what he was staring at. 'I used to live here,' he said. 'Well, I live here now, and I don't appreciate you staring at my house like that.' You know how nine-year-old boys can be, always trying to establish dominance with other boys." Justin chuckled. "He didn't say anything at first, then turned back to me and said, 'If you knew what happened when I lived there, you would understand.'"

Lexie's eyebrows climbed halfway up her forehead. "Holy crap."

"So now I think he's completely off his rocker, right? I said, 'What's your name, bro?' He looked at me again, then said, 'Michael.'"

Lexie's spine involuntarily straightened, causing her elbow to smack against the edge of Justin's desk with a bang. She winced and cradled it with her other hand.

Ryan was wide-eyed. "Michael? Michael Gilmartin?"

Justin shrugged. "He told me his last name was Madden."

"What else did he say?" Lexie was fidgety now; she wanted to get back to the house and look for that loose floorboard in the closet.

"He wouldn't say anything else; he just looked at the house for another minute or two, then walked back the way he came and disappeared around the corner. I tried to follow him on my bike, but by the time I got to the corner he was gone. The whole thing was very strange."

Lexie and Ryan stood.

"Thank you, Justin." Ryan said. "We really appreciate this."

"You have no idea how helpful you've been," Lexie said. "I think you might have just given us the key to figuring out this whole mess."

Justin stood and nodded. "You're welcome. I hope you find what you're looking for. Will you let me know how it all shakes out?"

"Of course," she said with a smile.

They both waved, then were gone.

Justin sat back down and stared at his computer, replaying the entire conversation in his mind. He'd started out thinking Lexie's haunted house theory was at least partly bullshit, and ended up being glad for his own family's run-of-the-mill suburban house.

I guess sometimes history comes back to haunt you, Justin thought, then turned his concentration back to his paperwork.

28

Lexie's heart pounded as she and Ryan approached her house. *I don't want to go in there.*

But at the same time, she did; she desperately wanted to find the doll and the photograph Justin had told them about. She was convinced that the photograph was evidence that the little girl who had been haunting her nightmares had actually existed. And maybe, just maybe, the doll belonged to her.

She was glad to have Ryan with her.

Lexie unlocked the front door and cautiously entered the quiet house. Ryan was right behind her. Nothing had changed or moved since she was last here on Friday morning, but Lexie could feel that presence. It was already starting to work on her consciousness, with the first signs of a foggy headache brewing behind her eyes.

"Come on, we gotta hurry," she said quietly, grabbing Ryan's hand and leading him down the hall to Ava's bedroom. The wood floor creaked under their feet as they walked.

In Ava's room, Lexie flipped the light switch and beelined for the closet. She opened the door, and she and Ryan crowded shoulder-to-shoulder in the doorjamb so they could see inside. It was still mostly empty; she hadn't yet had a chance to unpack

Ava's clothes and hang them up, or unpack Ava's toys and lovingly arrange them in the closet. All of Ava's stuff, save for her toothbrush, her nightlight, and her princess bedding, was still in boxes.

"Which floorboard do you think it is?" Lexie asked, keeping her voice low as if she could keep the presence from hearing her.

Ryan, who had plenty of experience with this kind of thing after six years spent renovating his own house, spied the loose floorboard immediately. He pointed to the back corner. "That one. See how the seams are a little bigger around that plank?"

She had to blink a few times, but she finally saw it. "Yeah."

Ryan entered the closet and kneeled on the floor. He pulled a pocketknife from the waistband of his shorts – Lexie had no idea there was anywhere to even put a pocketknife in athletic shorts – unfolded the blade, and carefully teased it into one of the seams. Lexie crowded in to watch as he levered one corner of the wood plank up, separating it from the rest of the floorboards and revealing a black space underneath.

Lexie drew air in through her mouth.

Ryan lifted the oak plank, roughly five inches wide by eighteen inches long, off the floor and leaned it against the wall. He pulled his cellphone from the pocket of his shorts and used it as a flashlight so they could see inside the gaping hole.

Inside, just as Justin Betz had described, lay a filthy old rag doll with long orange yarn hair and one missing button eye. Next to the doll sat a three inch by five inch photograph; its colors had drastically faded over time until the photo had a distinct yellow-orange hue. She reached in and picked it up, bringing it closer to her face so she could inspect it.

It was the same little girl from her nightmares, complete with bowl-cut blonde hair, expressionless face, white dress with cherries on it, and overturned tricycle. She half-expected the little girl's eyes to move like they had in her dream, staring at her with the same vitriol.

Instead, a white-hot bolt of pain shot through Lexie's head, causing her to cry out and clutch her skull. The photograph floated to the floor beside her.

"Lex?" Ryan's eyes were full of concern, but Lexie didn't see that; all she knew was the bright, intense pain that pulsed in her head. She could do nothing but lie on the closet floor in a fetal position, head in her hands, and sob uncontrollably.

"Lexie!" Ryan's voice sounded miles away.

The voice of a small girl – quiet, slightly muffled – floated to Lexie through the pain. "Mama."

Lexie didn't think she could speak, but somehow she managed. "Who – who are you?" she sobbed.

"Lexie, talk to me. What's happening?" She could hear Ryan's voice, but couldn't respond. She couldn't even open her eyes. The pain was unbearable.

A few beats, then: "Why did you hurt me, Mama?" The little voice inside the pain was louder now, urgent, demanding.

Lexie pried her lips apart and croaked, "I – I didn't mean to hurt you."

Suddenly the pressure in her head doubled, maybe tripled; the pain was unlike anything Lexie had ever experienced. Even childbirth couldn't compare. She screamed, holding her head, and actually wished for death.

"YOU DON'T LIE, MAMA! THAT'S BAD! MAMAS ARE BAD!"

The pain in Lexie's head was so acute, so bright, that she struggled to draw enough breath to speak.

"YOU HURT ME! AND MICHAEL TOO! IMMA KILL YOU MAMA!"

"No..." Another shot of hot pain through her brain. "I – I'm – I'm sorry," Lexie managed to get out before another scream escaped her. She held her hands against her head to keep her skull from exploding like a rotten Halloween pumpkin.

And then, suddenly, the pain was gone; it disappeared as quickly as it had come on. Panting, nose dripping snot, face covered in sweat and tears, Lexie slowly released her head and opened her eyes.

Ryan's frantic face was inches from hers. "Lex. Say something. Please, tell me what's going on!"

She gradually removed her hands from her head, ready to clamp them down again should the pain return. It didn't. She took a deep breath and, with Ryan's help, slowly sat up. Ryan made sure she was firmly lodged against a wall, then scooted so he was sitting right next to her.

"What was that?" Ryan asked, his voice low and slightly trembling. She'd given him a bad scare, and it was a herculean effort for him to stay calm for her.

"I – I think I just had a visit from this little girl." Her voice shook as she picked the photo up from the floor next to her and handed it to Ryan. He examined it closely. "She wanted to know why I hurt her and Michael. I heard that same voice the day after we moved in here, and somehow I forgot all about it." She sniffed to clear her nose and wiped her hot and wet face with her hands. "That little girl is Melissa Ann Gilmartin. And I think her mother did something to her."

Ryan looked up from the photo. "Holy shit."

Lexie leaned against the closet wall and closed her eyes, trying to keep her breathing steady. She kept expecting the unbearable pain to come crashing back in; every little noise made her flinch.

"I guess there really is a presence in this house," Ryan remarked, staring again at the photo of an innocuous-looking four-year-old girl outside this very house, marveling at how such a little thing could cause so much trouble over so many years.

"I think our research is pretty much done, save for one very important person we need to find," Lexie said, head still leaning against the wall and eyes still closed.

"Who's that?"

"Michael Madden."

PART THREE:
MICHAEL & MELISSA ANN

29

Michael was tired. But he took comfort in the knowledge that the battle was almost over. After thirteen months of fighting, he understood now that he would not emerge victorious. The cancer would win.

He eagerly anticipated the sweet relief that death promised. He hated to leave Amber behind; it saddened him that after walking step-by-step, hand-in-hand with him through this journey, she would endure even more pain. But he knew she could move on and build a new life.

Michael had no options left. The tumor in his brain was back, had grown to about the size of a lemon in the space of a month – and it was spreading. His oncologist had recommended hospice care. His time was limited now.

He had overcome a lot of adversity in his life. More than most people. He lost his entire family by the age of four and was raised by a couple who did the best they could in spite of their advanced age. Chronically depressed, he battled alcoholism and then an addiction to painkillers, which nearly cost him his life. Twice. He was a lost soul that was burdened with a constant indescribable sadness and had no direction, no purpose.

Until he found Amber. He was at one of his lower points when he met his future wife, drinking heavily, crashing in a room in his buddy's house, without a pot to piss in or a running car. He was at his favorite local watering hole one Saturday night, nursing his tenth or eleventh beer, when the most beautiful woman he'd ever seen, with ivory freckled skin and long auburn hair, sat on the barstool next to his and ordered a shot of rye whiskey. He was smitten. She raised her shot in a toast. "Here's to tomorrow," she said, and tossed it back. He'd never spent much time thinking about tomorrow; he was mostly concerned with just getting through today. But at that moment, tomorrow seemed more important than anything – and he hoped his next tomorrow would be spent with her. It turned out that she would be there for all the rest of his tomorrows.

He had no idea what she saw in him. "You can do better than me, Amber. When you leave me, can you just tell me first?" he used to say. She always laughed him off and told him to quit joking, but he was actually dead serious. And she never left him. She believed in him. This beautiful woman helped him help himself and learn how to live life right.

Just over a year ago, his life was at one of its higher points. He had a great job as a financial advisor, a shiny new house in the suburbs, a wife he was madly in love with, and a twelve handicap in golf. Then he had a seizure at work, and everything changed in an instant. Michael was diagnosed with glioblastoma multiforme, an aggressive brain cancer, and the fight to save his life was on.

The tumor had so rudely invaded Michael's brain, and the immunotherapy drugs, chemotherapy, and radiation treatments had utterly ravaged his body. Now, he couldn't feel his legs, and on the increasingly rare occasions he needed to go somewhere, required a wheelchair. His vision was currently at less than fifty percent, and getting worse by the day. He hoped he'd be gone before he went completely blind. His fine motor skills were shit; Amber had to feed him because he couldn't hold a spoon. He spoke slowly because it took him longer to remember the words he wanted to use. He'd lost so much weight that they could put his picture next to "skin and bones" in the dictionary.

Before hospice, he slept about fifteen hours a day. Now, with the help of a steady morphine drip, it was eighteen or more. His body was starting to shut down.

After all he'd been through, having it end like this pissed him off. But death was coming for him. And he was ready.

30

"Here goes nothing," Lexie muttered, and pressed the backlit button set in the frame surrounding the solid wood front door. The bell inside the house dinged.

"Nice neighborhood," Ryan observed.

"I guess so," Lexie said noncommittally. She wasn't impressed; the neighborhood looked just like her parents' in Minnetonka, only the houses were much newer and the trees were much smaller. It was shortly after noon on a Thursday, so the street was relatively quiet. Michael's house was a two-story white stucco structure with a three-car garage and a freshly sealed black asphalt driveway. It was surrounded by houses that looked just like it, with others under construction down the street.

The door opened. The most exhausted-looking woman Lexie had ever seen stood there. *I can't imagine what this poor thing has been through,* Lexie thought, and offered a smile. "Hi, Amber?"

Amber nodded. "You must be Lexie." She stood back from the door. "Come on in."

Lexie stepped inside and gestured toward Ryan, who was right behind her. "Thanks. This is Ryan."

Amber nodded, then turned and led them through the house. It had the lived-in look of a regular house, but had the antiseptic smell and the chilly air conditioning of a hospital. Lexie shivered despite the ninety-degree temperature outside.

Everywhere Lexie looked she saw clues to what life in this house had been like over the last year or more: a folded wheelchair sitting in the front entry, a mess of prescription bottles on the kitchen counter, a blue canvas bag that held some sort of medical contraption on the kitchen floor, a chrome IV pole on wheels next to the sliding glass door that led to the back deck. Sheets had been hung over the door that connected the kitchen to the dining room, and also where the dining room met the front entry. Lexie guessed the dining room was where Michael was staying, since there were no bedrooms on this main level.

Amber led Lexie and Ryan to the family room toward the back of the house, where she gestured toward a couple of comfy-looking couches. "Can I get you anything?"

Lexie and Ryan both shook their heads. "No thank you," Lexie said as they sat side-by-side on one of the couches.

Amber sat on the other couch, tucked her feet under her, and pulled her oversized University of Minnesota sweatshirt over her knees. Her auburn hair was pulled back into a tight bun. The emotional toll of caring for her dying husband was clear on her face; deep purple bags sat under her blue eyes, and deep lines creased either side of her mouth and the delicate pale skin of her forehead. Lexie's heart went out to her.

"Thanks for meeting with us," she said. "I can only imagine what a difficult time this is for you and Michael."

Amber shrugged. "When I told him after you called that you wanted to talk about his sister, he insisted that you come over."

"Did you know about Melissa Ann?" Ryan asked.

Amber nodded. "He told me when we were first married that he'd had a sister who disappeared, but he hasn't talked about her since. Honestly, I'm not sure how much he remembers. He was so young." She paused. "Although I've recently heard him say her name a couple times in his sleep."

"How old was he when Melissa Ann disappeared?" Lexie asked.

"He and Melissa Ann were both four years old. They were twins."

Lexie nodded, remembering that tidbit from George Gilmartin's obituary.

"What happened to her?" Ryan asked.

Amber shook her head. "He has never said. That's why I think he maybe doesn't remember."

"Where did Michael go after his mom died?" Lexie wanted to know.

"He went into foster care for a little bit, because he didn't have any close family left. Then they were finally able to track down a great-uncle on his mom's side who lived nearby, in Falcon Heights. Dick Madden and his wife Carol. They took him in and eventually adopted him."

"They must have changed his name from Gilmartin to Madden," Lexie mused.

Amber nodded. "It was just easier that way, I guess. Back then it wasn't so common for parents and their kids to have different last names."

"Are Dick and Carol still around?" Ryan asked.

"Dick passed away about ten years ago, and Carol went just a couple years later." Amber paused. "Michael's never been what you'd call a happy-go-lucky kind of guy, but he went through a really dark period after they died. 'Everybody close to me dies,' he said once. I was terrified he might try to kill himself."

"It sucks that he's experienced so much loss in his life, and then this happens." Lexie gestured toward the several dozen prescription bottles on the kitchen counter. "What do the doctors say?"

Amber's shoulders sagged slightly, and she sighed. "Dr. Radcliff thinks it's down to days now. Maybe a couple of weeks if we're really lucky. I – I look at him and it's like I'm watching his body giving up. Shutting down." She blinked back tears. "He didn't deserve this."

"I'm so sorry," Ryan said. Lexie had to blink back tears of her own.

Amber stood. "Let me see if I can wake him. I know he really wants to talk to you." She stopped just short of the curtain and turned to give them the full weight of her exhausted, worried face. "I'm always afraid I'm going to walk in there and find him dead." She took a deep breath and disappeared behind the curtain separating the kitchen from the dining room, then stuck her head back out. The relief on her face was clear. "He's awake. You can come in."

Lexie grabbed Ryan's hand as they approached the sheet curtain. They stepped inside the dark dining room; while her eyes adjusted to the dim light, Lexie noticed that the antiseptic hospital smell was much stronger in this room, mixed with the scent of stale urine. There was something more sinister in the air as well: the smell of death. It was faint, but it was unmistakable. She had to breathe shallowly for a minute or two until she got used to the odor.

Lexie had seen her fair share of death on the job, but her position in the operating room meant she didn't have to watch people die slow, lingering, painful deaths like Michael Madden was. When she could finally see him, her grip on Ryan's hand tightened until he winced. Michael lay on a hospital bed; Amber adjusted it to sit him up a bit. An IV pole stood next to the bed, a clear plastic tube snaking from the bottom of the bag to a needle inserted into his left hand and taped in place. He had wasted away to the point that Lexie could see the outline of every individual bone in that hand, and marveled that anyone was able to find a vein for his IV. His entire head, including his face, was smooth, free of any hair. His cheeks and brown eyes were drastically sunken, and his gray skin hung from every angled bone in his face like sun-warmed putty. Lexie knew he was only forty-four years old, but he looked decades older than that.

He managed a low-energy smile, pulling his thin lips back to show his teeth. Lexie was struck by how out-of-place those teeth looked in his wasted face. "Hi," he whispered.

Lexie and Ryan sat in sturdy wooden dining room chairs next to his bed. Ryan's face remained somber, but Lexie managed to smile back. "Hi, Michael. It's really nice to meet you."

"Michael, these are the people I told you about. They called earlier and asked if they could talk to you about your sister." Amber said, her voice slightly louder than it had been when they were talking in the family room.

"Melissa," he whispered, and sighed.

Lexie understood that he would not be able to talk to them for long, but there was one thing she wanted to do before they started in on the questions. She pulled a plastic zipper bag out of her purse, opened it, and removed its contents. She held the newly – and carefully – cleaned doll with the long orange yarn hair up so Michael could see it. "Ryan and I found this at the house, Michael. We think it belongs to you."

Michael's sunken eyes widened, then blinked, and his breath caught in his throat. He lifted his bony hands and gently took the doll from Lexie. "Dolly!" he said in a raspy voice. He held the doll against his face and began to cry.

"Oh, honey," Amber stroked his forehead.

They all watched him with concern, waiting for the tears to pass. Finally they did, and when he seemed to have collected himself a bit, Lexie gave him the photo. "We found this in the house too. That's Melissa Ann, isn't it?"

Michael's ruined face softened, and he gently stroked the photograph. "Yes." A watery sob-sigh escaped him. "Wasn't she beautiful?"

"She was," Ryan affirmed. "What happened to her, Michael? Do you remember?"

Still clutching Dolly, Michael took a deep breath. "We were living in the house on Washburn Avenue," he rasped.

31

Michael's heart beat a little faster; he dreaded talking about that house, and especially about Melissa. He'd spent his entire life trying to just move on from all the tragedy and live a good life. It took a long time, and he mostly succeeded -- but Melissa's shadow was always right next to him. This was his last chance to tell her story. *Their* story. And he felt as if it might burst from him.

"My parents moved into that house in 1976, just before Melissa and I were born. It was their first real house. My father owned a service station north of downtown Minneapolis, on Washington Avenue. He worked as a mechanic for the Burlington Northern railroad until he decided to take a chance on an old auto repair shop that was for sale."

Michael paused and took a sip of water from a cup with a flexible straw that Amber held for him. "Business was good, and it wasn't long before Gilmartin's Garage built a second garage stall and hired another full-time mechanic. That was when things got even better for the George Gilmartin family. My dad bought a brand-new 1979 Chevrolet Monte Carlo convertible. It was bright blue. My earliest memory is of cruising up and down the road in the backseat of that car. It felt like flying to me. My sister and I just couldn't stop laughing at how the wind felt against our faces.

"Dad worked and made good money. Mom stayed home and raised us kids. I mean, life was damn near perfect." Michael paused. "Until January of 1980."

"That's when your father died," Lexie said sympathetically.

"Yes," Michael said. "One of the pumps was leaking gas all over the ground outside, but nobody knew it. Al stepped out the front door and lit a cigarette."

Michael paused for a moment and took another sip of water. His raspy voice was starting to sound rougher, but he kept talking.

"There was a hell of an explosion. Al was burned beyond recognition, damn near incinerated. My dad was still inside the building, almost decapitated by a big chunk of flying glass from the window." He sat quietly for a moment, then said, "At least, that's what my Papa Dick told me much later. I don't remember any of that. Melissa and I were three years old when we lost our dad."

"I'm so sorry," Lexie whispered.

Michael closed his eyes and didn't speak for several minutes. Lexie, Ryan and Amber looked back and forth at each other, trying to decide what to do, when suddenly Michael rasped, "My mother went crazy after my father died."

"Crazy how?" Ryan asked.

Another sip of water from the straw. "Mama Carol told me that my mom was always emotionally fragile, even when she was young. I think the stress of losing my dad and raising us kids by herself was too much for her. She started hearing voices, talking to herself. Had nightmares. At first, right after my dad died, she fretted over Melissa and me, wouldn't let us out of her sight. But as time went on, it got to where she stopped taking care of us, and then she just ignored us completely.

"Once or twice I caught her looking at Melissa and me with this...this hungry look on her face. I thought she wanted to eat us." Another pause. "Those were her very bad days."

Lexie's eyes widened. "What did you do?"

"We learned to take care of ourselves. Stay out of her way." Michael's eyes closed again as he remembered. "There was nobody around to help us. Or our mom."

Ryan watched Michael intently. "What was your mother doing while you and Melissa were fending for yourselves?"

Michael's eyes opened and snapped back into focus. "The only way she knew how to cope was to drink...and that's what she did. All the time. She would sit at the kitchen table in her bathrobe, staring out the window, drinking bourbon. She always had a big butcher knife sitting on the table next to her, just in case." A deep breath. "In case of what, I don't know, but it scared us. She took it with her everywhere she went in the house. She even stashed it under her pillow while she slept."

If I do it quickly, she won't feel a thing. Lexie thought she could see where this was going; a pit opened in her belly and her heart started pounding. But she remained silent so Michael could talk while he was still able to.

"You didn't want to piss her off. One time I slammed my bedroom door, and she freaked out. I hid, and she searched for me all around the house with that butcher knife." A pause. "Another time, when Melissa accidentally said a curse word, my mom picked her up and tossed her down the basement stairs. It was a miracle she survived that fall with just some bumps and bruises; I am convinced my mom meant to kill her."

Silence followed this. Lexie sensed that Michael was running out of steam. "Michael, what happened to Melissa?"

Michael closed his eyes again and took a deep breath. He brought the doll up to his face again and clutched it under his chin, as if for comfort. A single tear made its way down his cheek. "I don't really know," was all he said.

"How can that be?" Ryan asked.

Michael was silent for a few beats. "She disappeared one night in August of 1981. My mother had had one of her good days, and put us both to bed. We shared a big bed. When I woke up the next morning, Melissa was gone. And so was Dolly. Melissa took Dolly with her everywhere she went."

"Gone?"

"Yes. I got up and walked all around the house looking for her. Hoping she was just playing hide-and-seek or something." Another, longer pause. "She was nowhere in the house. I found my mother sitting at the kitchen table, leaning over it so that her hair covered her face, holding a half-empty bottle of bourbon in both of her hands. At eight o'clock in the morning. I stood in the kitchen doorway and asked her where Melissa was. I was scared."

A deep breath, eyes still closed. "Mama looked up at me through her hair. Her eyes were dead. She said, 'I don't ever want to hear you say that name again, Michael.' She looked back down at her bottle, and I started to cry." A sip of water from the straw. "I screamed at her, 'Mama, what did you do to Melissa? Where's Melissa? I want Melissa!' My mother chucked the bourbon bottle at me, and it hit me square in the head. I fell flat on my back in a pool of liquor. Suddenly my mother was standing over me, pointing her butcher knife at me and yelling, 'I won't hear that name spoken in my house ever again, do you understand me? Never EVER!'"

Michael stopped talking for a moment, then took another tiny sip of water and continued. Lexie admired his chutzpah; she could only imagine how exhausted he must be.

"She picked up the bottle, carried it and the knife back to the table, and went back to her drinking like nothing had happened. I knew my mom had done something to my sister. But she would never tell me." Michael drew a deep breath and let it out in a near sob.

Lexie and Amber both wiped tears from their eyes. Amber laid her hand on Michael's, which rested just below his chin, still clutching Dolly. Lexie took Ryan's hand again and held it tight.

Michael continued, eyes still closed. "I missed my sister terribly. I cried a lot for days and days after she disappeared, and to this day I have never stopped thinking about her. She was my twin sister, and my only friend. I never felt whole again."

"What was life like for you after Melissa was gone?" Lexie asked.

"Lonely." Michael sighed. "My mom only got worse after that. She laid in bed all the time, cried all the time. Two months later she killed herself. I woke up in the morning and eventually found her in the attic, hanging by the belt from her bathrobe."

Lexie and Amber gasped and Ryan shuddered.

"I think she was haunted by my sister's memory, and by whatever it was she had done." Michael mumbled. His eyes were still closed, and his body had started to relax. His hands fell to his sides. He allowed himself to succumb to the deep darkness of sleep – the one place where there was no pain.

31

Lexie took one of Michael's hands – the one without the IV stuck in it – in her own and gazed at his skull-like face. His sunken eyes were closed, his thin mouth was slightly open, and he breathed slowly and deeply. "Thank you, Michael. I know that was a huge effort for you. We are going to find out what happened to your sister. I promise." She laid his hand on the bed next to him, and she and Ryan left the room.

Amber made sure Michael was comfortable, then stepped out from the curtained dining room and walked with Lexie and Ryan to the front door. "He'll probably sleep for two days after that," she remarked. "We've been married for fifteen years, and I didn't know any of that about his sister and his mom." She dabbed tears from her eyes with the sleeve of her sweatshirt. "Now I know why he never wanted to talk about it."

They stopped in front of the heavy wooden front door. Lexie laid a hand on Amber's arm and looked directly into her tired face. "You're doing a really great job of taking care of Michael."

Amber's china doll face crumpled, and she covered her face with her sweatshirt sleeves to hide her tears.

"Do you have help?" Lexie asked.

Amber uncovered her face, leaving big wet spots on her sleeves, took a deep breath, and nodded. "A hospice nurse and a medical assistant stop by every day to check on us, refill his meds, and clean him up. My mom and my sister come over most days too, for moral support. Michael sleeps most of the time now, so it's become a little easier. The physical part of caregiving, anyway." Amber sighed deeply. "Watching him go through this has been so hard." She wiped her face with her sleeves again.

Lexie touched Amber's arm. "I'm a nurse, and if there is anything you need, please call me. Anytime, day or night. It's the least I can do for you after what Michael did today. I know it wasn't easy for him."

"Cancer's a bitch," Ryan observed.

Amber nodded and opened the front door. "Yes. Yes, it is."

Lexie and Ryan both thanked Amber and ducked out the door.

32

Lexie's phone rang as Ryan drove them back to his house in his pickup truck. She dug it out of her purse and saw "JANE" flashing on the screen. She tried not to roll her eyes, and didn't quite succeed. She answered. "Hi Mom."

"When do you suppose you'll be coming to pick Ava up?" Jane's voice was impatient. Lexie could hear the TV in the background, and in her mind's eye she saw Ava twirling around her parents' posh living room.

"Mom –"

"Don't you 'Mom' me, Alexis. It's been almost a week. I'm beginning to wonder if this is your way of getting out of your motherly responsibilities."

Lexie blinked. "Excuse me?"

"Perhaps it's time we agree that Ava is simply better off here with me and your dad," Jane said. Her tone could have shaved ice.

"I will agree to no such thing!" Lexie shouted. Ryan glanced over at her. *What's going on?* he mouthed.

Scowling, Lexie gave a brief irritated shake of her head. "Fine. Have it your way. If having Ava at your house is such a damn inconvenience, I'll come pick her up today. Dad said she could stay as long as I needed her to, but I don't have the strength or mindspace to play these fucking games with you, Mom."

"What are you doing that's so important?" Jane demanded.

"I've been trying to figure out what the hell is wrong with my house. You remember, the house you swore you'd never come back to after you personally experienced the crazy things that happen here. Frankly, Mother, I'm surprised you're in such a hurry to send Ava back."

Silence from the other end.

"I need Ava to stay in a safe place until I get this figured out. If you're so fucking sure she's better off with you, what's your hurry?"

"Of course I'm happy to have her here." Jane's tone had changed; she was no longer confrontational. She sounded...defeated?

"Then what's the problem?"

From the background: "I WANNA SAY HI TO MY MOMMY!" There was some rustling on the other end, and then Ava was there. "Hi Mommy!"

"Hi pumpkin," Lexie said. The sound of Ava's voice brought tears to Lexie's eyes. "I miss you."

"I miss you too, Mommy. When are you coming to take me home?"

"Soon," Lexie promised. "Do you remember the little girl in our house?"

"Yeah," Ava said. "She said that mamas are bad and she gave us headaches and stuff."

263

"I know her name," Lexie said.

"You do? Is it Holly Golightly?" Ava wanted to know.

Lexie chuckled. "No, her name is Melissa Ann."

"Oh," Ava said in an awed tone. "How old is she? Is she four, like me?"

"I think so, babydoll. Ryan and I are going to try and find her. We met her brother today, and he really misses her."

"She misses him too. His name is Michael."

Lexie's breath caught. "How – how did you know that?"

"She told me, silly Mommy."

Lexie turned and stared at Ryan, wide-eyed. "How many times did you see Melissa Ann, Ava?"

"One time. She was in my closet."

"How come you never told me that?"

"She told me not to, cuz mamas are bad," Ava said.

"What else did she tell you?"

"Um..."

"You know what, baby? Ryan and I are coming over to Gramma and Grampa's house right now." Lexie made an incomprehensible gesture with her hand to let Ryan know that their plans had suddenly changed. "You can tell me when we get there, okay?"

"YAY!" Ava bugled, forcing Lexie to pull her phone away from her ear like she'd done with Lynn on Saturday.

Lexie smiled, and her eyes prickled. *God, I've missed this kid.* "Maybe I'll even bring you an ice cream bar."

"Well, okay, but it's gotta be a strawberry one," Ava said, pretending to be serious. Then she laughed. "Bring Gramma and Grampa chocolate ones!"

"I will, babydoll. I'll see you in a little bit." Lexie rang off and, while still holding the phone in her hand, began chewing the nail on her thumb as she stared out the window.

"We never thought to ask the kid," Ryan said.

"Yeah," Lexie said. "She mentioned the little girl, but I assumed she was just seeing her in dreams, like I was. She never said anything about seeing Melissa Ann in her closet. Sweet Jesus."

"That's where we found the photo of Melissa Ann," Ryan pointed out. "And her doll. I guess it makes sense that she'd appear to Ava there."

Lexie set her phone on her thigh, pulled her ponytail out, and ran her fingers vigorously through her hair. "Turn here, then get on the freeway heading south. Why would it not occur to me to ask her?" she asked.

"Because you were not exactly in your right mind," Ryan pointed out.

Lexie felt like the wind had been knocked out of her. "Like Michael's mom wasn't in her right mind. What was her name?"

Ryan merged onto the freeway, then said, "Lucy, I believe."

"Right. Lucy Gilmartin. Do you think I was out of my mind like she was out of hers?"

Ryan looked sidelong at Lexie. "Not at all. You're fine when you're not in the house. That tells me you were being influenced by Melissa Ann. Based on what Michael said, it sounds to me like Lucy was genuinely mentally ill and had no support system."

Lexie thought about that for a moment. "That poor woman."

Ryan shrugged. "I think it's more her poor kids."

Lexie nodded and stared out the window.

They swung in the drive-through of the ice cream shop closest to Paul and Jane's house, and Lexie directed him to a cul-de-sac less than a half-mile from Lake Minnetonka. Lexie watched Ryan's face closely as they slowly drove down the street and pulled into the driveway of the Novak residence. His eyes were wide as he scanned his surroundings: large multi-story houses with stone facades, long, elegant driveways, lush trees, expensive cars, riding mowers burring around expansive lawns. "Boy, you weren't kidding when you said you came from money."

Lexie shrugged and opened her car door. "My dad's a doctor. And my mom has an image to uphold."

"MOMMEEEEEEEE!" Ava came barreling out the front door of the house, wavy blonde hair bouncing against her back, and was in Lexie's arms before she'd even had a chance to grab the bag full of ice cream bars from the backseat.

Lexie closed her eyes and hugged Ava tight. The girl's hair smelled like expensive salon shampoo. "Hi pumpkin." She opened her eyes and leaned her head back so she could get a better look at Ava's face. She looked well-rested and back to her old self. "I missed you. How are you?"

Ava's arms rested on Lexie's shoulders, her hands behind Lexie's head, playing with her hair. "I'm good. I missed you too." She grinned at Ryan, who was approaching tentatively from the driver's side of the truck, ice cream in hand. "Hi Ryan! I missed you!"

Ryan smiled and tousled Ava's hair. "Hey kiddo, I missed you too."

Jane made her way down the front walk, pulling a light sweater around her tiny frame. "Hello, Alexis."

"Mom," Lexie said coolly. She pointed at the bag in Ryan's hand. "We brought ice cream." Then she gestured toward Ryan's face. "This is Ryan. He lives next door to me."

"Nice to meet you," Ryan said, offering his hand. Jane didn't take it, dipping her head in a nod instead. Ryan awkwardly shoved his hand in the pocket of his black athletic shorts.

"Ryan likes mac and cheese too!" Ava trumpeted from the middle of the expansive lawn, where she was running around in circles with her arms extended, making airplane noises.

"Are you here to take Ava home?" Jane inquired.

Lexie sighed. "Mom, we talked about this –"

Ryan interjected before Lexie could get too wound up. "I'm sorry, what would you like me to do with the ice cream bars? They're melting fast."

"Let's take them inside." Jane relieved Ryan of the bag and led everyone to the front door.

"Where's Dad?" Lexie asked.

Jane ignored her. "I didn't know you were coming –" Lexie heard the reproach in her mother's voice – "so I haven't packed any of Ava's things up yet." Jane's voiced echoed in the high-ceilinged entryway as she walked toward the kitchen. Jane favored Italianate finishes, including stone and wrought iron, and expensive art in her home decorating. Even though the woodwork was deep and rich and the walls were painted a warm shade of yellow, Lexie had always found her parents' house to be rather cold and museum-like – a place to be admired, not touched. *I like to be able to live in my house,* she thought.

Ryan and Lexie stood at the ornate kitchen island while Jane put the bag of ice cream bars in the freezer side of her massive refrigerator. Once that was done, Jane turned around, patted her hair, and gave Lexie a head-to-toe inspection. "You're looking a little chunky, Alexis. Maybe it's time to start another diet?"

Stunned and horrified that Jane would have the gall to say something like that in front of Ryan, Lexie could only stand there, tears spilling down her cheeks.

Ava, who was coloring at the breakfast table at the back of the kitchen, heard every word. "Gramma!" the girl shouted. She dropped her crayons on the floor and marched to Lexie, hugging her protectively around the thigh. "That is not nice! My mommy isn't chunky, my mommy is pretty!"

"Oh, honey," Jane cooed. "I didn't mean anything by that. I'm just worried about your mom, that's all."

"No, Gramma. You wanted to make my mommy feel bad."

A noise escaped Ryan's throat, and Jane's face turned bright red. *Busted*, Lexie thought.

"When we say mean things at daycare, Cindy says we have to say we're sorry," Ava said sternly. "Say you're sorry, Gramma."

"I really think you're overreacting, Ava," Jane said, her voice trembling. "I –"

"You say you're sorry." Ava's voice had taken on a distinctly adult-like tone of warning. "And then you have to give my mommy a hug."

Jane's eyes, fully made up to hide as many of the lines around them as possible, blinked. Then she turned briskly and headed toward the stairs, which were covered in plush carpet and swept up from the entryway to the second level, where the bedrooms were. "Well. I'll just go gather up Ava's things."

Ryan, Lexie, and Ava stood rooted in the kitchen, looking at each other uncertainly for a moment. Lexie dabbed at her eyes with a paper towel, and Ryan squatted so he was at Ava's level and smiled at her. "You did a great job sticking up for your mom, kiddo." He held his hand up in a high-five gesture.

Ava smiled back and slapped his hand. She held his gaze with her big, earnest blue eyes and asked, "But...why was my gramma being mean to my mommy?"

"Well, sometimes people who feel bad about themselves want to make other people feel bad too," Ryan said.

"They do?"

Ryan nodded. "Yeah."

"Why does Gramma feel bad, Mommy?"

Lexie shook her head. "I don't know, sweetpea. I think she just doesn't ever feel like she's good enough. That's why she works so hard to make sure her hair and her makeup and her house and everything looks perfect."

Ava, who had endured numerous admonishments throughout her short life for not using a coaster or leaving toast crumbs on the table, nodded. "But…Gramma is good enough for me," she declared.

"You should tell her that," Ryan said.

"Okay."

"You know who else feels bad and wants to make others feel bad too?" Ryan asked.

Ava shook her head.

"Melissa Ann."

Ava thought about this for a moment, then said, "She told me she's mad at her mommy. She's mad at all the mommies."

"When was this, babygirl?" Lexie asked.

"After our sammich picnic. I was sleepin and then I woke up and she was there. Standing by my closet." Ava paused, remembering. "She was wearing a pretty dress that had chorizos on it."

"I think you mean cherries," Lexie said, grinning. To Ryan: "That was our first night in the house."

"Yeah, cherries. I don't like cherries very much, they have rocks in the middle of them."

Something occurred to Lexie. "Oh my god. I heard strange creaking noises that night, like someone was tiptoeing on the wood floor. That might have been her!"

"Ava, what else did Melissa Ann tell you?" Ryan asked.

"She said that her mama hurt her and then hid her away so nobody would ever find her."

"Hid her away somewhere in the house?" Lexie asked, startled.

Ava shrugged, then moved a few steps away so she could practice her ballerina twirls on the smooth wood floor.

Ryan stood from his squatting position, and he and Lexie looked at each other with wide eyes.

Jane appeared, the plastic soles of her slippers click-clacking on the floor, carrying Ava's packed unicorn suitcase and a plastic bag from a children's clothing boutique nearby. "All right, I have everything together," she announced. She looked directly at Lexie; her eyes were ringed with red from crying. "I picked up a few new outfits for her, to replace some of those rags you sent her in."

Lexie blinked. "There's nothing wrong with her clothes. Are you kidding me right now?"

Ava stopped doing her ballerina twirls and went to Jane. "Gramma."

"Yes, Ava?" Jane didn't break eye contact with Lexie.

Ava took Jane's hand and pulled. "Gramma, come sit on the couch, okay?"

Jane maintained eye contact for one more beat as she turned, then did as her granddaughter asked. Ava climbed up and sat next to her. She took Jane's hand and said, "Gramma, please stop being mean to my mommy."

Jane snatched her hand back and started to stand. "I don't have to take –"

"Jane. Sit."

Everyone turned to see Paul standing in the doorway to the mudroom, which connected the kitchen to the garage. He was dressed much like Ryan in athletic wear and tennis shoes, and was covered in sweat from his daily run.

"Dad! How long have you been standing there?"

"Long enough. Your granddaughter has something to say to you, Janey. You sit and listen to her."

Chastened, Jane sat.

Ava took Jane's hand again. "I don't want you to feel bad anymore, okay? Cuz you're good enough for me and I love you."

Jane lowered her head and sat in silence for a moment. The tension in the air was so thick, so electric, that nobody dared move or speak. Everyone watched Jane closely. She raised her head and looked at Ava, mascara streaked down her cheeks. "I – I love you too, Ava."

Lexie, who had never in her life heard the words 'I love you' from her mother, wiped away the angry tears leaking from her eyes and picked up the suitcase and plastic bag. She needed out of here. Whatever else her mother had to say, even if it was an apology, wasn't going to magically make up for a lifetime of emotional damage caused by this woman.

"Let's go, Ava."

"But –"

Lexie marched toward the front door, with Ryan trailing behind her. "Now, please."

"Oh-kay. Bye, Gramma." Lexie heard her feet running across the kitchen floor. "Bye, Grampa."

"Here, I'll help you get your shoes on," Ryan said.

Ava waved at her grandparents and ran toward the truck. Ryan looked back one last time to see Paul and Jane squaring up for what looked to him like a cataclysmic fight. He followed Ava out of the house and closed the heavy wooden door behind him.

33

Lexie was already sitting in the front seat of Ryan's pickup, sunglasses on and arms folded across her chest, when he and Ava walked out the front door of Paul and Jane's house. Ryan buckled Ava into the back seat and then slid in behind the wheel.

"What was that?" Ryan asked, starting the engine and reversing out of the driveway.

Lexie didn't dare answer. She could feel her lips trembling, and she feared that if she opened her mouth, she might start bawling and never stop. So she just shook her head.

"Mommy's sad," Ava observed.

That did it. Lexie yanked her sunglasses off, covered her face with her hands, and wept.

"See?" Ava said matter-of-factly.

Ryan placed a warm hand on Lexie's leg as he pointed the truck toward home and said, "Lex."

This only made Lexie sob harder.

Ryan and Ava gave Lexie a few minutes to let the tears out and compose herself. Finally she got there, her face hot, her eyes puffy, and random hiccups escaped her.

"Are you okay, Mommy?"

Lexie turned toward the back seat so that her clearly concerned daughter could see her mess of a face. "Yes baby, I'm okay."

"Lex," Ryan said again, squeezing her leg. She sat back in her seat and looked at him. A watery sigh escaped her.

"It seems to me your mom took a big step today."

Lexie snorted. "Oh. Sure. She and Ava are in a great place with their relationship now."

"What does that mean?" Ryan asked.

"My mom has never told me she loves me. Not once." Lexie slid her sunglasses back on. "And she had no intention of saying it just now, either. She tries to couch the hurtful things she says to me in motherly concern, but none of it's real. Truth is, she never should have become a mother. She cares about nobody but herself, and that's a fact."

"What about your dad? He seems to be a genuinely good guy."

"He is," Lexie said. "And he's the only reason I'm not completely insane. I don't know how he puts up with her." Lexie snorted again. "He told me last week that she's sad that we moved out on our own. I felt kind of bad at the time, but now I call bullshit. I've always thought she resents me for ruining her perfect doctor's-wife life, and she's made me pay for refusing to be her perfect trophy daughter every single day of my life." Another sigh. Ryan took her hand and gave it a gentle squeeze.

They drove in silence for awhile, barreling down the freeway toward the city. Lexie felt better with every mile Ryan put between her and Jane.

"Mommy?"

"Yes, pumpkin?" Lexie turned in her seat so she could see her daughter better.

"You say you love me all the time."

"I sure do."

Ava hesitated, then said, "Do you do that because your mommy didn't?"

Lexie looked at Ava's sweet face for a long moment. She thought her heart might burst with love for this kid. "Yes. I don't want you to ever wonder if your mommy loves you, like I did."

"Okay." Ava settled deeper into her booster seat and leaned her head back. Lexie thought she might fall asleep before too long.

"So. Lucy hid Melissa Ann somewhere nobody would ever find her," Ryan said quietly.

Lexie turned her head and looked at him. "I can't decide if she's hidden inside the house, or maybe buried in the backyard, or out in the garage, or what."

"If she's even on the property," Ryan said. "I mean, she could be anywhere."

Lexie pondered for a moment, remembering their conversation with Michael earlier. "Michael said she was in bed with him that night, and gone the next morning. And Lucy was there and already wasted when he got up in the morning. I'm not sure Lucy would have been able to go very far."

Ryan nodded. "That makes sense. Chances are Melissa Ann is in the house somewhere."

"I don't know how she could be inside the house, though. There have been –" Lexie counted on her fingers – "six owners since the Gilmartins, plus the entire house was completely renovated before I bought it. How does nobody find the body of a little girl in nearly forty years?"

"Well, if she's buried in the concrete basement floor, she could go forever without being found."

This struck Lexie as exceptionally morbid; she also didn't think it likely that Lucy just happened to have a jackhammer and a concrete mixer on hand the night Melissa Ann died. "I think it's time to search the house." She gritted her teeth, expecting Ryan to protest again.

He didn't. "Yeah, it seems that way. But it'll have to wait until tomorrow." He grinned and cocked a thumb behind him.

Lexie glanced in the backseat; Ava was sound asleep in her booster seat, head lolling, mouth open. Then she looked at the clock; it was only dinnertime, but sheer exhaustion was starting to settle in her bones. She could use a nap too.

And that's exactly what she did when they arrived at Ryan's house. He carefully extracted Ava from her booster seat, carried her inside, and laid her in his bed. Lexie crawled in beside Ava and, feeling whole again with her daughter next to her, promptly fell asleep. Neither of them woke until the sun came up the next morning.

34

The scents of bacon and coffee beckoned Lexie out of bed. She stumbled into the kitchen to find Ryan and Ava already up and enjoying a big breakfast in front of the TV.

"Morning, sunshine. Your plate and your coffee are on the counter." Ryan pointed.

"Thank you." Her first sip of coffee sent a rush of warmth all the way to her toes. She picked up her plate and joined Ryan and Ava at the table.

"Hi Mommy," Ava said. "Did you sleep good?"

"Yes I did, babygirl. Did you?"

Ava pointed a strip of crispy bacon at her mother. "Yes, but you snore."

Lexie looked at Ryan for confirmation of this outrageous claim. "Is that true?"

He shrugged. "I plead the fifth on that one, man."

Lexie chuckled. "Okay, fine. Be that way."

They ate in companionable silence while animated royalty capered and sang in the background. The eggs were savory, the bacon melted in her mouth, and the coffee was life itself in a cup. She gazed at Ryan, and then Ava, and smiled to herself. *I could get used to this,* she thought. Together like this, they felt like a family. More so than her actual family.

"We should probably go over to the house today," Lexie said between bites.

"All of us?" Ryan asked, nodding his head toward Ava, who was still holding the piece of bacon, completely engrossed in her show.

"I think so," Lexie said. "She might be able to see things that we can't."

"What if we find something? Are you prepared for your kid to see her first dead body?"

Lexie gazed at Ava while she turned this idea over in her head. *She's already seen Melissa Ann's ghost and seems to have taken that in stride. If we find a body, she'll already know whose it is and has an idea of what happened to her. And, based on how she handed her grandmother yesterday – better than I did – she clearly has the emotional wherewithal.* "Yeah. I think she can handle it."

"That's an amazing kid you have there," Ryan said fondly.

Lexie grinned. "Yeah, she is."

"It's because she has an awesome mom." He met her gaze and held it. "You know that, don't you?"

Lexie's face heated up. "Oh. Well. I mean, I don't –"

"You do, Lex. You *do.* You've persevered through some really challenging circumstances and are singlehandedly raising a happy, confident, well-rounded kid. I can't imagine what it takes to do that. Own it." Ryan's eyes burned.

Memories swirled in Lexie's head like dry leaves kicked up by a cold November wind. Her mother saying *You're pregnant? My god, Alexis, how could you be so stupid?* Jake saying *Keeping this baby is not an option, you know that, right?* Holding her tiny, perfect baby girl in her arms for the very first time and whispering *You will never wonder if your mommy loves you.* She nodded. "I never felt like I had a choice, but okay – I'll own it."

Satisfied, Ryan pushed his chair back and started clearing the table while Lexie finished up her breakfast. He plucked the slice of bacon from Ava's fingers on his way by.

35

After Ava's late morning nap and a lunch of soup and grilled cheese sandwiches, the three of them ventured next door to Lexie's house. Lexie had learned a lot about 4741 Washburn Avenue North over the past week, and none of it good. The house looked innocuous from the street, just like every other house in the neighborhood – but the closer she got, the more sinister and foreboding it felt to Lexie. All five of her senses tingled. "I can feel her watching us, even out here," she whispered.

"Me too," Ava whispered back.

Ryan stopped them halfway up the walk. "Listen. I don't think Melissa Ann wants to be found, so she is going to fight us every step of the way. You both need to try really hard not to let her take over your heads, okay?"

Lexie and Ava both nodded.

"If she gets too strong, just go outside."

"Cuz the zaps means she's not in our brains anymore," Ava said.

Lexie's eyebrows shot up. "How did you know that, babygirl?"

Ava shrugged. "I dunno."

"Okay, let's go." Ryan took one of Ava's hands and Lexie took the other. Together they ascended the front steps and Ryan unlocked the door with the key Lexie had given him.

The house was quiet. They crept through the main level of the house, looking to see if anything was out of place. Everything was as Lexie had left it a week ago.

In the living room, Ava's DVD case sat on the wood floor in front of the darkened TV.

In the dining room, labeled boxes that Lexie hadn't yet unpacked still sat in the corner.

In the kitchen, her bag of licorice sat open on the counter. A week ago the thought that Ryan might see evidence of her terrible eating habits and think she was unredeemable would have mortified Lexie, but now she barely noticed. The dishwasher yawed open, the top rack pulled out. The fridge kicked on with a quiet *whirrrr*, making the adults jump.

"My head hurts, Mommy," Ava whispered.

Lexie realized she too had a headache building behind her eyes. Melissa Ann was here. "I know baby, mine does too. Just try to ignore it, okay? Don't let her in."

"Okay," Ava said.

A quick check of the bathroom and bedrooms revealed nothing. Ava pointed at the closet in her bedroom "That's where I saw Melissa Ann," she said.

"That's where we found her picture and her doll too," Ryan said. "Do you think she's in there now, Ava?"

Ava's brow furrowed in concentration. "No."

"Okay, then we keep going." Ryan led them back through the kitchen and down the basement stairs.

Lexie hadn't spent any time in the basement after moving in; she and Ava hadn't even generated a full load of laundry yet. It was clear that Jason, the guy who renovated the house and sold it to Lexie, hadn't spent any time or money down here either. In fact, Lexie guessed the basement hadn't been touched since it was first finished sometime in the late 1960s. The floor in the large main room was cold brown linoleum, the walls were covered in horrendous dark faux wood paneling, and the water-stained drop ceiling was missing more than a few tiles. The entire basement smelled of sixty-five years' worth of must.

The pain behind Lexie's eyes had started to pulse. Ava, normally bubbly and noisy, had grown quiet over the last few minutes; Lexie guessed she was feeling the same way.

"Okay, your basement is laid out basically the same as mine," Ryan observed, turning in circles to get a 360-degree view. "Although you have more closets than I do." He pointed at two sets of dark-stained pine louvered closet doors at one end of the room. "What are the chances she's in there?"

"Slim to none," Lexie said, thinking back to when she first toured the house. "I looked inside those closets, and they were empty."

"Let's take a look at the laundry room." He stepped through an open door and into an unfinished room that held a new washer and dryer, as well as two large sets of storage shelves. The small window set high in the foundation was covered with a brown and orange plaid curtain. The cinderblock foundation and concrete floor were plainly visible.

"Unless Lucy had a way to bust up concrete by herself without waking Michael, I just don't think Melissa Ann is down here," Lexie said.

Ryan nodded. "Let's head back upstairs."

They trudged up to the main level, through the kitchen and dining room, and up the stairs to Lexie's attic bedroom. Her headache worsened with each step, until halfway up she stopped. "Hang on, Ryan."

"What's up?"

"We'll be right back." Lexie took Ava's hand and led her to the front door. "You ready?"

Ava nodded, scowling.

They both stepped through the door; a tremendous electric ZAP shot through Lexie's head, causing her to sit hard on the concrete stoop. Ava cried out and fell on top of her mother, unconscious. The screen door slammed shut behind them.

"You girls okay?" Ryan asked from just inside the door.

Lexie leaned against the screen door, feeling like she could lay down and sleep forever. "We will be, just give us a second." She took a deep breath. "That was a big one. Melissa Ann is especially strong today."

Ava stirred in Lexie's lap, and her eyes fluttered open. "My head doesn't hurt anymore, Mommy."

"That's good, pumpkin. My head feels better too. Should we go back inside?"

Ava sat up, gave her head a small shake, and then stood. Lexie levered herself to standing as well so Ryan could open the door for them.

Holding hands again, Ryan leading the way, they went back to the attic stairs and ascended. He flipped the light switch and the room illuminated. Nothing looked out of place to Lexie.

Ava let go of Ryan's and Lexie's hands and started moving slowly past the bathroom and toward Lexie's bed. The little girl's eyebrows were knitted together with concentration.

"Where are you going, babygirl?" Lexie asked.

Ava didn't answer. She walked around the end of Lexie's bed to the right, and stopped next to the bedside table. *She stood in that same spot and threw an everloving tantrum about a picnic on our last night here,* Lexie thought. *Well, I guess it was Melissa Ann who actually threw the tantrum.* She shivered.

Brow still furrowed, Ava simply stood there and stared at a spot on the smooth knee-height wall that joined the sloped ceiling to the floor. "She's here."

"What?" Lexie and Ryan both crossed the room in record time.

"Hold my hand, Mommy. You too, Ryan," Ava instructed, and reached toward them.

They did as they were told. Ava slowly reached out and touched the wall. A ZAP not unlike the electric sensations Ava and Lexie experienced coursed through all three bodies, causing them to stand at attention. The room around them changed. The perfectly finished and painted walls faded to expose wood framing and dusty insulation. Lexie's bed and dresser disappeared, replaced by torn old boxes and broken furniture. All the lights went out...except for one: a single bulb with a pull chain at the top of the stairs. They heard voices coming up the stairs; careful not to break contact with the wall, all three turned to watch the events of August 21, 1980 unfold through the eyes of Lucy Gilmartin, who had been left alone, afraid, and falling ever deeper into the clutches of psychosis.

36

"Where are we going, Mama?" Melissa Ann's voice was rough with sleep, her purple nightgown twisted around her waist. Her mother had lifted her out of her bed, leaving Michael sleeping soundly, and was carrying her down the hallway toward the attic stairs. She held Dolly against her chin.

"Up to the attic," Lucy said. Part of her – the small and shrinking part that was still somewhat sane – dreaded what she was about to do. The other part was positively giddy.

"Why?"

"Because you and I are going to have a little picnic," Lucy said, her breath labored as she carried her daughter up the stairs. "Doesn't that sound like fun?"

"But it's the middle of the night," Melissa Ann protested. "I was sleeping. I'm too tired for a picnic."

The little bitch's whiny voice grated on Lucy's already frazzled nerves. She crested the stairs and carried Melissa Ann to a red and white checked blanket that had been laid out on the attic's creaky plywood floor. A picnic basket held one corner of the blanket down. An old cedar chest, open and empty, sat near a small door set in the short wall of the half-story attic. Lucy had pulled it out of the dank storage space behind the door earlier in the evening. *She'll fit perfectly,* she thought.

She set Melissa Ann on the blanket and sank to her knees, hiking her own nightgown up to free her legs for the task at hand. The warm attic air was dry and dusty. The only light came from a weak bulb at the top of the stairs. "See? We're even using our special picnic blanket."

"But Mama," Melissa Ann said, her little face troubled. She looked at Lucy with earnest brown eyes. For a moment Lucy was sure that Melissa could see right into her soul, and a brief pang of guilt shot through her heart. Dolly dangled by an arm from the girl's chubby hand. "We can't have a picnic without Michael."

"Sure we can," Lucy crooned. "It'll be our little secret."

The familiar anger abruptly washed over Melissa Ann's face. "NO WE CAN'T MAMA!" the little girl screamed, enraged at the very idea of doing something as fun as a midnight picnic without her twin brother. "THAT'S MEAN! I HATE YOU!"

Before Lucy quite knew what was happening, her hands shot out and wrapped themselves around the little bitch's neck. Melissa Ann's eyes widened and she made a strangled *urk* sound as Lucy squeezed with all of her strength. The little girl dropped her Dolly and clawed at Lucy's hands, trying to loosen her grip. She left scratches deep enough to bleed. Her lips moved soundlessly, forming the word *Mama* over and over again.

Lucy guided Melissa Ann from standing to lying down on the blanket. Melissa Ann jerked violently in a desperate effort to dislodge her mother's hands. Grimacing, struggling to maintain control of her daughter and finish the job, Lucy straddled Melissa Ann's little body for better leverage; she straightened her arms and put all her weight on her hands, letting gravity do the work. The girl's entire head turned purple. As blood vessels in her corneas ruptured, Melissa Ann's bulging eyes, desperate, pleading, and confused, never broke contact with Lucy's. The little girl's soul, her essence, her very being, slowly faded away. Not fast enough for Lucy.

"Why. Won't. You. DIE," Lucy grunted and pushed harder. After several minutes, Melissa Ann's small body, starved of oxygen, could buck and flail no more; all of her muscles relaxed spontaneously, her tongue protruded from her purple lips, and her bulging eyes froze in place.

She was dead.

Sweating, breathing hard, her nut brown hair hanging in clumps over her face, Lucy cautiously let go of Melissa Ann's neck. She was ready to grab again if the little girl moved, but there were no signs of life. No fluttering of eyelids, no gentle rising and falling of her chest. Nothing. Lucy leaned back on her haunches and took a deep breath. *Take care of her, my love,* she thought.

Lucy stood and pushed her hair back from her face. Melissa Ann's little body lay splayed out on the attic floor, her fine blonde hair – so like her father's – in a messy pile around her head. Lucy squatted and wrapped the body in the red checked blanket. Then she slid one arm under Melissa Ann's knees and the other under her back, and lifted the little girl's still-warm body into the cedar chest. She did indeed fit perfectly.

Lucy pulled two boxes of mothballs out of the picnic basket and scattered them over the body, then closed the chest and maneuvered it on its hand-carved wooden casters through the small door. She had already scattered mothballs in the storage space in the eaves, and their pungent odor wafted out. She tossed Dolly into the space and pushed the half-sized door shut. The triangular space under the sloping rafters of the roof was the perfect place to hide the chest; now that George was gone, nobody came up here anymore.

She moved a broken old dresser in front of the door, then clapped the dust off her hands. *It's done,* Lucy thought. *It's just Michael and me now.* She went back downstairs, changed into a clean nightgown – and slept like she hadn't slept since George died.

37

"NO!" Lexie screamed. She let go of Ava's hand; instantly the room went back to the way it was supposed to be, but Lexie didn't notice. She covered her face, sobbing. "No, my god, no...how could anybody do that?" she wailed, moving her hands from her face to her hair. "How could any mother not love her own child?" She sank to her knees, weeping for poor, innocent Melissa Ann Gilmartin...for Lillie, Liesl, and Britta Gustafson...for Shirley and Abigail Krueger...for Kathryn Dormeister...and for herself. For all the years she spent trying and failing to form some kind of bond with her own mother.

Ryan and Ava kneeled next to Lexie and put their arms around her. Ava cried right along with her mom – and tears coursed down Ryan's face too.

"Lexie." Ryan moved in front of her and took her face in his hands. She continued to weep, eyes squinched shut against the horror of what she'd just seen. "Lexie." His voice cracked with the emotion he tried to hold back in an effort to be strong for her. For both of them. "Do you know what this means?"

"Wh-wh-whaat?" Lexie wailed.

"We found her!"

The wails tapered to hiccups. She cracked her wet and swollen eyes open. "W-we did?"

"She's right there, Mommy." Ava pointed at the spot on the short wall where she'd placed her hand.

Lexie's eyes, still framed by Ryan's hands, widened and she grasped his wrists. "Oh-oh m-my god, w-we have to tell Michael! We have to call Amber! We don't have much time!"

Ryan kissed her and helped her stand up. "Yes. Let's go downstairs. You call Amber, and I will run home and grab a few tools. I have to open up that wall so we can get Melissa Ann out."

"Don't open the chest until I can figure out a way to get Michael here," Lexie said. "He needs to be here for that part."

"Agreed," Ryan said. "You want to come with me, kiddo?"

"YAY!" Ava screeched, and led them down the stairs.

Lexie pulled her cellphone from the back pocket of her denim shorts as she descended the stairs and sat on her living room couch. There was no trace of a headache, save for the remnants of her earlier tears. There was only a palpable sense of relief. It was like Melissa Ann knew she would be seeing her brother soon. "I'm working on that, kiddo," she said into the empty room.

Amber answered on the second ring. "Hi, Lexie."

"Amber, how is Michael today?" Lexie asked.

"It's the strangest thing," Amber said. "He's awake, he's talking, he's even trying to move. He has more energy than he's had in several weeks."

Lexie knew what that meant; in the medical profession this surge of energy prior to death is referred to as the "end of life rally." It meant that Michael's time was very short now...but was the perfect time to do what they needed to do next. "That's great to hear. Is he in good enough shape to travel, do you think?"

"I don't know...I doubt it. Why?" Amber asked.

"We found his sister. And he should be here when we pull her from where she's been hidden for the last forty years."

Amber was silent for a moment. "Is she in the house?"

"She is," Lexie confirmed.

"Holy shit," Amber whispered.

"I know," Lexie said. "Can you bring him here? Or can I come and pick him up?"

"I'll bring him," Amber said immediately. "The hospice nurse is here right now; she can help me get him into his wheelchair and loaded into the van. I'm sure I'll get an earful for this, but I don't care. She couldn't possibly understand how important this is."

Lexie gave Amber her address.

"We'll be there within the hour," Amber said.

"I'll be ready to help you get him in the house," Lexie confirmed.

"Lexie?"

"Yeah?"

"Thank you. So much."

Tears popped up in Lexie's eyes, and she blinked them back. "See you soon."

38

By the time Amber's white van pulled up in front of Lexie's house, Ryan had cut a sizable hole in Lexie's bedroom wall with his reciprocating saw and cleared it of insulation, exposing the triangular prism-shaped space behind the wall. The space was formed by the sloped roof meeting the plywood-covered floor joists, and closed off by the short wall that had once held a small door which allowed access to the space. At some point between Melissa Ann's murder and the discovery of her body, the attic was finished and the door removed, but nobody had bothered to look inside the mysterious cedar chest. Not even Justin Betz, the curious lad who found Dolly in the storage space.

The chest was dried out, cracked, and covered in a thick sheet of dust. Dozens of warped old mothballs were scattered on the floor all around it. Ryan had left the chest in its place for now; both he and Lexie wanted to wait until Michael arrived before finishing the job of recovering Melissa Ann's remains. Ava sat cross-legged on Lexie's bed, staring earnestly at the chest.

Lexie saw Amber's van pull up and went out to meet her. Amber got out of the driver's seat and moved to the side door. She opened it and pressed a button to extend Michael's wheelchair ramp.

"Need any help?" Lexie asked, peering into the van. Michael looked at her with bright, sunken eyes from under a baseball cap that was too large for his head. He held Dolly tightly in one hand. "Hi Michael. Thanks for coming. We have something for you."

His thin gray lips stretched across his teeth. "Amber says you found my sister," he rasped. "I want to see her."

"You will," Lexie said, unfastening the restraints that kept his wheelchair firmly locked in place in the back of the van. "We're ready for you."

Amber climbed into the van and carefully eased Michael's wheelchair down the ramp and onto the sidewalk, pulling his IV pole along with her, then pushed him slowly toward the house.

Lexie watched Michael's face. His eyes, shaded from the bright sun by the brim of his ballcap, stared unblinkingly at the house. *No doubt he's sorting through all the old memories*, she thought.

"It's been a long time," Michael said quietly, to nobody in particular. His eyes glittered with tears.

"The house isn't wheelchair-friendly, so Ryan is going to carry you inside. Amber will follow with your IV pole, and I will fold your chair up and carry it up to the attic. It might be a bit of a bumpy ride," Lexie said. "Okay?"

Michael nodded.

Ryan appeared at the front door. "Hey Michael," he said, smiling. "You ready?"

"Let's do this," Michael rasped. He seemed almost sprightly, which was a strange contrast to his wasted appearance. Ryan slid one arm under Michael's knees and one behind his back, and carefully lifted him from his chair. Amber was right there to make sure the IV lines didn't get tangled or caught on something.

Ryan shot Lexie an alarmed look that said *My god, he doesn't weigh anything* before carefully turning and walking inside the house.

Lexie nodded sympathetically. She guessed Michael was down to less than a hundred pounds now – severely underweight for someone of his height, which Lexie estimated to be about six feet. She folded Michael's chair and rolled it up the front steps, then hoisted it into the entryway. Ryan and Amber were slowly making their way up the stairs to the attic; Lexie followed them, walking backward, pulling the chair's large rubber wheels up each individual step.

Finally they reached the top. Lexie rolled the chair to the open space between her bed and the stairs and unfolded it, and Ryan carefully set Michael back in it. Amber rearranged IV lines and bags, locked the chair's wheels in place, adjusted Michael's baseball cap, and made sure he was secure in his chair.

"Would you like a blanket?" Lexie asked.

"Yes please," Michael said. The room was warm, but they all felt a bit of a chill.

Lexie retrieved a soft fleece blanket from her bed, where Ava still sat quietly, and laid it across Michael's lap. She squatted next to him and took his bony hand. "Are you ready?"

Michael brought Dolly up to his face and nodded toward a spot directly above Lexie's bed. "That's where I found my mom," he rasped.

Lexie gently squeezed his hand. "Now you know why she chose that spot." She stood and looked at Ryan. "Okay, let's do this." Amber stood bchind Michael and draped an arm protectively over his shoulder. Lexie and Ryan ducked into the hole in the wall and started moving the chest out into the room.

"I can feel her!" Michael called. His voice sounded...younger. "She's here! My god, she's here!"

"She's happy you're here, Michael," Ava said. "She missed you verrrrry much."

Lexie and Ryan manhandled the chest into the main room, and rolled it across the wood floor on its wooden casters to where Michael sat. Ava climbed down from Lexie's bed and followed closely.

Ryan made sure the chest was positioned so Michael could open the lid, and they all gathered around. Ava sidled up close to Lexie and took her hand. Lexie's heart pounded like it was trying to escape the prison of her ribcage.

Still holding Dolly, Michael leaned forward and hooked his shaky fingers under the lip of the chest's lid. He didn't quite have the strength to heave it open himself, so Ryan helped. Dust billowed. Rusty hinges screeched. The lid opened. They all gasped.

There she lay. A tiny skeleton with a few fine blonde hairs, wrapped in a stained red checked blanket. The sockets where her big brown eyes, so like her brother's, used to be were dark and unseeing. Her jaws were slightly separated, as if she were simply sleeping rather than forty years dead. Old mothballs littered the inside of the chest around her.

A sound unlike anything Lexie had ever heard came from Michael; it was an anguished sound, emotion and regret and fear and powerful love escaping his throat in a wave. He couldn't even form words; all he could do was throw his head back, clutch Dolly to his face, and wail.

Alarmed, Amber moved in front of him and bent to peer at his face. "Michael. Michael, honey, talk to me."

"Melissa!" Her name stretched into another anguished cry. Then: "Why didn't she take me too?"

Amber stood and gently cradled Michael's face in her hands. Tears rolled freely down her cheeks. "Michael. Listen to me."

Michael lowered his chin; his eyes were desperate, anguished. "All these years, Amber. She's been here all these years. Killed by our mother –" his voice began to shake "– and abandoned by everybody. She was my best friend. She was loved. How could my mother do this to her? To me?"

"I know, baby. I know," Amber whispered. "But look." She gestured to the open chest. "You're together now."

Michael's breath caught in his throat.

"And pretty soon you'll both be free," Amber said. A sob escaped her. "You and Melissa Ann will never be apart again. I promise."

Michael dropped Dolly in his lap and threw his emaciated arms around his wife.

"Mommy?"

Lexie, face covered in tears and snot, looked down into her daughter's enormous blue eyes. "Yes, babydoll?"

"I love you."

Lexie knelt so she was at Ava's level and smiled through her tears. "I love you too." She hugged Ava tightly, then stood. She looked at Ryan, who was watching her affectionately, and smiled.

Amber and Michael had finally composed themselves. The unusual energy Michael had when he arrived had clearly left him, and his eyelids seemed to grow heavier by the second. Amber looked at Lexie anxiously. "I need to take him home now. What do we do next?"

"Well, we need to call the police and start the process of getting Melissa an official death certificate," Ryan said. He'd done some research. "Once you have that, you can give her a proper burial."

Amber nodded. "Thank you. So much."

Lexie and Ryan helped get Michael back down the stairs and into the van, then stood back and watched Amber close the van's side door. She approached them tentatively. "I have no idea how to thank you. You've given him such a gift."

"Seeing him reunited with Melissa Ann was thanks enough for us," Ryan said. "Really. This was a gift for us too."

Amber hugged him. "Thank you." Then she hugged Lexie. "So damn much. He – he can go peacefully now." She took a few steps toward the van, then turned back. "It's funny, but I feel better about his death knowing that someone will be waiting for him there. He won't be lonely." She gave them a brief wave, then got in the van and drove away.

Ryan's arm circled Lexie's waist, and he pulled her to him. He gazed at her, smiling, and said, "Lexie?"

Lexie wrapped her arms around his neck. "Yes, Ryan?"

"What should we do with our scrapbook?"

Lexie laughed. "You have a fire pit, don't you?"

Ryan grinned. "You know I do."

"Then we'll burn it. I think that's the perfect way to close this chapter and start a new one together. Don't you?" Her heart skipped a beat at the thought of "together" with this man.

Ryan nodded and his face turned serious. "I love you."

A thousand-watt smile stretched across Lexie's face. "I love you too."

Ava came barreling out the front door. "Me too! Me too!" She crashed into them and wrapped her arms around their legs, beaming.

They were together. They were family. They were home.

www.startribune.com:

Madden, Michael Allen

Gilmartin, Melissa Ann

Michael Allen Madden, age 44 of Blaine, lost his battle with brain cancer peacefully on June 21, 2020. He was preceded in death by parents George and Lucy Gilmartin, adoptive parents Dick and Carol Madden, his grandparents, and his twin sister Melissa Ann Gilmartin. He is survived by his beloved wife Amber and many friends.

Melissa Ann Gilmartin, age 4 of Minneapolis, was lost on August 21, 1980 and found on June 19, 2020. She is reunited in death with her twin brother Michael Allen (Gilmartin) Madden. Special thanks to friends Alexis and Ava Novak and Ryan Laughlin for bringing our twins back together.

Private services have been held. Michael and Melissa Ann are interred together forever at Crystal Lake Cemetery in Minneapolis. In lieu of flowers, donations preferred to National Alliance on Mental Illness (NAMI) Minnesota. Arrangements entrusted to Johnson McNair Funeral Chapel, Blaine.

THE END

ACKNOWLEDGMENTS

My undying gratitude goes out to the following people, who continue to support me as I chase my crazy dreams:

My parents, Joel and Penny DeVries, who gave me the gift of words, shared with me their love of reading, and believed in me when I didn't always believe in myself.

My brother, Benjamin DeVries, my first best friend and my biggest fan.

All of my family, friends and colleagues who have offered kind and supportive words throughout my journey, and asked "When is your second book coming out?" I'm thrilled to finally deliver!

My fellow former City Limits Publishing authors, employees, and vendors, who escaped a nefarious small press and banded together to support each other -- I'm so fortunate to call you all my new friends.

And finally, my son Price and my daughter Kendall...everything I do, I do for them. Always.

ABOUT THE AUTHOR

Brenda Lyne is the pseudonym of author Jennifer DeVries. Jennifer lives just outside Minneapolis, Minnesota with her two busy kids, two cats, two fish, and probably a partridge in a pear tree. She is living, breathing proof that it is never too late to follow your dreams. *Sister Lost* is her second novel.

ALSO AVAILABLE FROM BRENDA LYNE:

An unexpected fall through a mysterious mirror
transports Sara Sullivan thirty years in the past,
where she has the chance to save dozens of innocent
young lives.

Can she unmask the Library Mall Bomber before
it's too late?

Available at select bookstores and
online at Amazon and Barnes & Noble.